Bear Creek

By Dan Arnold

I shot him as he was getting off his horse.

I'd just had breakfast with Tom and Becky at the Bon Ton and was walking out the door. I barely noticed a man at the hitching rail, just starting to step off his big bay horse. I wouldn't have paid any attention to him except his body language changed the minute he saw me. When I turned my head to look at him, he was reaching for his gun.

All in a flash I realized he was Ed Rawlins and we were firing at each other.

BEAR CREEK

1.

Bear Creek, Colorado was a fairly peaceful town considering how fast it was growing. What with it having its own railway depot, and it being a cross roads for the region and all, we had a lot of people passing through. Some were hoping to find a spot to settle down, others came for other reasons. Everyone brought their troubles with them.

As town Marshal in Bear Creek, I enjoyed a relatively easy life. I had my own room at the Marshal's office, free meals at the Bon Ton (paid for by the city of Bear Creek) and a fair bit of leisure time. This way of life was a far cry from my days breaking horses, herding cattle, and doing any hard or dirty job that came to hand. In my younger days I had traveled far and suffered more than my share of hardship.

I had become pretty fond of Bear Creek, and the folks there had come to respect me and accept me as part of the community. We all got along pretty well.

How I got to be the town Marshall, and what happened after, started with a runaway horse.

***

I'd come there that day just passing through, on my way from Texas to Wyoming. I'd taken the Union Pacific train from Fort Worth to Kansas City, then on to Denver. I changed trains again in Denver, catching the train north to Cheyenne. Bear Creek was one of the stops along the way.

I stepped down off the train that evening with no idea it would be a long time before I left this town again. I just wanted to stretch my legs and breathe some cool, high country air while the passengers and freight were loading. I was thinking back to the first time I'd been through this part of the country.

As a very young man, right after the War Between the States, I'd made a couple of cattle drives through this area. I'd helped push herds of wild cattle to Wyoming from Texas, with Yellow Horse and Charlie Goodnight. I never saw this town back in those days.

I was standing there on the railroad station platform, half day dreaming, remembering that time, back in 1869 when I'd tried to...

My memories were cut short, as I became aware of a ruckus in a livestock car.

Suddenly all hell broke loose.

Actually it wasn't all hell, not at first. It was just one horse.

A railroad hand had just led the saddled bay gelding up the ramp into a livestock car when the horse spooked. It crashed around in there, got turned around and came flying back down the ramp with the railroad hand limping and stumbling behind it. "Loose horse," he yelled, as he realized he was hurt and couldn't hope to catch it. The big bay had taken off at a full gallop, charging up the dirt street toward the main part of the town.

I took off right behind it, and so did another man.

The horse was fully saddled, and dragging his bridle reins as he ran. When he got to the main street with all the lights and activity, he slowed to a nervous walk.

The main street of Bear Creek was noisy on that Friday night. There was music playing in a couple of saloons, horses and buggies were tied to various hitching posts, and people were moving about. There was loud talk and even louder laughter.

When the horse pulled up, walking forward unsure where to run. I slowed to a walk myself, as I didn't want to scare him further. When I looked over at the other man, I could tell he had the same thought. We were easing up on the bay horse from both sides when another man stepped out in front of him and caught hold of his bridle reins, just as smooth and natural as could be. He put his face right up to the horse's muzzle as though he were going to kiss him.

"Gimme my horse you half breed son of a bitch," the other man who had come up from the depot hissed.

He was furious and had a gun pointed at the young man holding the horse. The young man seemed hurt by the other man's cruel taunt. Clearly he was only trying to help. He stepped back from the horse and calmly held the reins out toward the man with the gun.

The man thumbed back the hammer of his gun.

"Whoa now," I said. "There's no need for trouble here.'

The man with the gun took the reins from the kid while still holding the gun on him. "You made a bad mistake, boy," he said, and shot him right in the chest.

The sudden roar of the gun was startling. The young man collapsed as if all the air had been let out of him.

The gunman whirled on me, catching me flat footed and completely shocked.

"Mister, you really ought to mind your own damn business," he spat.

He was trying to keep his gun leveled on me, but the horse was having none of it and was trying to get away from him. People were coming towards us, drawn by the gunshot. He holstered his gun and focused on trying to get his horse under control, holding the reins with both hands. For a moment there, I'd been certain he was going to shoot me. If I had reached for my gun, it could have gone either way.

A man hurried through the growing knot of people. I saw the star on his chest, and he was moving with a purpose. He looked down and saw the boy on the ground gasping and choking, his shirt nearly soaked through with blood.

"You men stand right there," the lawman said. He was now holding his own gun, pointed in our general direction.

"Somebody go and get Doc Johnson, now!" he barked, never taking his eyes off the two of us.

"What the hell happened here?' he asked.

Before I could say a word, the man who now held his horse more calmly said, "Bastard redskin tried to steal my horse."

I was dumbfounded!

"Who are you?" The lawman asked him.

"Why, I'm Ed Rawlins," the gunman replied, as if he expected everyone within earshot to already know who he was.

"And you are…? The lawman asked, looking at me.

"My name is Sage, John Everett Sage"

"Well gentlemen," he said, "I'm Jack Watson, the town marshal here in Bear Creek. You boys will have to come with me so we can get this thing sorted out."

A younger man came running up. He was carrying a double barreled twelve gauge shotgun. He was also wearing a badge.

"This is my deputy, Tom Smith." The marshal said. "Tom, you keep these boys under your gun."

When the deputy cocked that sawed off twelve gauge, everyone near us stepped back.

"Now then, Mr. Rawlins, I'll have your pistol…real slow like, with just your left hand," the marshal said, with a smile on his face. His gun was steady in his hand.

Rawlins stared at him cold and hard but didn't move at all. He was still holding the bridle reins with both hands.

I heard the train whistle blow.

After a moment Rawlins sighed, twisted his neck a little and released the reins with his left hand, slowly moving it down to the gun on his right hip.

He eased it up out of the holster and with the barrel pointed at the ground, very slowly handed it to the marshal. The marshal held it down at his side.

"Somebody take this horse to the livery stable." He said.

A man stepped forward, took the reins from Rawlins and led the horse away.

The marshal spoke to me.

"I'll have you to hand your gun to my deputy there, same way...real slow."

It was a testimony to the man's powers of observation. I wear my .45, in a cross draw holster on my left hip, where it isn't immediately obvious, being covered by my suit coat.

The marshal was still holding his Colt, now leveled at me, just as steady as ever.

I did; I handed over my gun, with my left hand, slow and easy, just the way he asked me to.

A man came and knelt over the boy who had become still. I figured he was the doctor. He got busy trying to save what was left of the young fella's life.

As we were walking farther into town, on our way toward the Marshal's office, I heard the train leave the station.

2.

The center of town was a big square. I was reminded of the old Spanish *plaza majors* often seen in larger cities. I wondered if Bear Creek had started out as a Spanish settlement.

There was a brand spanking new, two story brick courthouse occupying the middle of the square, surrounded by grass and trees. There was colorful bunting hanging from the windows and a little bandstand or gazebo at the top of some stairs, raising it high above one corner of the square. Everything I had seen so far spoke of growth and prosperity.

The Marshal's office was built entirely of granite blocks, with a big porch on the front. It was set in the middle of the block on the north side of the square. Unlike most of the other buildings around the square, the Marshal's office sat alone and did not share any walls with any other building.

Inside the front door was one large room with a black pot-bellied stove, a desk, a gun rack on one wall, a safe, and two doors, one at the back and one on the other wall. We went through the door at the back of the office, into the jail. There were six cells, three on each side with two bunks in each cell. There was another door at the back of the jail. I figured it led out to an alley and the privy.

Marshal Watson and his deputy locked us up in separate cells, side by side. None of the other cells were occupied.

The marshal stood facing us in the open space between the rows of cells. He crossed his arms and looked up at the ceiling.

"OK," he said, "let's go over this again."

"I told you, that redskin stole my horse" Rawlins yelled.

"Mr. Rawlins, I heard you the first time. Now you just be quiet for a minute. I want to hear from this other fella." He looked at me, and so did Rawlins.

Rawlins glared at me. "I told you once already, mister; you really ought to mind your own damn business"

Marshal Watson uncrossed his arms and pointed at Rawlins. "That's enough out of you. You open your mouth again, and I'll come in there and shut you up myself."

He turned to me.

"What did you say your name is?

"John Everett Sage"

"Mr. Sage, what brings you to Bear Creek?"

"The train from Denver," I said, dryly.

Rawlins snorted at that.

The marshal looked down at the floor for a moment and when he looked back up at me, I could see he was not amused.

"Where are you from and why are you here in Bear Creek?"

I felt kind of bad about my first answer.

8

"Marshal, I'm on my way to Cheyenne. I came in on the train that just left. I don't know Mr. Rawlins over there at all."

"I didn't ask you that. Let's try this again. Where are you from and why are you here, in Bear Creek?"

"Yes, sir, I understand. The last few years, I've been living and working in Texas. I'm on my way to Wyoming to see my folks. I don't have any business in Bear Creek."

That last part came out wrong.

It made Marshal Watson smile, though.

"Why *are* you here in town, then?"

So, I told him the whole story about the loose horse. When I got to the part where Rawlins pulled his gun, Rawlins took a step toward me, grasping the bars of his cell with both hands.

"He shot the boy for no reason," I said, looking Rawlins in the eye.

"Will you testify to that?" The marshal asked.

"Yes, sir, I will."

"You are one dead son of a bitch." Rawlins said.

The marshal shook his head.

"No sir, Mr. Rawlins. If the boy dies, when the jury gets done with you, you'll be the one hanging from the gallows. That boy is well liked in this town. One way or another, I'm personally going to see you pay for what you've done."

He unlocked my cell and indicated I should follow him back into his office.

"You're both dead men!" Rawlins yelled from behind us.

We just ignored him.

The deputy, Tom Smith, was sitting on the edge of the desk.

"Tom, go see the Doc and check on Willy," Marshal Watson said.

Tom nodded and left, as the Marshal stepped behind his desk.

He motioned for me to have a seat in the chair in front of the desk. Tom left, and we both sat down. The Marshal rested his hat on the desk top.

"What were you doing down in Texas?" He asked.

He put on a pair of glasses and opened a desk drawer. He took out some "wanted" posters.

"I was a Texas Ranger. They wanted to make me a Captain, but I would've had to re-locate down to the border lands. I've been there and don't care to go back. I decided to take some time off and find my family, up north."

He looked up and nodded.

"I figured you for some kind of lawman. You don't look like a drifter or a business type."

He took my Colt out of another drawer in the desk and handed it to me.

"Well, I'm sorry you got mixed up in this," he said. "Generally, we don't have people carrying guns in town, so shootings don't happen often. Since you're a peace officer, I'll let you have your weapon."

"Thank you. I must say this town appears to be booming. That's an impressive courthouse you've just built."

"Rawlins' trial will be the first one we have in our new county courthouse. Tomorrow is Founders

Day for the town and we're going to dedicate the building."

"That explains why there are so many people on the streets. If you don't mind me saying so, you look under staffed."

He nodded again.

"Tom and I can handle most of the routine stuff, drunks and petty crime, or at least we used to be able to," he sighed. "We have enough problems with the locals, but there are scores of people passing through. We need at least two more deputies. This town has grown so fast; it's getting away from us."

He narrowed his eyes at me.

"I don't suppose you'd be interested in a job?"

I held up my hands and shook my head.

"No, sir, I'm just passing through, on my way to Wyoming."

"Well that's going to be a problem for you. You've missed your train, and you'll have to miss a few more."

"Why's that? I figured I'd just catch the next train to Cheyenne. I'll come back for the trial."

He shook his head.

"You're the only witness to the shooting. I can't have you leave the state. Something could go wrong, and that fella would go free," he said, jerking his head toward the jail. "No sir. I won't let that happen."

"Are you planning to lock me up?"

"No, I'm asking you to stay. We'll arraign him before Judge Tucker, on Monday. The trial will be scheduled as soon as we can get him an attorney and gather a jury. The city and county will stand your expenses."

That brought to mind a question.

"Don't you have a County Sheriff?

He sighed again.

"We just had the election. He gets sworn in tomorrow. We just formed Alta Vista County. There used to be just one giant county up here, but it has recently been reorganized into three separate counties, and we haven't had a county sheriff till now. Ten years ago, there wasn't even a town Marshal here."

"Well, now that you have a county sheriff, it will help get you more man power," I said.

"Sure. Eventually, but it's a political thing. Both the guys who ran for the position are local big wigs, with no law enforcement experience at all. The guy who won the election is named Clay Atwater. He owns the freight line"

I nodded. I'd heard of Atwater Freight.

"All my gear was on the train. All I have is the clothes on my back," I said.

"Mr. Sage, I promise we'll make you as comfortable as possible. I wish you'd take the job as a deputy."

I thought about it for a second. I figured I didn't really have a choice. I wasn't expected at any particular time, and I couldn't let a murderer go free. I would have to stay for the trial. I might as well get paid for staying around.

"I tell you what, Marshal. I'll think it over. Call me John," I said.

"Call me Jack" he said, standing up.

I stood up as he reached across the desk to shake my hand.

We talked for a while about Bear Creek, how fast it had grown, how prosperous the town was, and how the county commissioners would be raising and spending revenue.

"We've even got a fire brigade with a building and a brand new pump wagon and team."

He reckoned there were more than a couple of thousand people in the county. Most of them lived in or near Bear Creek. There were three or four outlying towns in the county and any number of farms and ranches. Bear Creek was the center of commerce.

I told him about the first time I'd come through this part of the country, driving cattle to Wyoming.

"It's a wonder to me, a community this big could have grown out of nearly nothing, in just a couple of decades," I concluded.

"Well, it took a lot of hard work by men of vision. We're real proud of the town. Now that Colorado is a state and Bear Creek is the county seat of Alta Vista County, I guess the sky's the limit."

DAN ARNOLD

3.

Tom came back and informed us Willy Walker had died.

"He was a good kid. I've known him all his life. His mother was Ute, and his father helped start this town. Both his parents died in a fire, last year. Willy worked at the livery. He was real good with horses. This is the first murder we've had."

Jack shook his head.

"Sure, we have our share of drunks, some fights and shootings in the saloons, some domestic issues, even a couple of killings, but Rawlins shot down an unarmed boy in cold blood. What kind of man can do a thing like that?"

Just then, a man came hurrying in off the street. He was wearing a suit with tails and he had on a silk, "stove pipe" top hat.

"Is it true? I just heard somebody killed Willy!" He cried, wringing his hands.

"Yes, sir, I'm afraid so." Jack confirmed, as he stood up.

The man looked at me.

"Bob, this is John Sage. He was a witness to the shooting. John, this is Bob Larkin, our Mayor." Jack said.

We shook hands.

"Well, I guess that explains the hat," I said.

Later on, as Tom was taking me to the hotel, he told me why he figured the Mayor was so upset.

"He sees having a cold blooded murder, on the eve of the festivities, as a black eye for the town. Its bad enough Willy is dead. Having all these dignitaries coming into town tomorrow, and then talking about the murder, all over the state, it sure worries him. "

When we got to the hotel, we learned there were no rooms available.

"Every room is booked or occupied; most of them have three or four people in them," the clerk said. "Even the Governor is coming here tomorrow, though I hear he's staying with the Courtney's, out at the Bar C."

"Of course," Tom said. "I wasn't thinking. What with all the festivities, even the boarding house is full. Every bed in this town is spoken for, one way or another."

"I can sleep in a cell at the jail," I offered.

"No sir. I wouldn't ask you to do that. It wouldn't be right…for a whole bunch of reasons."

We had just stepped out of the hotel, when he turned and said;

"Listen, if you wouldn't mind, I can put you up at my house. I can offer you a place to wash up, and my wife made a peach pie today. Let's go there."

I tried to bow out, not wanting to inconvenience his family, or get into an awkward situation, but he insisted it would be no trouble.

Tom's house was a few blocks northwest of the square. As we walked down the hill, we passed a number of homes of various design. Some appeared to have been here for years. Others were clearly newly built. We passed a very nice, whitewashed church with stained glass windows, a tall steeple and enough room on the grounds to park several buggies. The church and grounds occupied a whole block.

The deputy lived at the very end of a street, a fair distance from the square. It was a tidy, whitewashed single story house, with a wrought iron fence around it. It had a big porch on the front with rose bushes on both sides of the steps. There were lamps lit inside. The whole effect was cozy and I found it pretty inviting.

I heard a good sized creek running, back behind the house somewhere. The smell of cottonwood trees was heavy in the night air. Tom told me the creek was called Bear Creek, from which the town had derived its name.

Tom's wife Becky met us at the door. She was as cute as a button. Her strawberry blonde hair was pulled back in a single long braid, with a big bow tied around it. She was wearing a blue gingham dress that matched her eyes. She got busy getting us peach pie and coffee, as Tom explained the situation.

"Mr Sage, if you don't mind staying with us, we can make you reasonably comfortable in my sewing room. Now don't you try to say no, I won't hear of it!" Becky said, planting her fists on her hips.

I could tell she meant it. So that, settled that.

Tom had to leave to get back on the street, until the town started to settle down for the night. I offered to go with him, but Becky insisted I stay and keep her company, until he returned from his duties.

As we sat and talked, I learned she was Jack Watson's daughter. Her mother died a few years back, leaving Jack and her alone in the house. When Tom finally figured out that he was in love with Becky, and she with him, Jack had given them the house as a wedding present and moved himself into the Marshal's office.

"One or the other of them always stayed at the jail overnight anyway. This worked out nicely for Tom and me."

She showed me the "sewing room," and sure enough it had one of those new-fangled sewing machines, bolts of fabric, a big table with paper patterns, scraps of gingham, spools of thread, scissors, and so on. There was also a frilly looking bed, with bolts of cloth piled on top of it.

"This was my room before we got married. We hope it will be the baby's room, eventually. For now, it will be your room."

We went back out into the front room (she called it the "parlor") and spent a pleasant couple of hours talking, until Tom came home.

***

Later, when I was settled into the sewing room, I reflected on the events of the day. I thought about what kind of man Rawlins was. I thought about what kind of man I was.

I wondered what it would be like to be married and own a home. I'd tried it once, a very long time ago.

It hadn't worked out.

Other than that one failed attempt, I'd lived virtually my whole life traveling from town to town. Everything I owned could pretty much travel with me on horseback.

At this point, I didn't even own a horse.

Some people enjoy freedom. Other people enjoy belonging to someplace or someone. I didn't owe anyone anything, and I sure had my freedom.

Then again, if Rawlins had killed me on the street corner, it would be a long time till anyone who cared about me even learned I was dead.

I had no legacy.

If I died that night, it would be as though I had never lived at all.

DAN ARNOLD

4.

I got up early, lit the fire in the cook stove and had coffee on by the time Becky came bustling into the kitchen that Saturday morning. I asked Tom and Becky to let me buy them breakfast if there was a place in town that served it. They tried to talk me out of it, and Becky was horrified I would even suggest such a thing. Tom said there were three restaurants in Bear Creek, if you counted the Cantina as one of them. Only the Bon Ton served breakfast. It was where Jack got his meals when he wasn't with Tom and Becky. It was right next to the hotel. There were also three saloons in town but only the Palace and the Cantina served any real food, and that was only in the evenings. Tom told me the Palace Saloon was the best restaurant in Colorado.

I talked them into it, and we walked up the hill to the café.

There was a two sided sign hanging above the door. On both sides, in fancy script, it said, "Le Bon Ton Café." Under that, it said "Henri Levesque, Proprietor."

I didn't know it that day, but having breakfast at the Bon Ton on Saturday morning with Tom and Becky, was going to become a fairly common occurrence.

After breakfast we went to the Marshal's office.

"Gonna be a big day in Bear Creek," Jack said. "We've got horse racing, pie eating contests, there'll be speeches from the Governor, the Mayor and the newly elected Sheriff. There'll be a big parade, with a marching band. We'll honor the civil war vets and some of the old timers that settled this area. It'll be a big Whoop ti doo," he grinned. "Hell, we've even got a carnival."

My ears pricked up at that.

"What kind of carnival?" I asked.

"Oh, well, you know…all the usual stuff, jugglers and acrobats, knife throwers, games, fortune tellers, and dancing girls flashing their legs." He shrugged.

Becky blushed when he said that.

"Where is this carnival?" I asked.

"They're set up right outside town, on the east side. Some of them will be performing in the parade."

"Jack, there's too much going on. There's no way you and Tom can cover all of this by yourselves." I said.

Jack leaned back in his chair.

"Well, I have six guys with the Fire Brigade in their red shirts and helmets, to help keep things in order at the parade. Tom will have to stay here with the prisoner. I'll be busy with the activities on the square and everything else. The big problems probably won't come until tonight, when all the drinking and celebrating gets out of hand."

He looked at me.

"You sure you don't want a job?"

I really didn't want a job. I needed to find my family. It was bad enough I had to stay for the trial of Ed Rawlins. Committing to help protect the community of Bear Creek wasn't something I wanted to do. Then again, I saw a need and I knew the work.

I sighed. "Jack, I'll put on the badge, but just to help out until things settle down."

Tom and Jack looked at each other and grinned.

Jack reached into his vest pocket and tossed me a badge.

"I cleared it with the Mayor last night," he said. "I also sent a telegram to Cheyenne. Your gear will be coming in this afternoon on the 12:10 to Denver."

"Tom if you'll hold down the fort here, I need to take John to meet some people. Then I have to get to the depot to meet the Governor's train."

Becky kissed Tom goodbye and left with her dad and me.

The streets were crowded as we made our way over to the courthouse. Most of the women wore the latest fashions with hats and parasols. Most of the men were in suits and children were running around playing tag. We climbed up the wide granite steps at the front of the building, the tiny crystals in the granite flashing like diamond chips, in the sparklingly clear morning sunlight. Once inside, Jack took us through a polished oak door, with opaque glass, into one of the offices. The Mayor was there with two other men.

Jack made the introductions.

"John, you know Mayor Larkin."

We shook hands.

"Judge Tucker, this is John Everett Sage, lately of the Texas Rangers. Today he's working for us."

When he added that last part, he was looking directly at the third man, to whom I had not yet been introduced. That man was the biggest man in the room. He would have been the biggest man in most any room, most anywhere.

I shook hands with the judge and turned to the big man.

"John, this is Clay Atwater, our new County Sheriff."

"Pleasure," he said shaking my hand.

His grip was firm, maybe just a little too firm, but then he was clearly a powerful brute of a man.

"You all know my daughter, Becky," Jack said.

Becky smiled and gave a little mock curtsy.

"Gentlemen…" She started to say something else.

"I guess we better get over to the station," Atwater interrupted, rudely.

"Oh, the train isn't due for nearly an hour. I think we have time to have a look around this new building. Would you folks like a tour?" Judge Tucker offered.

"Yes, please," Becky said. "This building is huge!"

"Fine," Atwater said. "You go ahead and do that. I'll be at the Station."

He pulled his hat on and walked out of the office leaving the door open.

"I guess he's as nervous as a long tailed cat in a room full of rocking chairs," Mayor Larkin said. "It's a big day for him, he has to give a speech and he's being sworn into office by the Governor himself."

Jack and I looked at each other.

Judge Tucker took us upstairs to the courtroom which occupied the entire top floor. He showed us his chambers behind the bench. It was a small office, richly appointed with lots of polished oak in evidence. He was especially proud of the narrow, secret stairwell that would allow him to come and go from his chambers, without having to go through the courtroom or the hallways.

He took us down those hidden stairs, all the way to the basement. It wasn't really a basement, as it was only about half underground and had narrow windows just above ground level.

This space was the Alta Vista County Jail. There were eight big cells with four bunks in each. The narrow windows had bars set into the walls on the inside. On the outside, steel shutters could be opened to allow light and air in, or closed to keep out bad weather.

He showed us the County Sheriff's office, right next to another set of stairs that went up to a door in the side of the building that could be barred from the inside. This was the place where prisoners would come and go, in and out of the jail.

At the end of the basement were a couple of rooms with three bunk beds in each. These were for sheriff's deputies to sleep in and for the occasional jurors, when a trial lasted more than a day or there weren't enough rooms available at the hotel.

He took us up another flight of stairs at the end of the building, which brought us back to the main floor.

Later, at the train station, the judge and the Mayor excused themselves and went over to join the Sheriff, up on the railroad platform.

There was a band assembled there at the depot, and a huge crowd of people. Bunting was decorating every surface in sight and was prominent on several wagons. I noted the fire brigade in their yellow painted helmets and red shirts, with their fancy pump wagon and team of matching grey horses. There were a number of older men in the familiar uniforms of Blue and Gray, with the flags of North and South. Some uniforms still fit, some didn't. Former officers were mounted on horses; the rest were all on foot. I was hoping they all knew the war was over. Children raced around a juggler walking around on stilts.

Clearly, this was where the parade would start. It also ensured a large and colorful crowd would be on hand to greet the Governor. We heard the train whistle blow, and the crowd cheered as the train rounded a bend.

When the band started playing, I excused myself and took the distraction as an opportunity to head back into town.

5.

This was my first chance to really walk around in the town. When we'd been up on the second floor of the courthouse, I'd been able to see the general layout of the town was four square, with the streets running north/south and east/west.

Line Street came in from the west, ran by the square on the north side, crossed Main Street and ended a few blocks later at the railroad depot. The parade would come from the depot, west on Line Street to the square. The dignitaries would leave the parade at the courthouse, to dedicate the building, swear in the new County Sheriff and make their speeches. The parade would turn south on Jackson Street, to go around the square and then head back east on Omaha Street, ending at the freight yard.

I figured the parade wouldn't get started for at least a half hour, what with the Governor being greeted and then getting the parade lined out. Already the whole parade route was lined with people. The street corners were blocked with barrels and bunting to keep traffic away from the square.

I wanted a shave, but the barbershop on the corner of Main Street and Line was closed.

I stopped and looked around, realizing this was the corner where Rawlins had killed Willy Walker. It looked cleaner, safer and happier, on this festive morning. All sorts of finely dressed people were talking and laughing. Most or all of them, were unaware a young man had spilled out his life's blood into the dirt at the edge of this very boardwalk, just hours before.

I walked south on Main Street, observing all the buildings in this block were built of brick. The First National Bank was in the middle of the block. The Hotel was on the North side and the Bon Ton was right on the corner. On past the bank, on the south corner, was a dry goods store. I turned the corner and headed east, back toward the tracks. I passed a hardware store, and directly across the street, the doctor's office, with his residence on the second floor. Next, I came to one of the three saloons, this one called the Ox Bow. It was clapboard, painted bright yellow, with a big porch out front. There were several people on the porch and on the board walk in front of it, waiting for the parade. The crowd here was a little different from the folks all around the square and at the depot. The people here were dressed for work. They were just taking a break from doing the things they had to do, to watch the parade when it passed their way.

The folks on the square, at the depot and along the main parade route, were making a day of it, all decked out in their finest.

I'd seen it before. It seems odd how just a couple of hundred yards, or turning a corner, can change the very nature of a community.

Even though it was just past nine O'clock in the morning, the Ox Bow was open for business. I went inside.

The place was half dark and smelled of stale beer, sweat and tobacco smoke. There were only a few men sitting at tables, and no one was standing or sitting at the big bar that ran the whole length of the back wall. I figured once the parade was over, business would probably pick up.

Behind the bar, a bartender was polishing glasses and trying not to stare at my badge, as I walked up to him.

"What'll it be?" He mumbled, not meeting my eyes.

I smiled my friendliest smile.

"Nice place you've got here," I said.

"Uh huh," he nodded.

He looked like any one of a hundred bartenders I had seen. He was of medium build with a bushy mustache, a fairly clean white apron, and he had thin, dark hair, which he had slicked down over the top of his head with some kind of hair grease.

I tried again.

"My name is John Sage..." I started.

"I know who you are," he said flatly.

I was wondering how the word about a new deputy could possibly have gotten around town, so fast. Maybe he knew about Rawlins and the shooting.

A man seated at one of the tables stood up and started across the room toward us.

"Hold on there, Bob," the bartender said.

I turned to meet the man. He was built like the proverbial brick outhouse, about two hundred and fifty pounds of solid muscle. He had a handgun in a holster, pulled high up on his hip. On him it looked like a toy.

He was looking me over pretty good.

"Hmmm, you must be new," he said. "I know the big dog; Marshal Watson and his puppy, Smith. But you, I don't know."

The other men who had been seated at the same table, stood up.

"Now wait a minute, Bob. Don't start any trouble here," the bartender said. "He's a heller with a gun," he glanced my way, indicating me. "In Tascosa, I saw him shoot three men down, as easy as counting to three. He's a Texas Ranger"

"Well that don't mean squat to me," Bob growled, looking at the bartender.

He turned back to me.

"Is that right?" He sneered. "You a gun hand?"

"No, I'm not a gunman, or a Texas Ranger. Here in Bear Creek, I'm just a deputy marshal," I said, pointing at my badge.

The other men sat back down.

"Huh!" he snorted. "That don't carry no weight. My boss is the new County Sheriff."

"I met Mr. Atwater this morning!" I beamed. "He seems like a real nice fellow. You remind me of him"

He turned his back on me and went back to his table.

"We'll see about that," he growled.

I looked over at the bartender. He was as white as his apron.

I rapped my knuckles on the bar.

"Y'all have a nice day," I said.

I walked out through the swinging doors.

Outside the Ox Bow, I looked down the street toward the railroad tracks. There was a lumber yard on one side of the street and a brick yard on the other. Down a ways, was a wagon yard for the freight line and on the other side of the street, right by the tracks, was the freight yard and a warehouse. I headed that way. As I did, I heard the band at the depot strike up a march. I figured the parade was getting started.

Ever since walking by the corner where Rawlins had killed the boy, I'd been thinking about Rawlins and his big bay gelding. I decided to cut across the freight yard and go back past the depot to the livestock pens. Then I would come back into town on Line Street, past the livery stable and the blacksmith's shop.

As I was cutting through the freight yard, I noticed two men who looked like they were guarding the warehouse. Either that or those shotguns were handy for scaring away pigeons.

My timing was good; the last wagon in the parade was just leaving the station. There were several women standing on the wagon. The sides of the wagon had signs promoting women's suffrage, and there were several women and children marching along behind it. Some of them were holding up signs, demanding a woman's right to vote.

If that happened, the next thing you knew, women would be serving on juries, too. I'd read in some newspaper, in Wyoming, women were already allowed to serve as jurors.

How was that working out?" I thought.

As I followed along behind the parade, I checked out the livestock yard.

Several horses were in one of the livestock pens, and a bunch of cattle were in another, but the big bay gelding was not to be seen. I wandered down to the livery stable. There was an office at the front of the barn, and there was a man standing there, watching the Suffragettes go by. He saw me coming down the boardwalk and smiled.

"Howdy," he called. "Don't you just love a parade?"

When I got closer and he saw my badge and gun, he raised his eyebrows.

"Howdy," I said. "I'm John Sage."

As we shook hands, he told me his name was Alexander Granville Dorchester, the third!

"You can call me 'Al'," he said.

It turned out he owned the livery stable and had been Willy's boss. More than that, he had probably been Willy's closest friend. His eyes welled with tears, when I told him I'd been a witness to the killing.

"Willy started working here when he was just thirteen. I had him cleaning stalls, feeding the horses and so on. I saw he was really good with the horses, and it wasn't long until I found out he was also a really good rider. By the time he was fifteen, I had him starting some colts for me. He didn't snub em down and buck em out. He knew how to gentle em. The year he turned sixteen, his parents were killed in a fire. Willy moved into a room at the back of the barn, and he basically managed the stable, ever since. We were making money. I have an eye for good horseflesh. I would buyt the young horses cheap, and Willy would do the breaking and training. He did a damned good job of it, too. We've been able to sell horses for three times what I paid for em."

I asked about the big bay gelding.

"I have him inside, in a stall," he said. "Come on in."

Every stall was full of people's saddle horses, being boarded for the festive weekend.

The bay horse was calm and quiet in the stall, as I looked him over. He had a −C brand on his hip.

"Mr. Dorchester, did Willy break this horse?"

He shook his head.

"No, I have some horses Willie started, but this isn't one of em. Please, like I said, call me Al."

"OK, Al, have you ever seen this horse before?"

"Not this particular horse, but I see the brand all the time."

"Why is that?"

"The Bar C brand is the Courtney ranch. The Bar C is the biggest ranch in these parts. They ship cattle and horses all over the country. Mr. Courtney had the biggest and fanciest wagon in the parade just now. Hell, the Governor, the Mayor and all the big wigs, were riding with him on that wagon. Didn't you see the big Bar C brand painted on the side?"

I'd seen all that, including the gruff giant, with the gold County Sheriff's star, sitting right next to the mayor.

Mr. Alexander Granville Dorchester, III, took me to a corral behind the barn and showed me some of the horses Willy had trained. I liked them all, but I especially liked a big line-back dun gelding.

Al told me the dun was Willy's own horse, which he had been riding for about three years.

6.

When I arrived back at the square, the official activities had started at the courthouse. There were dignitaries sitting on chairs up in the gazebo. The band was assembled directly under them. Now I understood the purpose of the raised gazebo. It was both a platform for giving speeches and a covered bandstand.

The Mayor was standing, in the middle of giving a speech.

"…and these streets will be bricked by the end of the year!" He shouted.

The band struck up "The Bear Comes over the Mountain."

"We're looking into having the town wired for the new electric lights. Why in no time at all, Bear Creek will be as big as Denver!"

From directly under his feet, the band blasted away again.

"And speaking of Denver…without further ado, it gives me great pleasure to introduce to you, the man who has the vision to lead us into the next decade, should I suggest the next century? Ladies and gentlemen, I give you, the Governor of the great state of Colorado, the right honorable J. Huxley McGee!"

Again, the band gave it all they had. The crowd was cheering.

The Governor stood and shook the Mayors hand then put his arm around the Mayor's shoulder, smiling and waving at the crowd. They froze like that as a photographer held up his flash pan.

FLOOSH!

You've probably seen that photograph. I think it was printed in every newspaper in the country.

The Governor started speaking, and I found Jack at the west end of the courthouse, standing at the top of the stairs, with a small group of people. Becky was nowhere to be seen.

Since we were in public, I decided to be a bit formal.

"Marshal, I've been patrolling on the west side of town. If it's alright with you, I'll continue on to other areas, until it's time to get my gear from the station."

He nodded.

"That's a good idea, John. Get to know your way around town. I've got this covered. Check back with me in a couple of hours."

He glanced over at the gazebo and the Governor. He winked, indicating he might have to be there listening to speeches for that long.

Because the town of Bear Creek was built on the top of a hill above the creek, the highest point in town was the courthouse. As I worked my way across the street and through the crowd of people listening to the Governor's speech, I was amazed at how clearly I could hear him.

"…and today I am happy to announce …The city of Bear Creek, has been chosen as the location for the new college!"

I was on the south side of the square now, and all the buildings on this side were also brick. On the corner opposite from the barbershop was another bank. This one was the Farmer's Bank and Trust. I've always found a town that has more than one bank tends to be a pretty healthy place. It means there are enough people and enough businesses to support two banks. With more available money in circulation, more business can thrive.

Right next to the bank, on the other side of a narrow alley, directly in the middle of the block, was another saloon.

The elaborate sign above the double swinging doors said simply, "The Palace." It was open for business, so I went inside.

I think I was grinning as I walked in. As dark and shabby as the Ox Bow was, the Palace was just the opposite. The open doorway and all the windows let in quite a bit of light. That light was reflected by the giant mirrors behind the beautiful bar, which ran for about seventy five feet down the north side of the building. That light, was also reflected by all the polished brass and gilded fixtures. The bar itself was magnificent. It was a hand carved and lacquered marvel. The entire top of the bar was marble. The brick walls had been plastered over and painted to match the color of the marble. Every table, chair and wood surface was carved and lacquered like the bar. Even the wood floor was polished oak. At each window, damask drapes hung from ceiling to floor.

The ceiling looked to be twenty feet above the floor and was paneled in decorative tin. Hanging from it were beautiful chandeliers. I couldn't see a single bullet hole in the ceiling. Some saloons I've been in, leak like a sieve when it rains.

At the very back of the building was a stage.

Most startling of all were the well- dressed ladies sitting at the table with some of the gentlemen. In many towns I'd worked, ladies would not dare enter a saloon. Oh, there might be women inside, but they probably weren't ladies.

Every little thing about this place spoke of style and sophistication. It really was both a restaurant and a saloon.

I was self-conscious because my suit was rumpled and dirty from days of traveling. My shirt could no longer really be called white, and I hadn't shaved since I was in Denver.

"Howdy, sir" called the bartender.

I realized I'd been standing and gawking. I walked over to the bar.

"You must be a new deputy. I don't think you've been in here before." He said.

This bartender had a waxed handlebar mustache, and his hair was slicked down over the top of his head, with some kind of grease. His apron was as white as the snow on the mountain tops.

"No, I'm new in town." I replied.

"Well, then, welcome to Bear Creek, and welcome to the Palace, Mr…?"

"Thanks. My name is John, John Everett Sage."

"What'll it be, Mr. Sage.? The first drink is on the house." He smiled cheerily, spreading his arms wide.

I could see in the mirror the people at the tables were looking our way, with some curiosity.

"Could I get a cup of coffee?

"You surely can, and I'll join you. We also have tea, fresh lemonade, cold beer, or just about anything you can imagine."

"Just the coffee, thanks…Did you say *cold* beer?"

"I did. Would you rather have beer?"

No, I was just wondering how it could be cold."

"Oh, we keep the barrels and bottles on ice. The ice house is right behind this building. It's handy to both the Palace and the grocery store, next door. Would you like cream with your coffee?"

When I left the Palace, the speeches were over, the new Sheriff of Alta Vista County had been sworn in and the Courthouse of the County Seat was open for the public to tour.

I walked north past the grocery store, with rows of fresh produce on display out front, under a bright green and white striped awning. I turned the corner and headed south. Sure enough, the first and only commercial building on the south side of the street was the icehouse. It took up most of the back part of this block. Between it and the back side of the grocery store and saloon was an alley that was wide enough for delivery wagons.

I had noted earlier, there were pipes running down into rain barrels from the roofs of nearly every building in town. These barrels were readily available if they needed to be used to fight fire.

From where I was standing, I could look down the hill at several blocks of homes. The nearest, were beautiful two story houses, many built of stone and brick. They had a variety of fancy gingerbread decorations with rambling porches, fenced yards, flower beds and trees. They all had carriage houses behind them. I guessed this was where the rich folks lived.

I heard a train whistle blow, reminding me it was time to go back to the railroad depot to get my things.

When I got to the platform, the train was still in the station. The clerk at the depot informed me my gear had been shipped as freight, so I would have to go to the freight office to get it.

As I headed north to the freight office, the train whistle blew, and a few minutes later it chugged off for Denver.

At the freight office, the clerk looked over his manifest and said, "Yes, sir, Mr. Sage, we have your things right here. That'll be one dollar. Sign here, please."

"A whole dollar!" I exclaimed. "That's a lot of money just to send it back here from Cheyenne."

"Well, if you don't want your baggage, we can just sell it or dispose of it in some other way." He said crossing his arms and leaning back in his chair.

"No, no, I want it. Thank you."

I slapped a shiny silver dollar down on the counter, and grudgingly signed the manifest. The clerk took me through a door into a big empty room, and there, piled on the floor, were my saddle and saddle bags, my rifle in the scabbard and my valise.

"I can't carry all this into town." I said.

"Well, we can send it to the hotel or wherever you want it delivered."

"Is there an extra charge for that?'

"Yes, ordinarily there would be, but seeing as how you're a Deputy Marshal, we'll just chock it off as a professional courtesy. Where do you want it sent?"

I had him send my saddle and rifle to Al, at the livery stable. I picked up my saddle bags and valise and carried them back into the freight office.

"If I wanted to go to Cheyenne, and ship my saddle horse on the same train, how would I do that? I asked.

"Oh, that's easy," he said. "You just go to the depot, buy your ticket and pay the shipping fee, right there. They'll have somebody go to the livery stable and get your horse, when the train comes in."

"What if it was a last minute thing? You know-like if I just barely got to the station in time to catch the train, and I had my horse with me."

"No problem, as long as there's room in a livestock car…and you pay the shipping fee."

I went back to the railroad depot with my saddle bags slung over my shoulder and my valise in my hand.

"Hello, again" said the clerk. "How can I help you, Deputy?"

"Can you tell me how many passengers boarded the train for Cheyenne, yesterday evening?"

He got out his manifest and looked it over. As he was doing so, he mused;

"Yesterday there weren't many departures at all. We had people coming in for the festivities, but not many leaving, only two, in fact. Well, one really. You know the guy they say shot Willy? He never got on the train to Cheyenne."

"Yeah, about that guy…did he pay to have his horse shipped?"

"No, sir, he didn't. He didn't pay for his ticket either."

"Well, that's odd. I saw his horse being loaded on the train."

"Oh, you probably did, but I hear that horse off loaded himself." He grinned.

"I don't understand how he could have his horse loaded on the train, without buying a ticket or paying the shipping fee."

"That's because he just had the whole thing put on the ledger."

"Pardon me…what ledger?"

"The Bar C keeps an account with us, the freight company does too; because they both do so much business with the railroad, we keep account ledgers for them. Anyone who works for either the Bar C or the freight company can just add something on the account."

7.

I went straight to the Marshal's office. When I arrived, I found Jack sitting at his desk.

"I sent Tom out to get some lunch for himself and our prisoner," he said.

"What about you?"

"Oh, you might say I've eaten. I had to judge the chili cook off!"

I laughed. Then I remembered what I wanted to ask him.

"Jack, when you brought Rawlins and me in, you asked me where I was from and what I was doing here in Bear Creek. Did you ever ask Rawlins those questions?"

"Yes, I did, after you and Tom left. I asked him a lot of questions, not that it did me any good. I won't bother telling you what he told me I should do to myself."

I told him what I had learned at the railroad depot.

"That *is* interesting. I don't see how it has any bearing on the murder of Willy Walker, though."

"Rawlins put his train ticket and the shipping of his horse, on the Bar C account. His horse carries the Bar C brand. I don't want to jump to conclusions, Jack, but it might be interesting to ask Mr. Courtney if he knows Rawlins."

"I can do that," Jack said. "I'll see him again at some point, later this afternoon. There is another thing that's interesting. When we were at the courthouse this morning, a local attorney, named Frank Perkins, came to me and informed me he would be the defense counsel for Rawlins. He wanted to bail him out of jail. I told him he would have to wait till after the arraignment."

"Hmmmmm…that *is* interesting. We need to find out who this guy Rawlins is."

There doesn't seem to be any paper on him. If he's wanted, I haven't seen a poster.

"I need to ask a favor," I said.

"What is it?"

"I haven't had a change of clothes, a bath or a shave in days. Could I maybe take an hour or so, to go and get cleaned up?"

"You bet, take all the time you need. Go to the hotel, and tell them what you need, and have them charge it to the city. Check in with me later. You'll have to find me though, this afternoon I'll be out and around."

At the hotel, the clerk told me one of the guests had checked out, and there was now a room available. I was able to get a room upstairs that looked out at the courthouse. The use of a bath tub and hot water was arranged, and in short order, I was clean and shaved. I had my suit and hat given a good brushing while I was bathing, and with the addition of a clean shirt, I felt like a new man.

While it was nice the city was standing my expenses, it wasn't that much of a necessity. I had somewhat more than two thousand dollars in paper money tucked into my gun belt.

I was planning to give some of it to my folks, when I saw them. I was hoping that was going to happen sooner rather than later.

When I went back down to the hotel lobby, I asked the clerk if they had recorded in the registry, at any time recently, a guest named Ed Rawlins. He looked through the book; they had no such name.

The lobby of the hotel had a number of people in it, and the streets were still crowded around the square. People were visiting the courthouse, kids were playing games and vendors were selling everything from handicrafts to harness. The air was filled with the sounds of light banter and laughter, and the smells of cooking food.

I was starving. As I wandered past several food vendors, I found a Mexican vender.

"Quisiera el carne asado a la parilla en una tortilla, por favor."

"Si senor, y que mas?" he replied.

"Nada mas, gracias."

He handed me my lunch, and I handed him a dime. I took a bite, worth every penny!

I wanted some cold beer to wash it down, and I knew where to go to get it, but I decided against it. Instead,I headed over to the Marshal's office.

I found Tom in the Marshal's office. He told me Jack was at the horse races, over on the other side of the tracks.

"Have you been over there?" He asked.

"No, I've only been to the depot and the freight office, on that side of town. I haven't had occasion to cross the tracks."

"Well then, let me tell you a little bit about the layout of the town and why Bear Creek is such a boom town. West of here, if you go down Line Street, the road follows the creek up into the mountains. You'll find a couple of towns up there. The first one, North Fork, is a wide open, hell on wheels source of entertainment for the miners. Higher up, is Flapjack City, a smaller mining town, with nearly a hundred miners. Everything either of those towns needs to survive comes from, or through, Bear Creek."

"…and is handled by the Atwater Freight Company," I interrupted him.

He nodded.

"The mines ship the ore through Bear Creek, and the miner's payroll comes from the First National Bank of Bear Creek," he added.

I nodded my understanding.

"North and south of town is mostly farmland and ranches, irrigated by the various smaller creeks. There's a tremendous amount of produce, hay and even fruit, grown in this county. We could grow anything you can imagine, if the growing season was longer. We ship produce all over the region."

"…and it's all handled by the Atwater Freight Company?" I raised my eyebrows by way of a question.

He nodded again.

"East of town, going down, out onto the plains, there are several farms and ranches along Bear

Creek. The Bar C is out there, and a couple of small towns.

On the east side of town, just on the other side of the tracks is where most of the laborers live. There's also a Mexican community. That's where the Cantina is. Good food and good people over there. The old Spanish mission is now the Catholic Church. There wouldn't be a town of Bear Creek, if the old mission hadn't been here."

"But," he held up his finger, "that side of town is where most of the trouble happens, or comes from. The Spanish speaking folks stay pretty much to themselves, and we don't have much trouble with them, but there is a rough crowd over there on the other side of the tracks.

If you take Omaha Street east, out past the freight depot, then on across the tracks, you'll go through there, to get to the rodeo grounds, where the horse races are. Omaha Street is called that because it continues on east as a heavily used freight road. You can go from Bear Creek, across the plains into Nebraska, Kansas, or wherever. That road was part of the Santa Fe Trail"

"The Goodnight/Loving Trail also went by here. Bear Creek really is a cross roads." I mused. "From what you've said, it seems like this is the area center for mining, farming, ranching, shipping, banking and other service businesses."

He nodded and grinned.

"Well then," I said, as I opened the door. "I'm off to the races."

DAN ARNOLD

I didn't have any trouble finding the race track. It was only about a half mile on the other side of the railroad tracks. The race track went around the rodeo grounds, and the people could watch most of the racing from the stands. A little farther along the road, on a bend of the creek, I could see where the carnival was set up. There was a bridge across the creek at that point. I was amused by the fact that, down in Texas, this "creek" would have been called a river.

There was a pretty good crowd of people at the rodeo grounds. Rather prominent was a huge wagon, with bunting, an awning over the top, and a big Bar C brand painted on the side.

That's where I found Jack, and he introduced me to several people, William Courtney, his wife Annabelle, his lovely daughter Lacey and the Governor, among others.

"Marshal, I checked in with Tom, he told me you were over here. What would you like me to do?" I asked him.

"I need you to go over to the carnival and show the badge, just to keep everybody honest"

"Yes sir, I'll head on over there, right now."

From the moment I'd heard there was a carnival at Bear Creek, this was just what I had been hoping I would get the chance to do.

When I had first seen the carnival, even from a distance, I had recognized the tents and wagons. I had seen this carnival before.

There were horses, buggies, carts and wagons of various kinds, parked in the shade under the cottonwoods along the creek, where local people had tied them up while they went inside to spend their money. On the other side of the creek, just past the bridge, there was an encampment of the carnival people, with their wagons in a circle. I headed for the carnival entrance.

The area had been roped off, to guide people to the entrance gate. I went to the front gate, where the ticket salesman seeing my badge, waived me through.

There were various tents and partitioned booths lining both sides of a wide aisle. In some of the tents there were people performing acrobatics, pretty girls dancing, knife throwing, tight rope walking, and the like. Some of the booths had games of skill or chance. There was a juggler walking through the crowd and the man on stilts was selling balloons. Pretty much everything here was designed to provide entertainment while separating people from their money. I wandered around for a little while, just letting people see that the law was represented.

Eventually I came to a fortune teller's tent. I read the sign "*Madame Cleopatra, Sooth Sayer and Palm Reader; have your fortune told for twenty five cents.*"

I ducked inside.

There was a woman in a colorful dress, with a white, peasant style blouse. She was laying out the ever popular Tarot cards. She had her dark hair pulled back and tied with a bright silk scarf. Her back was turned as I entered. I had pulled my hat down over my eyes before I came in, and I ducked my head as she started to turn toward me, so when she turned to look at me, we couldn't see each other's faces.

"Hello mother," I said, spreading my arms and looking up.

She was still beautiful after all those years. Her dark eyes sparkled, as she broke into a smile, but the woman who stood before me wasn't my mother!

"Hello, John." Katya said.

8.

I was completely overwhelmed by the memories of our years together, of our years apart, of my time spent searching for her, and of all the changes that come with the experience of this life. I was at first, speechless, then simply at a loss for words. My mind whirled and when at last I spoke, I was only able to say four words.

"Where is our son?"

***

Decades had passed, since I had been the ten year old boy who staggered into their circle of firelight. I was nearly frozen, half naked, and covered in blood. Some of the blood was my own.

That group of Romani had saved my life, and since I had no one else, become my family. Sasha and Kergi Borostoya, were the leaders of this band of Romani. They had no children, so Sasha became my mother and Kergi became my father.

We had traveled thousands of miles together. The Romani are travelers, always on the move. Some are horse traders, tinkers, skilled laborers, entertainers, and the like. Over the years, I had learned many useful skills.

Katya was my first love.

When I was twenty, I took a job in one of the towns where we had been camped, and persuaded Katya to be my wife. I had tried to make a life with Katya, and she had tried to make it work. We had a son, who we named Nicolai. But life in a town, apart from her people, was not for Katya. She was heartsick and miserable.

One day, while I was gone driving a herd of cattle to Cheyenne, she took our son and joined a different band of Romani, who happened to be passing through. They were her people, and distant relatives, so they were happy to have her, I suppose.

By the time I returned to Texas, they had already been gone for a month. It took me seventeen more days to catch up with that band of travelers. When I did, Katya and Nicky were no longer with them. Pleading and threatening were of no use. No information about where my wife and son had gone was given me.

After months of searching and many false leads, I eventually had to stop looking for them..

I would go home to Sasha and Kergi, whenever I could, whenever their travels brought them close enough. Sasha always told me she had heard good things, and all was well with Katya and Nicolae, but she did not know where they were. I would leave money with Kergi, and he would see to it their needs were met, somehow. After many years, I eventually gave up any hope of finding them, and got on with my life.

As I was pondering these things, a man parted the curtains behind Katya, and held them open.

"John," Sasha cried, as she rushed into the tent and threw her arms around me. "My son is home again."

We hugged, and I held her out at arm's length. Her hair was more silver than black now, her face more deeply etched, but the tears in her eyes did not mar the beauty and the wisdom there.

"How long has it been, this time?" she asked.

"Too long, mother…about three years, I think."

"Three years, this month, it was in New Orleans, wasn't it? Thank God you were there."

"I'm so glad to find you here," I said. "I was on my way to see you; I heard y'all were in Wyoming."

"We were, but there were not enough towns, and it is time we are heading south, before winter comes."

"Will you be going to Texas?"

"No, John. We will go down into New Mexico and then head west."

She turned to indicate the man who had opened the curtains for her. She introduced us.

"John, this is Matthew Vilokova. Matthew, meet my son… John Sage."

I was aware of the way Katya was watching us. We shook hands.

"Matthew is our leader now, John," Sasha said, giving me a look I could not interpret.

"Oh? Where is my father?" I asked, hoping I was reading the whole thing wrongly.

Sasha put her hands on my shoulders.

"John, I am so sorry…Kergi was killed in a wagon wreck, coming down a mountain, back in the spring."

She put her face against my chest, and I held her. There were tears in my eyes now.

Katya motioned to Matthew, who silently stepped out of the tent, leaving the three of us alone.

We spent some moments with our grief, then Sasha sniffed and wiping her eyes, she motioned we should sit at the table.

She held my right hand in both of hers on the table top, and looked me in the eye.

"John, everything that has been done, has been done according to our customs, and the Roma Law." She said. "You have a right to know your son...and you have a right to claim leadership of our people."

I raised my eyebrows.

"You are the son of Kergi Alexiev Borostoya. You have the right to leadership of our people, by direct succession. Do you understand?"

"Mother, I was not born Romani..."

She made a cutting motion with her hand.

"According to our customs and Roma Law, John, it is your right. Among us, you are 'Vlad', a prince. Beyond that, everyone knows you and respects you. You have served and protected our people. What you did in New Orleans has become a story told among us, in every camp. Matthew was only chosen as our leader because you were not home with us."

I was again overwhelmed and confused.

"You need some time to think on this," She said.

She looked at Katya, and nodded.

"John, Nicky is here, with us. He is working now, but you can see him later." Katya said.

I looked at her.

"There is something else...Matthew and I, are married now. We have been for several years."

Sasha reached out and turned my face toward hers. She held my eyes,

"John, you must think and pray about these things. Go away from here, for a while. We will meet again to discuss your decision tonight, after the townspeople go home. Already they are leaving. Tonight, we will celebrate your return home, no matter your decision. Come back tonight and you will see your son."

It was the custom of our people, not to allow the "townies" to be among us after dark, nothing good could come of it. Over the centuries, we had learned the dangers associated with staying too long in one place, or of having townspeople get too close. They did not trust us, and we did not trust them. Most of the townies wanted to get home before dark, anyway.

I left the tent, and as I was leaving the carnival, I was watching everyone with new eyes. We all learned to juggle and walk on stilts. We all learned to operate all of the games. Many of us were trained in a variety of acrobatics, sleight of hand, or "specialty" skills, according to our talents. My son could be any of these Romani. Which one was he?

As I was pondering this, a commotion broke out in the tent where the girls who did the Kheliben dancing were performing. I ducked inside.

Roma Kheliben dancing is ancient. It is as old as the Romani. We brought it with us from the Middle East. To some it has been considered scandalous and lascivious. To us it is common and respected as a dance form. To many of the men in the towns, it is an exotic spectacle, for which they are willing to pay. Sometimes they make the mistake of thinking the girls are of questionable morals, or simply prostitutes. They are wrong. They might not make the same assumption about ballet dancers. Regardless; we protect our girls and do not tolerate lewd or offensive conduct toward them, from anyone.

Inside the tent, two of the Romani men were down and appeared to be injured. The cause of the commotion was the man from the Ox Bow, who had tried to impress me with his toughness.

He was pawing at the only girl who had failed to escape from the tent.

"Hey, Bob," I called as I approached him, "Where'd you find that gal?"

He crouched over her.

"Geshur own," he growled.

It was obvious he'd been drinking all day.

He narrowed his eyes when I got right up close to him.

"You that gummen," he slurred. "I'll brekyu laka twig."

I slowly held up both my hands, very high, so he could see that I was not reaching for my gun.

"Now, Bob, you know I'm your friend." I said, as I looked up at my right hand, just above his head

He looked up at it too.

I hit him in the throat with my left hand, and as he started to reach up to clutch his throat, I hit him with two hard blows to the midsection and one to the crotch. He doubled over. I only hesitated a second, then I brought my knee up hard, into his face.

He flew over backward, and crashed down on the platform.

Romani men rushed in, led by Matthew. They had daggers and guns in their hands.

I don't like to take advantage of a drunk. Bob was just too dangerous to take chances with. He was too big to fight. I would have had to kill him. The Romani certainly would have killed him.

I also don't like to injure my hands. So, if I have to hit someone, I generally hit them in soft tissue, or bend my gun barrel over their head.

The Romani men gathered around.

"His nose is broken," I said. "Make sure he doesn't choke to death on his own blood. Throw him in a wagon, and drop him off at the doctor's office."

I told them where it was.

"Tell the doctor *I* did this to him. Tell him why."

I walked out.

DAN ARNOLD

9.

As I walked back toward town, I noticed it had become cloudy, and the wind was picking up. The weather matched my mood. The horse races were over, and some folks with horses and buggies were headed east on the road, but I was part of a general migration back toward town. Now that all the festivities were over, people were going home.

I remembered the hotel clerk had mentioned the Governor would be staying out at the Bar C. I hadn't seen the big fancy wagon go by. I figured it had probably left earlier to get out to the Bar C, before dark.

Somebody once wrote: "It matters little where we've been, or where we're headed. It matters most, who we are." Somebody else said: "It matters not what road we take, but who we become, on the journey." I know the truth; the trail we choose, will greatly determine who we will become on the journey. The Christian life is a narrow trail and few there are who find it. One has to watch their step. Open roads are easy to find, and there is usually a lot of traffic. The road to hell is broad, well paved, and jammed with traffic. The narrow trail can be rough and lonely.

I had a lot to think about.

When I came to the Mexican quarter, I took my time and wandered around a bit. I heard beautiful guitar music coming from an old adobe building that had a fresh coat of whitewash. As I approached, I realized I had found the cantina. I listened to the guitar for a moment, but I didn't go inside.

When I got back to the Marshal's office, Tom was still there, alone. He said he hadn't seen Jack, all afternoon. I started to fill him in on my experiences of the day, when the door opened. Jack came in, carrying a covered tray.

"I stopped at the Bon Ton and had an early supper. Here's Rawlins grub," he said nodding at the tray. "Looks like it's gonna rain."

Tom took the tray back into the jail, to give to Rawlins. When he came back out, Jack told him to go on home, and have supper with Becky. He indicated we would both be needed on the street after dark.

"This town is getting too big, to walk a patrol from one end to another, or be able to get across in an emergency. The city council has voted to pay for two more deputies. I sure would like it, if you would stick around here and be one of them," Jack said, looking at me.

There was a knock on the front door, so Jack went over and opened it. Standing there was one of the Romani men. He had a big bruise started under one eye, and the eye was swelling shut. I recognized him as one of the two men who had tangled with Bob. He had his hat in his hand and he was fidgeting.

"What can I do for you?" Jack asked.

"Mr. Marshal, the doctor told me to come and tell you, Bob Maxwell will have to spend the night with him, for observation." He blurted.

He was staring at me, the whole time.

"OK, thanks," Jack said.

He started to ask a question, but the man turned and left, in a hurry.

Jack closed the door.

"I wonder what that was about," he said.

I gave him a rough account of my two encounters with Bob.

"Wow." Jack said. "That's good work. Bob Maxwell is one tough teamster, and the best muleskinner I ever saw. He can handle an ox team like nobody's business. That's why he's the foreman of the teamsters working for the Atwater Freight Company. He's usually not a problem, but when he gets his drink loaded on, he gets mean and somebody always gets hurt. Never him though."

He gave me an appraising look.

"I knew having that damn carnival in town was going to cause trouble. You just can't trust those gypsies. We'll have to run them out of town, tomorrow," he said, shaking his head.

"I'll go back out there tonight, and ask them to move on," I volunteered. "That way, there won't be anyone to file charges against our Mr. Maxwell. He won't be tempted to go back out there and start more trouble, either."

Jack looked at me.

"I hate to ask you to do that. It might be dangerous."

"Oh, I think I can handle it," I said, trying to keep a straight face.

"Yeah, you probably can at that." He nodded. "OK, be careful. It's Saturday night, and things can get rough on that side of town. I'll stay here with our prisoner. When Tom gets back, I'll have him hit the streets."

By the time I got back out to the carnival site, all the tents and booths had been taken down and packed up. There were cooking fires going, and the wonderful smell made my stomach growl with anticipation. We would be feasting on the fatted calf, tonight

Matthew took me to his brightly painted wagon. It was much like a sheepherder's wagon, only somewhat larger. It had a hard roof and walls, even windows with glass in them. There was a built in bed on each side that you could sit on, and a table with two chairs, even a small stove. The lamps were lit inside. It was getting dark because of the heavy cloud cover. We sat at his table and he brought out a bottle of wine. We talked and drank a little wine. We found common ground.

After a little while, he left. A moment later, a young man came into the wagon. It took me a moment to realize who he was. It was Nicolai, my son.

"Hello, sir," he said, somewhat formally.

I couldn't help myself; I got up from the table and embraced him

"Nicky, you're a grown man!"

It was all I could think to say.

"Father, I am so glad to finally see you again." He said, as though he were starting a well-rehearsed speech.

"Nicky, I couldn't find you…" I interrupted.

We stared at each other, for a moment.

"Let's sit down," I suggested.

"I know you were looking for us, sir. When I was a very small child, I never thought about not having my father with us. You know how it is, we're a tight community and we all raise the children as if each were our own. As I got older, I realized you were somewhere else. I heard stories about you, of course. Mother let me know who you were, and how proud I should be, to be your son. I know the things you have done for our people. For many years, we were with a different band of Romani. When we would occasionally see Grandmamma and Grand poppa, they told me stories of when *you* were a boy.

I smiled at the idea of calling Sasha and Kergi, by those childish informalities.

"Why wouldn't anyone let me find you?"

"It is…complicated."

He struggled for an appropriate word.

There are so many times when a single word, must be used to account for all the convoluted subtleties and brutal realities of a situation.

"I understand, some of it," I said. "It's partly my own fault. I left the family. I took your mother with me. I wasn't born Roma. I…"

"It was thought it would be best, for everyone, sir," He interrupted. "You must know, this is not the first time this sort of thing has happened. We are a nation of mixed blood. You are not the property of the Romani. You are not perfect. You are a man. You must do what it is, that God has put into you to do. Mother is not perfect. It is not your fault she could not stay away from our people, and it is not her fault, you could not stay with us. It is, what it is."

I was amazed at his logic and that he had thought it through so well. I was overcome with pride in him, and humility at the fact I had nothing to do with how well he had turned out. I found myself with tears rolling down my face.

He stood, as if to go.

"Wait,' I croaked

I stood up quickly.

We embraced. This time he hugged me.

"Father, I want you to meet my fiancée."

There were tears in his eyes, as well.

"What? You're getting married? Well, you really are a grown man," I grinned.

Her name was Rachel Tullosa, and she was a beauty. She had striking red hair and a dancer's grace. It was good to see my son had excellent taste!

We all sat together to eat at a table set up outside. There was a campfire and eventually everyone gathered around it. Some of the children looked at me shyly, half hidden behind their mother's skirts.

Soon the musicians began to play their violins, tambourines, balalaikas, guitars, castanets, drums and pipes. It was a magical time. For me it could not last long enough. This music was like the rhythm of my heart. It raced and danced in my blood. It spoke of joy and it spoke of sorrow. It spoke of inner strength and determination. It spoke of things long lost and things yet to be discovered. It was ancient and contemporary, this music of my soul.

As the mother's began to gather the little children for bed, I knew it was time for me to address the things which needed to be said. I caught Matthew's eye and he nodded. At the next break in the music, he stepped forward and motioned for the musicians to put down their instruments.

When I stood up, a hush fell over the people.

"I am, John Everett Sage, son of Kergi Alexiev Borostoya. I have the right to claim leadership of our people. After the death of my father, while I was gone, you chose Matthew to be your leader. That is good. He is a good man, and he has been a good father to my son.'

I looked at Matthew. He had his arms crossed and was looking into the fire.

"I am honored that you would even consider me for your leader, but I cannot leave this place. Not now. There is a thing I must do. I have asked Matthew to lead you, in my absence."

I looked around the group. Many were nodding and I could see relief on Katya's face.

"I cannot say when, or if, I will be able to return home to you. Matthew has agreed to lead, for as long as I am unable to. Upon my death, my son Nicolai will become the leader, as is his right as a direct descendent of his grandfather, my father, Kergi Alexiev Borostoya. This is my word and it is done."

I looked over at Nicky where he was standing with Rachel. He looked shocked. I looked at Katya, and although she was smiling, she was also crying. So was Sasha.

"Enough talk. Let's have some music." I said, not knowing how to move on.

There was dead silence.

Matthew walked over to me, with his arms spread and we embraced. Lightening crackled in the mountains and thunder boomed down through the canyons.

Then the music started up again.

Sasha came to me and led me back to her wagon. This was the same wagon, where as a child, I had lived in, played under, and even played on top of. It seemed to get smaller, every time I saw it.

We went inside and talked about many things. When it was time for me to go, we held each other for a long time.

"My son, you must be careful, there is a storm coming."

"I can see that mother, I'll be fine."

She clutched my hand and looked at me intently.

"No son, this storm is coming to you, in this place," she said, waving her other hand in a circle. "There will be bad trouble, soon."

"I'm a careful man, mother. Don't worry about me. You take care, as well.

I hugged her again and went outside.

Matthew and Nicolai were waiting for me.

10.

I'd stayed too long. It was late and about to storm. The wind had picked up and thunder rumbled, much nearer now.

There is always a storm coming. There will always be trouble in this life. My mother's warning was not prophetic, I thought, as we walked along. No tea leaves needed. No tarot cards or crystal ball, either. It doesn't take a fortune teller, to tell you what you already know. The past is a memory, the future is a dream and we only live in the moment. It is how we live in the moment that matters. The future is not to be found in crystal balls or tarot cards. It is determined by the will of God and the choices we make.

As we walked into town, we talked for a while. Finally, as we neared the railroad tracks, Matthew turned to me.

"As you and I discussed earlier, we will leave tonight. We'll go directly south from here, to avoid the town, and then work our way down to Denver, then on to New Mexico. I plan to take us all the way to California." He looked at me. "John, if you need anything, anywhere, at any time…" He trailed off.

"Matthew, I can never thank you enough, or repay you, for the way you have cared for my family and our people. Go with God"

We shook hands, and he turned back toward the campsite, leaving Nicky and me alone.

Nicky and I walked on in silence, for a little while.

Presently, he spoke up.

"Dad, I have to go back now."

"I know, son. Thank you for spending this time with me. Take care of your mother and grandmother for me." I paused. "Nicky, I am very proud of you." I rasped.

We were hugging, not far from the front door of the Ox Bow, when Tom walked up on us. The look on his face was priceless.

"I got worried about you." Tom said. "Jack told me you were going back out to the gypsy camp. When I didn't see you anywhere, I figured I'd better check on you. I was on my way over there, now."

"Tom, I'd like you to meet my son, Nicky." I said. I was immediately embarrassed, for having called him "Nicky."

"Nicolai, this is my friend, Tom Smith."

I saw Nicky looking at Tom's badge, as they shook hands.

"I'm pleased to meet you, Mr. Smith. My friends call me Nick." He said, looking at me.

I smiled and nodded. "Nick it is. Nick Sage. It has a nice ring to it."

Tom smiled.

"It's a small world, huh? Were you expecting to run into each other?"

Nick and I looked at each other, and grinned.

"…Not hardly," I said. "I couldn't have had a better surprise."

"Well, it's a night for surprises," Tom said. "It's been real quiet. There's been no trouble at all. Maybe it's because of the storm that's coming, or maybe everybody has had enough fun for one day. Whatever the reason, it's unusually quiet. I'm about ready to call it a night."

Nicky took that as his cue to leave.

"I'll say good night here then, Dad. You know where to find us. Don't be gone so long, next time. Nice meeting you, Deputy Smith." He started to walk off, but he turned and said. "Dad, be safe." He held up a hand, in a kind of wave and turned back down the street. In a moment, he was gone.

I was struggling with many emotions, but one thing was clear. He had called me, *Dad*!

"He looks just like you," Tom ventured. "Taller though," He added, grinning.

Tom and I walked over into the Mexican section and swung by the cantina. There was soft guitar music, being played inside, and no other sound. We went in and drank some lukewarm beer, in the soft light of the lanterns, enjoying the peace and the quiet sound of the lone guitar.

"It's almost eerie," Tom observed. "It's never this quiet on a Saturday night, or any other night on this side of town"

We left and walked back toward the square.

When we got to the square, we stopped and looked around. There was no one to be seen. The wind was blowing some trash around, and there was piano music coming from the Palace. It was subdued, popular music, and there was nothing else going on. It was apparent most people were sheltered from the storm.

"John, I'm gonna go home and go to bed. Will you do me a favor?" He asked.

"Sure. What is it?" I asked.

"Well, we like to go to church as a family on Sunday morning, and Jack won't leave the jail unattended, when we have prisoners. Would you hang out in the office, while we go to church?" He was very earnest.

"Of course, I'll be happy to. What time should I be there?"

We decided since the church service was at nine o'clock, I should get to the office at about eight thirty, in the morning.

"What about Rawlins breakfast?" I asked.

"Jack will get him fed, at about eight o'clock," Tom said.

We bid each other a good night.

I walked on down to the Marshal's office. It was dark. There was faint lamplight from behind the shade in the window of Jack's room. The front door was locked. It was starting to spit some rain. I went back to the hotel and found my bed.

I lay there thinking about the day.

Roma Law was developed as a system of self-governance. The Romani had started out in the Middle East or Asia, possibly northern India, and traveled throughout Europe. Because there was intermarriage, everywhere they traveled, perhaps the Romani were technically Eurasian. Over the centuries we had learned that laws changed with the national borders, even differing from town to town. We also learned, through horrible experience, travelers have no rights.

So, we have our own law.

I had only been with the Romani for a little over ten years, and there was far more about Roma Law I didn't know, than there was that I did know.

I was in no way qualified to lead the Romani. Oh, I might have learned, as I went along. Sasha and the other elders would have counseled me, but it was not my place. If I had claimed my right to become leader, it might not have been just the leader of our little band of forty some people. A leader of the Romani has many duties and functions. Matthew would be a good leader. He had traveled with other bands and was well known and highly respected. He was qualified, in every way.

Nick was, in some ways, more his son than mine. One day Nick would lead our people, having earned that right through both succession and apprenticeship.

Matthew had promised this to me.

I hoped I had gotten one other thing right. The money I placed in Sasha's care would be my wedding present to my son. Sasha would see that Nick got the money, and Matthew would help him choose and purchase a good wagon and team for himself and Rachel. There would also be enough money for Rachel's dowry. Matthew insisted on paying for any other expense. That left me with about five hundred dollars.

It had been very hard for me to stand in front of my family and all the people, and tell them that yet once again, I could not be counted on. Once again, I would not be with them. Once again, I would choose a different path.

It was clear to me I was, after all was said and done, still just another "Townie."

11.

The storm hit hard, just as I started to go to sleep. A flash of lightening and immediate crash of thunder rattled my window. Right behind that, a curtain of rain hit the town like a cow peeing on a flat rock. The electric fireworks passed over fairly quickly, but the rain continued in earnest. I fell asleep to the sound of pelting rain, but in my mind, I heard the music of the Roma people.

A little before eight o'clock the next morning, I hustled over to the Marshal's office. I wanted to give Jack the option of sending me to get Rawlins breakfast, so he wouldn't have to run that errand in the rain. Because my slicker was on my saddle in the livery stable I had to race through the rain, from one covered stretch of boardwalk, to an awning, then a porch.

When I made it to the office, I stood on the porch for a moment and drained most of the water off my hat.

The door wasn't locked, so I went inside expecting to find some hot coffee on the stove. I was disappointed. The stove had gone out and there was no coffee. Jack wasn't there, either. I figured he had already gone to get himself and Rawlins some breakfast.

I started a fire in the stove. There was some water in a pitcher, so I poured it into the coffee pot and got some coffee started on the stove. I sat behind the desk, putting my feet up on it.

It seemed odd that Jack had left the door unlocked while he was out…and why would he let the stove go out, when it was wet and cold outside? Something wasn't right.

I went to check on the prisoner. When I looked in the cell everything appeared normal. He was lying kind of curled up with his back toward me and he had the shabby blanket pulled over him.

"Morning, Mr. Rawlins." I called "Do you need to use the privy?"

No response.

I realized he was too still.

"Hey!" I yelled, banging on the cell door. It was now clear he was not going to move.

I ran back into the office and got the key off the peg. I ran back to the cell and unlocked it. Throwing the cell door open, I walked over to the man on the bed. When I touched him, he was cold and stiff.

It wasn't Rawlins body lying on the bed.

It was Jack and he was dead.

He'd been dead for some time, probably for several hours.

When I pulled the blanket back, it was apparent he had been stabbed, just under the breast bone. His shirt was stiff with drying blood, and the flimsy, straw stuffed mattress under him, was nearly saturated. He was lying in a pool of congealed blood. He'd been put on the bed and covered up, after he was stabbed. I looked at the floor and saw big drops of dried blood. I hadn't noticed them before.

I left the cell and wandered back into the office, in a daze. How had this happened? Where was Rawlins? What should I do? How would I tell Becky and Tom?

After a moment, I went outside, locking the office behind me. I ran to the doctor's office and raced up the stairs, to his residence. I pounded on his door and he opened it, almost instantly, startling me. He was obviously dressed for church.

"Doctor Johnson, I'm John Sage…" I began.

"I know who you are. What's the problem?"

I told him what had happened.

"Doc, I don't know where anybody lives, except Tom and Becky. I need you to find the Judge and the Mayor and meet me at the Marshal's office. I'll go tell Tom and Becky what's happened." I said miserably.

He put his hands in his pockets and thought for a moment.

"No." He said. "I'll send Bob Maxwell to get the Judge and the Mayor. You and I will go to Tom and Becky's house. Since we have to go right past the church to get there, we'll pick up the Pastor on the way."

I had forgotten all about Bob Maxwell.

He was downstairs, lying on a bed in a room behind the office, but he was awake. He looked like hell. Both eyes were going black and the doc had stuffed his nose with cotton, and taped it. I knew he was probably sick as a dog. He probably felt like he was going to die, just from the hangover.

"Bob, you have a bit of a concussion, from your, uh…shall we say 'encounter', with the deputy here. You need to take it easy for a few days. You can go on home, but first, the deputy needs you to do him a favor."

Bob looked at me and ducked his head.

"Listen, Deputy Sage, I sure am sorry about last night. I don't know what come over me. I know I shouldn't drink, but sometimes I do. No hard feelings?" He asked bashfully.

"OK, Bob. You were lucky this time. There will be no charges. Will you go to the Mayor's house and ask him to meet me at the Marshal's office in about an hour? I also need you to tell the Judge the same thing."

Doctor Johnson was looking at his pocket watch. As he snapped it shut, he said, "We'll find the Judge at the church. Bob, just have the Mayor meet us at the Marshal's office. That's all, Bob. Go on now," he waved Bob out the door.

"Come along, deputy, we want to get to the church before the service starts."

As we headed that way, sloshing through the rain, we could hear the church bell ringing. When we reached the church, Tom and Becky were already going inside with some other folks. With this weather, no one was standing around outside. They hadn't even seen us. We had to follow them inside.

That was one of the worst and best times I have ever experienced in a church. It was the worst because we had to tell Becky her dad was dead. It was the best, because the pastor and the entire congregation wrapped Tom and Becky in their love and support. The pastor's wife, Mildred, latched on to Becky and wouldn't let her go with Tom and me back to the Marshal's office. Becky wanted to see her dad, right away, but Mildred and others told Becky to wait just a little while and she could see him at the mortician's. I was grateful for that. Doctor Johnson stayed there with her, in case he was needed. It was clear he wouldn't be needed at the jail.

I hated to have Tom come with me, leaving his wife behind, but he was coming, and that, was that. The three of us, Tom, Judge Tucker and I, walked in silence through the pouring rain to the Marshal's office.

Mayor Larkin was waiting on the porch. I unlocked the door and we went inside. Only Tom, the Judge and I, looked at the scene of the murder. The Mayor did not care to see it, and I don't blame him.

We heard a knock on the back door of the jail. I walked over and unlocked it. There were two men standing there in the rain. I could tell by the rig behind them, they were there for Jack's body. The mortician had been at the church.

Back in the office, we started addressing the issues at hand. I looked in the drawer where Rawlins' gun had been, it was gone. He had taken Jack's gun as well. I wasn't surprised.

"How did this happen?" Tom asked. "How did Rawlins get a knife and how did he get Jack to open the cell door?"

I didn't want to tell Tom. Jack was not as careful as he should have been. When he disarmed us, he had let us touch our weapons. That shouldn't have happened. When he locked us up, he never patted us down, or had us empty our pockets. Rawlins had a knife hidden on him the whole time. I had one myself. I also had a hide-out .38 in a shoulder holster. Evidently Jack had been unaware of it, or had ignored it.

Rawlins knife must have had at least a six inch blade and he knew exactly how to kill a man with it, very quickly. He was patient and waited for the right opportunity. He waited and planned. Once the crowds emptied away and the rain came, he had his chance. Poor jack was compassionate, so it had been easy for Rawlins to fake being sick or hurt, luring Jack to his death. Rawlins was a cold and calculating killer. Jack never had a chance.

"I guess Rawlins had a knife hidden away somewhere. Tom, Becky needs you. You should go to her." I said.

"We have to find that son of a bitch." Tom swore.

"I understand how you feel, Tom, but he's probably long gone from here and in this rain, we can't hope to find any sign of where he went. We'll find him. Wherever he goes, we'll find him, but Becky needs you, now."

Mayor Larkin cleared his throat. "We have two men dead and a killer on the loose. I hate to bring it up now, but we need a new Marshal." He paced a little and we waited.

"Tom, do you feel like you should take over as Marshal?"

He looked at Tom, solemnly.

"No sir. I can't. I don't think I have enough experience…and, you know…" He trailed off, looking down at the floor.

"What," I asked, "did I miss something?"

There was an awkward silence. Then Tom sighed and looked up at me.

"I can't read. I mean, I can, a little. Becky is teaching me, but…"

He looked back down at the floor.

I thought about it for a moment. A Marshal had to be able to read and write. Tom was a good man, but he couldn't really do everything the job required.

The Mayor and the Judge looked at me. I knew what was coming.

"Mr. Sage, I can't think of anyone in this town, better qualified than you. Will you take the job?" Judge Tucker asked.

There was nowhere else I needed to be, no longer a reason for me to move on. We discussed a number of things, but in the end, I said "yes", pending approval of the city council.

We agreed on certain terms, which I hated to haggle over, under the circumstances, but I knew from previous experience that clarity was essential, right from the get go. I had a written list of rules that I always enforced in every town I worked. Back in Texas, my list of rules had come to be called "Sage Law."

The Judge looked over the list. He nodded his approval, telling me, most of the rules on my list were already ordinances in Bear Creek.

Finally, the Judge said, "Raise your right hand and repeat after me…"

12.

Tom took off, to go be with Becky. I told the Mayor and the Judge I needed to send some telegrams. I also had a possible lead to follow and I would be gone for most of the rest of the day. I took a moment to write a note, tucking it in my vest pocket.

The streets, which had been so heavily populated with families enjoying the festivities, were now completely empty, and had turned to mud.

By the time I finished at the telegraph office, the rain stopped.

I headed over to the livery stable. Just as I suspected, the latch and lock on the front of the barn had been broken away. Lying in the mud where he had dropped it, there was a long piece of pig iron. Rawlins had taken it from the side of the blacksmith's shop.

Inside the barn, I discovered that his horse and tack were gone. Again, this was exactly as I had expected.

He had ridden out of town several hours ago, covered by the rain and darkness. No one would have seen him go and the rain had erased any hope of tracking him.

I took the note I'd written at the Marshal's office out of my pocket. It said simply:

"*Al,*

Marshal Jack Watson has been killed. The killer broke in here and took his horse, to make his escape. I have borrowed Willy's horse, to pursue the suspect. Any charges for the rental will be paid by the city. Thank you." I had signed it, *"Marshal Sage."*

I stuck the note in the crack at the edge of the office door.

I found my saddle and gear where Al had put it, when it was sent over from the freight depot. I took my riata off my saddle and went out to the pens behind the barn. I found Willy's line-back dun and eased the loop over his head. I petted him some and talked to him quietly for a moment and then I took him back into the barn. I gave him a quick grooming to get him dry and fairly clean before I saddled him. After I saddled him, I checked my rifle, led him outside, tightened my cinch and mounted.

I walked the gelding up to the railroad depot and turned right. We walked on past the stage depot and the post office, to Omaha Street, and the freight yard.

I thought about how well the layout worked. The mail came in on the train with the passengers. The mail was sorted at the post office and then the stage line carried the mail and any passengers on to the outlying towns. The stages also brought mail and passengers back to the railroad from those towns.

We crossed the railroad tracks on Omaha, and I trotted him in the mud, on through that part of town and all the way to where the carnival had been. The dun gelding was relaxed and confident, and he didn't mind the mud.

When we reached the place beside the road where the carnival had been, there was no sign it had ever been there. The Roma have learned to leave nothing behind that could cause someone to come after them with a charge or a fine for littering or destruction of property.

At the campsite, the latrines had been filled in and the sod put back. The stones where the fire rings had been were returned to the creek and where the fires had been the sod had also been put back. Even the manure from the horses and mules had been scattered. The rain had done the rest.

I thought about Rawlins maybe coming this way in the rain. There was no sign of him either.

I was glad the Roma would have been gone for hours before he passed through here, if he had even come this way.

As the sun broke through the clouds, I turned the gelding back on to the road and we headed east.

We passed a couple of farmhouses along the road and then it was mostly open range for about three miles. I love open range. The road was fairly straight, only winding around and through some low hills. Much of the time it ran right alongside the creek. That ended when I came to a corner post of a barbed wire fence. The fence crossed the creek and disappeared off to the north over a hill. To the east, it continued in a straight line parallel to the road. Eventually, the creek wandered off somewhere to the north, somewhere on the other side of the fence and I couldn't see or hear it anymore. The barbed wire fence continued on for about a mile.

I hate barbed wire. I had seen it slowly boxing up the range land, all over Texas. It was a great benefit to some of the ranchers, but it changed a whole way of life. Now it was getting harder and harder to travel cross country. More and more land was bounded by barbed wire, keeping livestock in and everyone who didn't own the land, out. Back in Texas, there had been many men killed in the clashes involving barbed wire.

Free grazing on the open range was nearly gone. And that wire was brutal on any animal or person who tangled with it. I was glad there was still some open country here.

There had been range wars fought over the barbed wire fences, in various parts of the country.

I was thinking about all that, when I came to the gap in the wire at the entrance to the Bar C. It was a fancy entrance. On each side of the ranch road was a big flat stone, standing upright in the ground, with a Bar C brand carved into it. There were two tall poles, holding up a wrought iron sign, which arched over the entrance. Worked in the wrought iron, was one word. "Courtney."

"Yep, this must be it." I thought.

The barbed wire continued on east, for as far as I could see.

I turned the dun horse north, down the ranch road, with barbed wire on both sides, following it for about a mile. We stopped at the top of a hill and looked down on the ranch headquarters, at the end of the road. It was a beautiful sight.

Bear Creek, lined with giant cottonwoods, wandered along below a bluff. On this side of the creek were corrals and barns, and a single story, log and stone bunkhouse with a porch on the front. There was a stone bridge spanning the creek and on the far side of the creek, on the top of a rise, with the bluff towering above it, the big ranch house sprawled.

It was a two story house, made of peeled, lodge pole pine logs and stone, with a huge porch on three sides. The porch had a rail around it built of smaller pine logs and the roof was supported by stone columns. The house had been built on high ground, at the base of the bluff and there were various out buildings nearby. There wasn't much activity going on, it being late on a Sunday morning.

I rode on down the hill.

As I got closer, I could see there were some cowboys lounging on the porch of the bunkhouse. One of them stood up and walked out to meet me.

"Howdy," he said. "Can I help you?" He was eyeing my badge and gun.

I stayed up on my horse. "My name is John Everett Sage. I'm the new Marshal in Bear Creek. I need to speak to Mr. Courtney."

"OK. I'm the foreman, Glen Corbet," he said, reaching up to shake my hand.

"Is he expecting you?" He asked, nodding his head over toward the big house.

"No, he isn't. Can I ask you a question, Mr. Corbet?"

"Sure, go ahead."

"Has a man named Ed Rawlins been here, at any time you can recall?"

"Not that I know of," he said, thoughtfully. "Course, I don't meet everybody that visits."

That made sense.

"Let me ask you this then…did anybody ride in here early this morning, maybe about daybreak, on a big bay gelding?"

"It was pouring down rain at that time, and we were all pretty much still in bed. A couple of the boys were out feeding and doing some chores. Nobody mentioned a rider coming in. You're the only person we've seen coming down the road today. Now, let me ask you a question. Why are you looking for this fella?"

I told him the story.

"We'd better go on up to the big house and talk to the boss. I'll walk up there with you. You can tie your horse up here or you can put him in that empty pen over there, if you want." He indicated a nearby breaking pen.

I never tie a horse by the bridal reins if I can avoid it, so I was glad to be able to turn him out in the pen.

We walked across the bridge over the creek, then up the hill to the big house.

13.

The house was even more beautiful and massive from the bottom of the stairs. It was at least as big as, and probably bigger than the courthouse in Bear Creek. Just standing in the shade on the porch was like being in a pole barn.

Glen turned the bell crank by the enormous front door. After a few moments it was opened by a man in a tuxedo!

"Mr Corbet, how nice to see you, we were expecting you," he said. He turned toward me and raised his eyebrows.

"Fred, this is the marshal from Bear Creek. He needs to talk to Mr. Courtney," the foreman said.

"Oh, I see. Well then, do come in. I'll go get him."

We stepped into a big room with a flagstone floor. It took me a second to realize this was just the foyer. There was a long hallway off to our left, and a pair of double doors off to our right. On the far side of the foyer, was a broad staircase that divided, with one branch going up to the left wing, and the other to the right. The whole staircase was covered with a burgundy colored carpet. The stair rails were elaborately carved. We stood there, with our hats in our hands, on an oriental rug. I was aware of my muddy boots. Directly above us was a huge chandelier.

The man "Fred" left us there and walked over to the big double doors and knocked. We heard some sort of answer from within. He slid the doors open just enough to allow his entry, then turned and closed them behind himself.

"That's Fred, the butler," Glen Corbet said quietly, as we waited.

"Yeah, I got that."

Glen bobbed his head and chuckled.

The big double doors slid open and William Courtney came striding into the foyer. He left the doors open behind him.

"Howdy Glen, you're early. Howdy, Deputy Sage. Where's the marshal?"

He was dressed in jeans and boots, and had a pair of suspenders over a red paid shirt. He looked like he was ready to go chop down a tree.

"Mr. Courtney, Marshal Watson was killed by a prisoner at the jail, in Bear Creek, sometime last night. The prisoner escaped," I said.

"My God, no…not Jack! I can't believe it."

I could tell he was truly shocked.

After a moment he said.

"Surely you didn't ride all the way out here, to tell us that."

"No sir. I was hoping to find some sign of Rawlins. He's the man that most likely killed the marshal. When I got to the ranch, I thought I would come on down and ask if anyone had seen him."

It was more or less the truth.

"Rawlins? That's the name Jack mentioned yesterday. Didn't he kill young Willie? I'd never heard of him till then."

He turned to Glen.

"Has he been here? Has anyone seen him?"

"No Bill, at least not as far as I know. I'll ask the boys, but I'm pretty certain he hasn't been here."

"Glen has been very helpful, Mr. Courtney," I interjected. "It was just a hunch and kind of a faint hope, that he might have come this way."

"Glen, Deputy Sage, how nice to see you," Mrs. Courtney said, as she swept into the room. She stopped when she saw our demeanor.

"What has happened, what's wrong?"

She put her hand to her mouth.

"Gentlemen, let's go into the sitting room," Mr. Courtney said.

He took Mrs. Courtney's arm and led us through the double doors into the other room.

What a room it was. It had a river stone fireplace, so big; a buffalo could have slept in it. The mantle was about eight feet wide, with a lamp on each end and a beautiful gold clock, sitting in the middle of it. Hanging above the mantle, was a big buffalo head. I wondered if they had shot him for sleeping in the fireplace. There were several built in bookshelves that housed hundreds of books. Over near the windows, was a grand piano, at which Lacy Courtney was seated. The floor in this room was the same flagstone, and there were beautiful oriental rugs in each seating area. I say each seating area, because there was more than one. There was one seating area right in front of, and facing the fireplace. Another was over by the piano; a third was at the far end of the room. Each area had great couches and chairs, upholstered in the finest fabrics and leathers.

Seated in the area by the piano was the Governor, and as I mentioned, Lacy Courtney was seated at the piano. They both stood to greet us as we came in.

"Governor, you and Lacy know Glen, of course, and you may remember Deputy Sage." Mr. Courtney said, by way of introduction.

Glen and I shook hands with Governor McGee and said hello to Miss Courtney.

"Let's all have a seat. Deputy Sage has brought us bad news from Bear Creek," Mr. Courtney said, with a motion toward the furniture.

When we were seated, Fred the butler appeared from somewhere to offer refreshments.

"Would anyone care for tea or perhaps some coffee?"

We all declined.

"That will be all Fred. Please tell Melba we'll have one more for Sunday dinner. Thank you," Mr. Courtney said.

I attempted to decline, but was overruled.

"Glen almost always has Sunday dinner with us and it's a treat to have visitors. It's unfortunate it has to be under these circumstances. Ordinarily we would have been at church this morning, but the weather was not conducive," Mrs. Courtney said.

I thought about that. It would take them the better part of two hours to get to town, and another two hours to get back. Church would have to be a serious commitment. I doubted the weather would deter them. I figured they hadn't gone to church because they had the Governor staying with them.

I was especially grateful for the invitation to join them for Sunday dinner. I had only had coffee so far that day, and I was famished.

"Now tell us the situation, Deputy," Governor McGee suggested.

I told them the story from the beginning, including the fact I had been sworn in as the new marshal.

"Poor Becky," Mrs. Courtney said. "As girls, her mother and I were best friends. Now Becky has lost her mother and her father. I'm glad Tom is there for her."

The Governor had been watching me closely while I was speaking.

"Are you the same John Sage, who put an end to that mess down in Raton, New Mexico, a few years ago?"

"I wasn't alone, sir," I replied. "That was a long time ago and a long way from here. I'm surprised you would have heard about it in Denver."

"It was five years ago, and I was the Mayor of Trinidad, when it happened. I read that before it was over, there was a whole company of Rangers killed, and you were the only survivor."

"No sir, there were only five of us Rangers, not a whole company. A company could be anywhere from twenty to forty men. I wish it had been a whole company. The outcome would have been quickly assured. We were only five Rangers, and our tracker, Yellow Horse, was with us. Charlie

Goodnight had told us the Murdock gang was hiding out in the Palo Duro canyon. We figured if we surrounded the gang, we could easily take them. We figured wrong. When we went in to surround them, they slipped past us and ran. We pursued them out of the canyon up onto the high plains. We had kind of a running gun battle for six days, as we chased them north. By the third day, they had managed to wound two of my fellow Rangers. We sent them back under the care of one able bodied man. That left three of us, Billy Whitney, Yellow Horse and me, to maintain the pursuit.

We continued the running fight for three more days. We didn't know when we had left Texas and were in New Mexico. When we got to Raton, we checked in with the Sheriff there. Since it was his jurisdiction, he came with us. We didn't have time to waste forming a posse, so the four of us chased the remaining members of the Murdock gang up into the pass.

Now, when we started the pursuit in Texas, there were only seven men in the Murdock gang, and we had killed Joe Murdock and another man, in the fighting coming north. There were actually only five of them in the pass that last day, and they were shot up some themselves," I reflected. "They had the high ground and set an ambush. They shot our horses out from under us, killing first Billy Whitney, and then the Sheriff of Raton. Yellow Horse and I had to finish them off one at a time, on foot, and at one point, hand to hand.

"So, the fact is, two Rangers were badly wounded and they recovered. Only one Ranger was killed, plus the Sheriff, and Yellow Horse and I both survived. You can't believe everything you read in the papers," I concluded.

Fred came back into the room.

"Dinner is served," he announced.

We enjoyed a fine dinner, though I was ever mindful of the reason for the occasion. In fact, our conversation was mostly centered on it.

"…Well, that's not surprising, Marshal, a lot of horses around here carry the Bar C brand. Glen can explain it," Mr. Courtney said.

I didn't need an explanation. I had clearly seen how fond Mr. Courtney was of slapping his brand on everything in sight.

"We sell a lot of horses, but not all of them are branded, same with the cattle. We only brand the better quality animals. The culls carry no brand at all. We used to brand all of our stock, but now that we have fences, we don't need to. There isn't much chance our stock will get mixed in with anyone else's." Glen explained.

"Now, the big bay gelding you described sounds like a pretty good quality horse. We breed a lot of bays. How much white did he have on him?"

"He had two white stockings on the back legs and a blaze."

"Yeah, we would've probably branded a horse like that. If he had any more white on his legs, we wouldn't have done it. That's also why we gelded him. Good horse, just not good enough."

"A lot of our cowboys ride bay horses, and as I mentioned, we sell a lot of them every year. Of course, if he was an older horse, going back to the days when we were still branding everything…" He shrugged.

"Rawlins showed up at the railway station pretty much when the train arrived. He put his ticket and the freight charge for his horse on your account."

I wanted see if there was any reaction to that.

"That's a nuisance. We'll have to give the depot agents a list of authorized people. We've never had a problem before. I guess the word about us having an account has gotten around. Glen, you go to Bear Creek tomorrow, and get it taken care of," Mr. Courtney directed.

"Bill, we're going to the station tomorrow, to see the Governor off, on the 12:10 to Denver. Perhaps we can do it then," Mrs. Courtney suggested.

"Right, I wasn't thinking. Thank you mother," he beamed at his wife.

"Mr. Courtney, you might want to have Glen and a couple of your cowboys ride along with you on the way to town. Tell them to look to their guns. With a killer on the loose, it doesn't pay to take any chances," I noted.

He looked at me.

"Damned good idea, Marshal! You're welcome to spend the night, and ride into town with us tomorrow."

I was tempted, but I needed to get back to town. I thanked them for the offer, and the lovely Sunday dinner, and took the opportunity to say my goodbyes.

Glen walked back down the hill with me.

"Marshal, have you got any idea where that polecat is?" he asked, as we walked over the stone bridge.

"No, I don't," I admitted. "He could be anywhere."

I was not happy about the prospect of Rawlins having fled the area. Then again, I didn't like the thought he might still be around somewhere, any better.

As I rode back into town, I watched the country around me with care.

The dun proved a really good mount. I liked him a lot and decided to buy him.

When I got back to the livery stable, Al was there feeding the stock.

"Howdy Marshal, I found your note," he said, as I dismounted. "There is no charge for the rental. You can get the loan of a horse, anytime you need one. Any sign of the killer?"

I shook my head, as I loosened the cinch.

"Thanks for the loan, Al. What did Willy call this horse?"

"Willy called him 'Dusty'."

"I like that name. And I like this horse, a lot. Al, will you sell him to me?"

Al frowned.

As I led "Dusty" into the barn, I was thinking, *"Oh boy, here we go. He's going to get every penny he can."*

"I can't sell him," he said.

I thought about it for a minute, as I unsaddled the dun.

"OK, I understand. He was Willy's horse."

He smiled sadly, "Yeah, that's just it. He was Willy's horse. He's not mine to sell. I think Willy would have wanted him to go to someone who really appreciated the horse. I can't think of anyone better than you."

"I couldn't..."

"I insist. It's perfect. You were there when Willy was killed. You're working to catch Willy's murderer. You have a connection to Willy. You need a horse and I can see you and Dusty are a good match. I think Willy would be proud for you to have Dusty, and I sure don't need another mouth to feed. He's yours," he concluded, reaching out to shake my hand.

I was humbled and very thankful.

We arranged boarding for Dusty, and I was glad to know Al would be getting some compensation for his generous gift.

14.

I walked over to visit Tom and Becky. They were getting through it. They had arranged to have the viewing at the mortician's on Monday evening and Jack's funeral at the church on Tuesday afternoon. Tom told me he would be at work first thing in the morning. I told him to take as much time as he needed.

When I got back to the Marshal's office, I took the ruined mattress and bedding out behind the jail and burned them. Then, I scrubbed up the dried blood from the floor of the cell.

That night I did the rounds, checking locks and making sure everything was secure and quiet. It was Sunday night and quiet was the norm in most towns. Even the saloons were closed on Sunday night. When I was sure there was nothing else that needed to be done, I climbed up the stairs to my room at the hotel and surrendered to my exhaustion.

Monday morning found me having breakfast alone, in the Bon Ton. I met with the owner, Henri Levesque, to explain the situation and arrange for an account.

"Oh Monsieur Sage, thees is terrible." He said that last word like 'ter reeb luh', but I knew what he meant

"We weel mees heem so."

Yeah, I got that too.

After breakfast I unlocked the Marshal's office. I went into the room that had been Jack's. It was cozy. There was a sitting area with a bookcase, a table with a lamp and a big wingback chair upholstered in leather. The lamp had burned out. The globe was darkened with soot. Jack's reading glasses were on the table.

From the chair, if the shade was up, you could see out the window. There would be a view of the square. The shade was still pulled closed now. There were only two books on the shelf. One was a collection of Shakespeare's plays; the second was a reading primer.

It seemed Becky was not the only one helping Tom with his reading.

On the floor by the chair, a Bible lay open to the book of 1st Corinthians. There was a bed up against the wall that separated this room from the jail. If there was a commotion in the jail, he would have heard it. Against the remaining wall was a wardrobe with a couple of drawers at the bottom. When I opened it, I found some of Jack's clothes hanging; some more were folded in the drawers. The only other things in the room were a little wood burning stove in a corner and a cowhide rug on the floor.

The bed was still made. Added to the fact he was fully dressed when I found him, it indicated to me that Jack had never gone to bed. He still had his boots on.

He might have been reading when I stopped by the office late the previous night, or he might have already been dead. Maybe the storm hitting had roused him to go check on the prisoner. Maybe

Rawlins had cried out as though in distress. Maybe this, maybe that.

In the end, Jack was dead and Rawlins was long gone. I aimed to see he didn't get away with it.

Tom came in and found me standing there.

He looked like five miles of bad trail.

He surveyed the room and I could see him going through the process.

"He never even went to bed," he said.

I took him back out into the office. We sat down at the desk. I felt awkward sitting behind the desk with Tom in front of me, but there it was.

"Tom, I want you to keep your eyes open and be very, very careful."

"What...why?"

"Just because Rawlins is gone, doesn't mean he won't come back. When he killed Jack, he eliminated the arresting officer. When he escaped from the town, he eliminated the trial. He thinks I was just passing through, and the only reason I stayed in town, was for his trial. He'll figure I have no reason to stay. He probably believes I'll be getting on a train to Wyoming. That leaves you, as the only person who's a threat to him. No one else in this town knows who he is. If he comes back here, he'll probably be ready, willing and possibly even looking, to kill you," I added.

"Why would he even come back here?"

"I'd like to think he won't. You might not be aware of this, but criminals often like to return to the scene of a crime they believe they have gotten away with. He's the kind of man who might do that."

"I've heard that. It seems kind of stupid though."

"He isn't exactly stupid, Tom. It has more to do with his need to feel powerful. He believes he's untouchable, smarter than we are. He needs to feel superior. It's also just possible he might come into town today and attempt to catch a stage, or even get on the train," I mused.

"You've got to be kidding," he said.

"Remember, he thinks you're the only lawman left in town. There is no telling what he might try. Just be alert and watch your back. He probably won't come at you head on. He prefers to kill unarmed men and catch them by surprise, if he can. He will use any advantage he can get. I expect he's gotten away with this sort of thing before. We have a couple of advantages ourselves," I added.

"What are they?" He asked.

"Well, you're not alone. We're ready for him and…"

The door opened and in walked the giant of a man, who was now the new Sheriff of Alta Vista County.

"Good morning, Sheriff Atwater. What brings you by here?" I asked.

"Is it true you beat up my man, Bob Maxwell?"

"I had to subdue him. He was drunk and disorderly and he had assaulted a couple of people," I responded. "Do we have a problem?" I leaned back in my chair.

"There's only one other man who ever beat him, single handed," he started.

I was pretty sure I knew what he was going to say next.

"That man was me," he finished.

"It doesn't surprise me in the least." It was exactly what I expected him to say. "So, do we have a problem?"

"Naw!" He grinned. "I'm just glad the situation got handled. I've seen what happens when he gets drunk. He had it coming."

I was glad he understood.

"He might not be so lucky next time. There were no charges filed this time, but there sure could have been. He would have been facing some jail time and probably a hefty fine."

Atwater nodded his understanding and added,

"I reckon it's worse than that. One of these days he's likely to kill someone, or maybe get killed himself."

I nodded.

"So what can we do for you, Sheriff?"

Tom stood up.

"I'm going to go do my job." He held up a hand. "I know, I heard you, I'll keep my eyes open. Nice to see you, Sheriff," he said, on his way out the door.

The Sheriff took a seat in the vacated chair.

"Well, I'd like to kinda get some direction. I don't like to go down the wrong road. If you know what I mean," he said.

"No Sheriff, I'm not following you," I said, straightening up in my chair.

"You know, with the lawman stuff."

"Could you be more specific? Exactly what is it you want to know?"

He looked around the office for a moment, as he gathered his thoughts

"I come into this part of the country, right after the war, with a good wagon and a team of oxen. I started hauling freight to the mining camps. Pretty soon, I had enough money to buy another wagon and hire some help. I ran mule teams and jerk lines. After a few years, I found myself making a delivery to Bear Creek. The railroad was being built through here then, and I saw the possibilities, right off.

I decided to make my headquarters here and it worked out, real well. I helped build this town. Now, everybody on the Front Range knows Atwater Freight. I got warehouses in Denver, Cheyenne, even Omaha, now. If it gets moved, in this part of the country, Atwater moves it. I don't compete with the railroad, we work hand in glove.

"Yes sir, I'm aware of your success. What are you driving at?"

"I guess the point is, I won the election because everybody knows who I am, but I don't know nothing about being a lawman," he concluded.

I knew he wasn't bragging about his accomplishments. He was just stating the facts. I appreciated his honesty. I was also impressed he had the humility to admit his lack of qualifications. He wasn't the sharpest tool in the shed, but he understood his limitations. He had accomplished a lot, by hard work and determination. He was smart enough to know what he didn't know.

"What was your plan? You had to know if you won the election, there would be a lot you had to learn," I speculated.

"Yeah, I did. I figure to hire people who know what they're doing. I'm no great shakes with numbers and books, so I hired a book keeper. He keeps our accounts straight, so I don't have to. I expect to do the same thing, with lawmen."

I nodded.

"That's a really good plan and the sooner the better. How can I help you?"

We talked for a long time. I explained it was vital to get men who could be trusted. There were plenty of experienced lawmen out there, who were only about one step away from being outlaws. Others would be looking to steal his job. We talked about how important it would be, to have deputies manage the jail, placed in some of the outlying towns and patrolling the roads.

The door opened and a man stuck his head around the corner.

"Howdy" he said "I'm looking for Marshal Watson."

When he stepped into the room we saw that he was wearing a tin star.

I saw no reason to beat around the bush.

"Marshal Watson has been killed. I'm John Everett Sage, the new Marshal. This is Clay Atwater, the new Sheriff of Alta Vista County."

"Well then, I've come to the right place." He grinned.

15.

It turned out his name was Tommy Turner. He was the town sheriff of North Fork.

"I'm looking for a fella that caused some trouble yesterday evening, in our fair town. He rides a big bay gelding with two white socks," he said.

"What makes you think he might have come here?" I was thinking about Rawlins.

"Well, last Friday, when this guy passed through North Fork, he was headed this way. So I figure he probably came back here, after doing what he done."

"What did he do?" Sheriff Atwater asked him.

"He beat up one of my …uh…ladies of the evening, and shot a fella that tried to get in the way," he answered.

"You're telling us that you have a whorehouse in North Fork and he beat up a whore and killed a man last night?"

"Well, it ain't exactly a whorehouse. It's a saloon, with some girls who provide services. The fella he shot ain't dead, neither," he clarified.

I looked over at Clay, where he had moved to lean against the wall.

"Clay, did you know about Sheriff Turner's 'full service' saloon, in North Fork?"

He nodded.

"North Fork is where all the miners from Flapjack City go for entertainment. The mine owners won't allow any women up there," he said.

"It ain't legal here in Colorado, but neither the State nor the County, has any real law enforcement up in the mountains. They can do as they please in North Fork. Many of the miners have their families living there. Eventually, the wives of the miners will probably put an end to it."

I thought about that.

It is an unfortunate fact, so many young women with no education and no prospects find it hard to survive out here. Too many are left to make a living, doing what they can. It is a horrible life, mostly ending in sickness and despair.

"How do you know he was headed here, last Friday?" I asked the 'sheriff' of North Fork.

"The girl he beat up told me. She says he's some kind of hired gun. He told her he was going to Bear Creek, to catch the train, for some kind of job in Wyoming. But he came back to North Fork, yesterday." He shrugged. "I figured he ran down here, after."

I thought about Tom, out on the streets alone.

"Does this man have a name?" I asked.

"Goes by Ed…something. She couldn't remember his last name. He probably lied anyways," he speculated.

I stood up and headed for the door.

"Sheriff Turner, we'll have a look around. You hit the streets and the livery stable. See if you can find that horse. I'll send my deputy back here. If you find the horse, you come here and tell him.

Clay, you and I will go up to the depot to make sure he doesn't try to get on the 12:10 to Denver, or catch a stage."

I didn't think to make it a request or say "please."

We found Tom over by the 1st National Bank. I told him the situation and sent him back to the office. As we made our way toward the railroad depot, it seemed like every horse in town was a big bay.

Clay went to the Stage depot and I went up to the Railroad depot. As I walked by the telegraph office, the clerk called me over.

"We've had some responses to your telegrams" He handed me several telegrams.

The first one was from the sheriff in Cheyenne. It read:

"Have not seen suspect <stop> will be on the lookout <stop> Fred Barnes <stop> Sheriff <stop> Cheyenne, Wyoming <stop>"

The other telegrams from lawmen all over the area, said pretty much the same thing, except one. It read:

"Rawlins wanted <stop> murder suspect <stop> location unknown <stop> Maxwell Warren <stop> U.S. Marshal <stop>Denver, Colorado <stop>

The last telegram in the pile wasn't from the local area. It made me smile. It read:

"Yes <stop> See you soon <stop> Yellow Horse <stop>"

I asked the depot agent if he had seen Rawlins, but he had not. Clay came up and told me that no one matching Rawlins description had booked a ride on the stage.

We waited and watched for a little while.

At about 11:30 we saw a carriage approaching the depot with two riders ahead of it and two behind. Each man had a rifle across the pommel of his saddle. I recognized Glen Corbet the foreman at the Bar C, as one of the lead riders. In the carriage were Bill and Annabelle Courtney and the Governor, with a driver. I noted that the harness horses were a matching pair of bays. One of the cowboys rode a bay as well. When the buggy got to the station we greeted each other. The riders dismounted and tied their horses while the passengers stepped down from the buggy, then we all went back up on the platform.

The 12:10 to Denver reached the station at 12:06. The passengers boarded without incident. Once the baggage and freight were loaded, the whistle blew and the train chugged away at 12:17, after only eleven minutes at the station.

The Courtney group headed back to the ranch.

Clay and I went by the stage depot again, but Rawlins was nowhere around. We walked back downtown. We found Tom and the sheriff from North Fork, at the office. They had seen no sign of Rawlins, or his horse. The four of us went to the Bon Ton for lunch. It was the first time there had ever been four armed lawmen in the restaurant. We got some looks.

Later, after another fruitless search, we concluded that Rawlins probably hadn't come to Bear Creek after all. Maybe he was hiding somewhere in the town, but it was unlikely. He had to know people might be looking for him now.

The sheriff of North Fork went back into the mountains.

The rest of us went about doing our jobs, with a heightened sense of vigilance.

I didn't go to the viewing that evening. I had seen Jack both alive and dead. I preferred to remember him alive. Also, I was new to Bear Creek and not really a part of the community. I wanted the people who knew and loved him best, to have that time together.

The next morning when Tom came in, he was in a mood of some kind. I wondered if he might be unhappy I had not come to the viewing. Maybe it was losing his father in law and all the grief and sorrow for both he and Becky.

I was wrong on all counts.

We were walking through town together that morning when I asked what was troubling him.

"People," he said. "Stupid, small minded, morally corrupt, people."

"How's that?" I asked.

He stopped and leaned against a hitching post. We were on the west side of town, down near the creek, in front of someone's beautiful two story home, with a wrap-around porch.

He made a gesture with his hand, as if to include the whole area.

"We serve these people as protectors and enforcers of the law. Jack lost his life at the hands of a vicious killer, and some of these people…" He trailed off.

I waited and pretended to look around.

When I realized he wasn't going to complete the thought, I prompted him.

"…What about these people?"

He took a deep breath and rubbed his face.

"Last night at the viewing, Wilson Monroe," he looked at me, "you don't know him. He had the nerve to walk up to Becky and me and ask us if we had considered the possibility that *you*….had …murdered Jack, to get his job."

"Listen, Tom. People are people, wherever you find them. Good ones, bad ones and everything in between. These folks here are no better and no worse than anyone else. We all have our problems. I get it though. I understand how you feel. Let it go. There will always be some who insist on seeing everything through their own twisted and perverse imaginations. It's best not to dwell on it."

I was very close to being completely angry myself.

The front door of the house opened and a woman came out on the porch.

"Good morning, Mrs. O'Malley," Tom called.

"Hello, Tom. Is everything alright?"

"Oh, yes, ma'am. We were just enjoying the view of your garden."

The yard was surrounded by a white picket fence. Inside the fence were a variety of flowering plants, and a vegetable patch.

She came down the stairs and walked out to the gate. She was wearing a light blue dress that was made of a shiny fabric that might have been silk. Her long dark hair was pinned up behind her head. She was carrying a hand towel, indicating that she had been doing some sort of household chore

I was startled at how beautiful she was.

"Would you gentlemen like some lemonade or a cup of coffee?"

she smiled at me.

"I don't believe we've met."

I swept off my hat.

"No, ma'am, I'm quite certain we haven't. I mean….I would have remembered," I stammered.

Tom saved me further embarrassment.

"Lora O'Malley, may I present John Everett Sage. I'm pleased to report that John has been kind enough to assume the duties as Marshal of Bear Creek."

"I'm very pleased to meet you, sir." She turned back to Tom.

"Please tell Becky I was serious last night. I will be bringing food to your house for as long as you need me to. We will have a ton of food left over after the reception today. If there is anything else I can do…if she just wants to talk, I will be there for her."

"Thank you. She knows it, and you've been very kind," Tom said.

She turned back to me.

"Mr. Sage, can I interest you in some refreshment?"

"No ma'am, I mean…yes ma'am, but not at this time…" I felt my face going red.

"We have to get back to the office now, Lora. Right away, in fact," Tom said, sticking me in the ribs with an elbow.

"Well then, until we meet again." She smiled at me again and turned back toward the house.

Tom kind of pulled me away and directed me up the hill, toward the square.

"If I didn't know better, I'd think you were interested in her." He said, grinning.

"Good night, Tom! She's a married woman."

"Was," he said.

"Excuse me?"

"I mean, she *was* a married lady. Now she's a widow."

"Oh, I didn't know that."

He chuckled.

"Her husband died nearly two years ago. They didn't have much, except the house and land. She's had to take in boarders to make ends meet. I can tell you, she's a great cook."

He narrowed his eyes at me.

"You might want to consider moving out of the hotel," he grinned.

"Stop it!"

"That's too bad. I think she likes you."

"…Yeah? Well, maybe."

I'd have to see about that.

16.

I was pleased but not surprised to see so many people at Jack's funeral. Every seat in the chapel was occupied and a great crowd of people waited outside to accompany the hearse to the cemetery. Because I came in with Tom and Becky, I was able to sit with them.

Bud McAlister, the minister spoke about his long standing friendship with Jack. He reminded us that life on earth is temporary and that it is only a small part of eternity. He told of how he knew Jack had gone home to be with the Lord and be reunited with his lost loved ones. He talked about how our loss and sorrow were nothing compared to the joy Jack was now experiencing. He promised that one day, if Christ was our Savior and Lord, we would see Jack again. He said if we died without a personal relationship with Jesus, we would be dead and separated from God and our loved ones, forever. He invited anyone who was not a believer to come and talk to him or anyone in the congregation, about how to meet the Lord.

After the service we followed the hearse to the cemetery. We walked through the west side of town, down across a bridge over Bear Creek, and up to the cemetery on the top of a hill, dotted with pine and spruce. Along the way, as we passed through neighborhoods, many people came out to pay their respects.

I thought about how different this parade was from the one we had seen on Saturday.

There was a reception after the funeral. Because Tom and Becky's house was small, Jack had lived at the jail, and neither Tom nor Becky had any family to host it, the reception was held at Mrs. O'Malley's boarding house.

She was bustling about, seeing that everyone was taken care of. Tom and Becky were busy with people offering condolences and telling stories about Jack. I went out on the porch and walked around the house. Here on the porch and out in the yard, there were little knots of people talking and drifting. At the back of the house were two rocking chairs side by side. From here there was a view past the well house and the carriage house, down the hill to Bear Creek with the mountains towering up behind it. Between the house and the creek was a pasture with a couple of chestnut colored horses in it. I figured they were carriage horses.

"Are you enjoying the view?"

I turned at the sound of her voice.

She had come through a screened door at the back of the kitchen.

Her dark hair had just a tiny sparkle of silver. It was pinned up in a bun, but some of it had slipped loose and dangled beside her face. She was aware of it and attempted to put it back up, but it fell down again. She blew at it in frustration.

"Yes, I am," I said.

Obviously I was looking at her.

"Why Mr. Sage, are you being forward?"

"No ma'am," I smiled. "No offense intended, Mrs. O'Malley."

I held my hands up.

"None taken Marshal"

"Please call me John."

"Thank you, John. I will."

"I must say, you have a lovely home."

"Mmmmm." It was a thoughtful sound.

She went over and rested both hands on the porch rail. She was watching the horses.

"I never thought it would be turned into a boarding house, or that I would have to cook and clean for strangers. Oh, don't get me wrong, I don't mind the work. These things have to be done. I just wanted a family… I guess I'm just lonely," she frowned.

"Why Mrs. O'Malley, are you being forward with me?"

She laughed.

"No offense intended, John. Please call me Lora."

"Thank you, Lora. I will"

"Well, if you will excuse me, I have to get back inside."

She turned back to the screen door and paused. She looked back over her shoulder at me.

"I am very pleased to meet you, John."

"And I you," I said, bowing slightly.

A couple of days later, Tom packed up Jack's clothes. He told me he knew I needed to move out of the hotel and this room was available.

"If I was you, I'd be tempted to move to the boarding house though," he suggested, again.

"This will be more than adequate Tom. Thank you very much."

I glared at him.

He picked up the books and Jack's glasses.

"How's your reading coming along?" I asked.

"A little better all the time, I can mostly read the headlines in the newspaper and pick my way through some of the stories. I get stuck a lot, but Becky helps me along."

"Tom, that's great."

He shook his head. "Not really. Have you seen today's *Bear Creek Banner*?"

"Yeah, what can I say? They're right. We haven't found the man who murdered Willy and Jack. At least not yet," I added.

"I really liked the way they wrote about the funeral, though. It was a nice tribute to Jack."

Tom looked down at the books he was holding.

"I could leave these here, if you'd like."

"No thanks, Tom. Those were Jack's, and Becky should have them, especially his Bible."

"I want to be able to read the Bible myself, someday," Tom said. "I really have a hard time with it."

I thought about his statement. I thought about the fact so many people owned Bibles, knew perfectly well how to read, but didn't bother to read their Bible. Many other people had tried to read the Bible and just couldn't understand it. I figured I knew why that was. Most of them were unfamiliar with the author. For them it was probably like trying to read someone else's mail.

We heard the front door open, so we went out to see who had come in.

It was Yellow Horse.

17.

Yellow horse is a bear of a man. He's only about five feet, nine inches tall, but massive through the shoulders, with a barrel chest. He wears his hair long, in the manner of the Comanche.

Yellow Horse nodded when he saw me.

"John,"

"Hello, Yellow Horse."

"You owe me for the train"

"Yes, I do."

He nodded again. Then he grinned, white teeth flashing in his sun darkened face.

I grinned too.

He looked over at Tom.

"Tom Smith, meet Yellow Horse."

They shook hands.

"Tom is and has been, a deputy here in Bear Creek," I said, by way of further introduction. I was thinking about how to explain Yellow Horse to Tom.

***

Yellow Horse was born half Comanche and half Cherokee. His mother was stolen from her people by the Comanche. Like many Cherokee, she was fair skinned and had light brown hair with blue eyes. She was a great prize.

Yellow Horse has dark brown hair (now going grey) and grey eyes. He is darker than most white men, but there are some white men who, having been sun darkened, are darker than he is. He can pass for a white man.

He is not.

Because of his lighter hair, skin and eye color, he was seized by the army in a raid on a Comanche encampment. They thought he was a white boy that had been stolen by the Comanche. He was twelve at the time.

When no white family would claim him, he was sent to an orphanage run by the Roman Catholic Church. They tried to make a "decent" white "Christian" out of him. He ran away. They brought him back and gave him the name "James". He ran away. He was captured and returned. They taught him to speak English. He ran away. This process went on for a couple of years. He learned to read and write.

There was a war being fought among the white people. One day, he ran away and this time they didn't get him back.

He was far from his home and his people. It took him a long time, but he worked his way back toward home, passing for a white boy.

Right after the War Between the States, a couple of men in Texas decided to round up some wild cattle and drive them to New Mexico. There was no market for cattle in Texas, but they needed beef in the big cities. Those entrepreneurial men were Charles Goodnight and Oliver Loving. I was young, and needed work. They put me on the crew. They still needed a scout.

BEAR CREEK

James Yellow Horse was able to convince Goodnight and Loving he had traveled that way with the Comanche, spoke the language and would be a valuable scout. That's how I first met him. We drove nearly two thousand head of cattle to New Mexico, together.

A couple of years later, we all set out to drive a herd to Wyoming. One day, when we were still somewhere in New Mexico, Yellow Horse and Loving were far ahead of the herd, intending to make trade agreements with the Comanche, for passing through that country. They were attacked by a party of Comanche hostiles. Loving was badly wounded in the fight. Yellow Horse fought beside him, being gravely wounded himself. He managed to get Loving to Ft. Sumner, but Oliver Loving sickened and died there.

When Goodnight and the rest of us brought the herd to Ft. Sumner, we found Yellow Horse had been seized by men who intended to lynch him. We didn't let that happen. He and I have been friends ever since.

Yellow Horse and I took a few herds up the trail together, before the railroads reached Texas. My life eventually took me in other directions. We didn't see each other for some years. Yellow Horse was back among his people. He fought beside Quanah Parker at the second battle of Adobe Walls. I heard he was instrumental in getting the great chief of the Comanche to seek peace with the white man. When the last of the Comanche were all moved to the reservation in Oklahoma, Charlie

Goodnight took Yellow Horse under his wing. When I found myself in Texas again, I looked him up. Yellow Horse was scouting for the Rangers. I joined up.

***

"Yellow Horse is the best tracker I know. He's my friend and I've asked him to help us find Rawlins."

"Outstanding," Tom said.

I looked at Yellow Horse.

"I guess there've been a lot of changes, since you and I last saw this country together."

"More white people, less of mine."

I nodded.

He slapped me on the shoulder.

"Tell me," he said.

I told him how I had come to Bear Creek and met Rawlins in the street. I told him about the murders. When I finished the story, Yellow Horse said nothing.

I was used to that. I knew he was considering the possibilities.

"Where do I sleep?" he asked.

As I indicated, Yellow Horse has had trouble in some towns, with some white people. He doesn't like hotels.

"I have arranged for you to have a bed at the livery stable. It was where Willy Walker lived."

He nodded.

"He won't go far, John. He is hiding and waiting."

I knew he was referring to Rawlins.

"Yeah, I figured."

The next man to show up, within a couple of days, was "Buckskin Charlie" Owens. He was a colorful character I had worked with many years ago. Lately, he had been performing in some "Wild West" shows, back east. He was the real deal though. When he had still been little more than a wild kid, he and I had worked together to tame a couple of towns.

He was fond of wearing a buckskin jacket with fringes, over a maroon shirt with a bright yellow scarf. He wore a broad brimmed white hat, set at a rakish angle. He sported a walrus moustache and a narrow beard on his chin. If anyone thought of him as being a bit frivolous, they would be wrong. He was the best shooter with either a handgun or a long gun, I had ever met. He was ready, willing and able to shoot the eyes out of anyone, or anything that threatened him. Because of his flamboyant stage persona, his fans didn't think of him as a former lawman.

I knew better.

He had probably made more money entertaining, but he was ready to be "useful" again.

I made him a deputy Marshal of Bear Creek, Colorado.

At the end of the week, Hugh Lomax arrived. Hugh was the man who gave me my first job as a deputy, and rescued me in a tight pinch in Arkansas. He was steady as an anvil. When the War started, he was a no-nonsense, hard working farm boy, in

Missouri. When it ended, he was a one armed Lieutenant, in the Union army. He left the army and moved to Arkansas.

I had been his deputy, when he saved my bacon. At that time, he was the Sheriff in Cherokee County, Arkansas. We had followed a train robber named Billy Bob Johnson, into the Ozark Mountains. I was as green as a sprout. I was foolish enough to corner Billy Bob in a dugout cabin. His cronies got the drop on me. I had gotten myself trapped between the dugout and three of Billy Bob's hooligans.

When the shooting started, the one armed man came running down a hill, firing his .36 caliber, Colt Navy revolver, and saved my life. We captured Billy Bob and one surviving member of his gang. I had not seen Hugh for many years.

Those years had not been kind to him, but it didn't matter to me. I introduced him to Clay Atwater.

"Hugh, I'd like you to meet the Sheriff of Alta Vista County, Clay Atwater."

They shook hands a little bit awkwardly.

"Clay, Hugh managed to get himself elected to… Was it five terms?"

"Six," he rasped.

"…Right, six terms, as Sheriff in Cherokee County, Arkansas. He can advise you on anything you might need to know. I suggest making him your chief deputy and putting him in charge of the jail."

"Done," Clay said.

"Have you had any success finding other deputies?"

"I've been busy with the freight line, but I looked around. I can't find none with any real experience as law men, but there are a couple of guys I trust who work for Atwater Freight. They have experience as guards. They've brought the ore down from the mines, secured the warehouse and guarded the payroll."

"Good," Hugh rasped. "We have to start somewhere. They know that part of the county and the roads into the mountains. They are comfortable with their weapons. They can learn to wear the badge. No reason they can't continue to guard the ore as well."

"I thought I might get Bob Maxwell to be a deputy, too," Clay said.

"I don't know about that, Clay. Can you trust him? What about his drinking?" I asked.

"Aww, he only does it once in a while, and never when he's working."

"I hate to see you pulling so many people from your company. You'll have to hire people to replace them. Also, there is the public perception, you should consider."

"Waddya mean?" Clay asked.

I looked at Hugh. He just shrugged.

"The Sheriff's office can't be seen as a private company or personal empire." I said.

"Huh. I'll have to think about that."

I nodded.

"You've made a good start, Sheriff. If you'll get me settled in, we can discuss some options." Hugh managed.

As they were leaving, he rolled his eyes at me.

Now that I had two deputies, Yellow Horse and I were able to scout around. We rode up into the high country, hoping to cut Rawlins trail. Yellow Horse was concerned that Rawlins might be in one of the nearby towns, so we headed for North Fork.

North Fork proved to be a typical raw boned, frontier town. The road went right through the middle of the town, as the main street, and continued on up to Flapjack City. The commercial part of town lined both sides of the road, for about three blocks. There was a general store, hardware store, post office, barbershop, stage depot, and several saloons. It appeared the principle reason for the existence of the town was as a service center for the miners up at Flapjack City. The homes of the residents were scattered through the trees, on the mountain sides.

We found Tommy Turner, the sheriff of North Fork, in one of the saloons. He was the owner of that establishment. It looked to be the "full service" saloon he had told us about. I was pretty sure the other saloons in North Fork worked the same way.

He told us he hadn't seen Rawlins or heard any more about him. I had no reason to believe t he was lying, but we decided to search the town. A couple of saloon keepers and clerks said they had seen a man matching his description, there in the town on occasion, but not lately. The "working girls" said the same thing.

After we had searched the town pretty well, we headed home, sensing our man was still somewhere nearby.

DAN ARNOLD

18.

All of our searching and all of our vigilance, had not helped us find Rawlins.

It turned out I had been right about him coming to us. Rawlins and I found each other on a Saturday morning.

I shot him as he was getting off his horse.

I'd just had breakfast with Tom and Becky, at the Bon Ton, and was walking out the door. I barely noticed a man at the hitching rail, just starting to step off a big bay horse. I wouldn't have paid any attention to him, except his body language changed the minute he saw me. When I turned my head to look at him, he was reaching for his gun.

All in a flash, I realized he was Ed Rawlins, and we were firing at each other.

His first shot went past me, through the open door of the Bon Ton. My first shot went through his chest and hit the saddle on his horse. The horse jumped sideways, but Rawlins was already firing his second shot. It splintered the wood of the door frame, right by my ear. He didn't fire a third shot because when the horse jumped away, it caused Rawlins to fall on his butt in the street. He had barely hit the ground when I fired my second shot. I put that second bullet through his head. The big bay gelding had taken off, galloping down the street.

I didn't go after it this time.

Tom flew out the door, with his gun ready. I walked over and kicked Rawlins smoking gun out of his lifeless hand.

"Are you OK?" Tom asked me.

"Yeah. You?"

I emptied the two spent shells, reloaded and holstered my gun.

"We're all OK. Say, that's Ed Rawlins isn't it?"

"It was."

Fortunately no one in the Bon Ton had been hit. That was a relief. Becky and Mrs. O'Malley were among the people inside.

Tom turned and kept the people from crowding out. I asked for a tablecloth and covered Rawlins body with it. By now, people were coming from everywhere.

Buckskin Charlie and Hugh Lomax arrived on the run. I noticed that Hugh looked ashen and was having trouble catching his breath. He looked at me and shrugged.

"Not as young as I used to be," he rasped. "I'm OK, though."

I left them to handle the crowd.

I went over to the Marshal's office and washed my face. My hands were trembling.

The door opened and Clay Atwater came in. Yellow Horse slipped in behind him and closed the door.

"Well you got your man," Clay said.

"It was a near thing."

"Didn't look that way to me, I saw his body, you shot him twice."

"It was his horse that killed him. If he had been standing on the ground, I don't know."

I shook my head and rubbed my face with the towel again.

"Who fired first?" He asked.

"Does it matter?"

"It might. Maybe you shot first and he was just attempting to defend himself. For all we know, he was coming into town to surrender to authorities," he said.

I saw Yellow Horse's head whip around at that comment. He gave Clay a hard stare.

"I can tell you he drew first. I can tell you he probably came back here to kill someone. He was probably looking for Tom and was surprised to see me. He was armed and ready. It was a near thing. If his horse hadn't jumped, he probably would have killed me."

"That's your story, but there were no witnesses. By the time anyone realized what was happening, it was over. You've shot a man to death." Clay was glaring at me.

I took a deep breath.

"Sheriff Atwater, do we have a problem?"

"You're damned right we do. I know for a fact, you and this half breed," he glanced at Yellow Horse, "went hunting for Rawlins out in the mountains. You went to North Fork. You had no authority to do that. It's my juris...my...my area of duty." He concluded angrily.

If Clay Atwater had known how much Yellow Horse hates to be called a "half breed", or if he could have seen the fire in his eyes, he would have kept his mouth shut.

"Come on, Clay! Is that what this is about?"

"You don't even have the sense to deny it. We'll see what the Judge has to say about this." He slammed his hand down on the desk and stormed out.

I looked at Yellow Horse. He would not have been offended if Clay had called him an Indian, or even a redskin. He was proud of that heritage. He hated it when people thought he was half white. He will not be insulted. He will repay evil for evil.

This meant trouble.

"I'm done here. I'll go back to Texas. Buy my ticket." He walked out.

The door had barely closed, when it opened again.

In walked the newspaper man.

I was thinking I needed to lock the door and pretend I wasn't there.

Jerry Starnes was the publisher, printer, editor and principle reporter of the *Bear Creek Banner*. I say principle reporter, because it seemed like half the women in town carried stories to him. He tried grilling me about the shooting, but I had no comment. He was clever and tried several different tactics. He did manage to confirm that the "victim" in the shooting was a man named Ed Rawlins. Ed Rawlins was wanted by the U.S. Marshal in Denver, on suspicion of murder charges. Rawlins was also wanted locally for jail breaking, theft of property, breaking and entering, and suspicion of murder in the deaths of town Marshal, Jack Watson and local horse trainer, Willy Walker. He learned that Ed Rawlins had been armed and he had fired on the new town Marshal, John Everett Sage. He learned all of that, without me ever making a statement. There was not one thing he could quote me on. I had mostly just made faces or nodded my head in response to his questions. I noticed my hands had stopped shaking, but I was very, very tired.

"Well then, do you have any comment on the theft of the payroll?" He asked.

I know I shot forward in my chair. I'm pretty sure I was about to say something stupid like, "What payroll?"

Somehow I managed to avoid it.

"Perhaps I can confirm the information you already have." I speculated.

"OK. Is it true the payroll for the mines has been stolen?"

"You'll have to confirm that with the mining companies and the bank."

"Is it true Preston Lewis, the bank officer was killed?"

"That name is not familiar to me, personally. I'm new to Bear Creek."

"Is it true the County Sheriff's deputies, who were guarding the payroll, are missing?"

"Mr. Starnes, if you'll excuse me, I have to go. Your questions would be better answered by Sheriff Atwater."

I stood up and grabbed my hat.

"I tried that."

"When did you talk to him?" I was headed for the door.

"I was interviewing him just before the shooting at the Bon Ton cafe."

"What did he tell you?"

"Nothing, he seemed very angry and confused."

I found the Sheriff of Alta Vista County at the courthouse, sitting behind his desk in the Sheriff's office. I suppose he could tell by the look on my face that I had learned about the robbery.

"I guess you heard about it. You know everything, don't you?"

He looked like he might cry.

"Tell me all of it."

He took a deep breath.

"Friday is payday for the miners, once a month. The payroll never showed up in Flap Jack City, yesterday. They sent some men out to look and they found the body of Preston Lewis in the buckboard by the side of the road. There was no sign of the payroll or the deputies. They sent a rider down here to tell me. He got here late last night."

He was running his hands through his hair.

"What are you going to do?"

He covered his face with his hands for a moment.

"What can I do? They were my men, my deputies. I hired them. I look like a fool."

Suddenly I couldn't take anymore; I was mad, straight through.

"I'll tell you what you can do. You can start by getting over feeling sorry for yourself and your precious position. You need to be thinking about how to get the mine payroll back and catching whoever killed the bank officer."

"How can I do any of that?"

He was running his hands through his hair again.

"You've got resources man, use them!" I shouted.

He scowled at me.

"I've got nothing but one old deputy, and he really works for you."

"I'm placing all the resources I have at your service, including the best tracker I've ever known. You can start by apologizing to Yellow Horse."

"That'll be the day,"

"It will be today, right now in fact," I snapped.

"You can go to hell, both you and Yellow Horse."

I slapped him.

He lunged up, tossing his desk off to the side, as if it were an empty crate.

He froze when he heard me cock my Colt, which he was surprised to see, was now pointed at the tip of his nose.

"You will apologize to Yellow Horse, you sorry son of a bitch. If you're lucky, very lucky, he'll let you live. If he feels like it, he might even agree to help us clean up this mess."

I took a step back, then another.

"I'm going to wait for you on the courthouse lawn. When you come out, you'll either be ready to apologize to Yellow Horse, or use that pistol on your hip."

I turned and walked out.

I chose a place outside where I could see both ends of the courthouse and the door to the Sheriff's department. I swept my coat tail back on the left side. I'm right handed and I carry my Colt on the left side in a cross draw holster. I do this so I can easily reach it whether standing, sitting, or on horseback.

While I was standing there, my anger melted away. Every thought, word and deed has consequences. The Bible says every way of a man is right in his own eyes. I couldn't justify my words or my actions this time though. I had allowed my temper to get the best of me.

Sin is sin. The wages of sin is death.

Yellow Horse is no Christian. He is proud. He will not be insulted. He always gets even. I couldn't have him doing that. I had dangerously placed myself in the middle.

I wondered if I was about to reap the reward for sewing the wind.

From where I stood, I could see that the crowd was drifting away from the Bon Ton. Rawlins body had been carried away. I saw Tom, Buckskin Charlie and Hugh coming my way. They passed by the workmen who had gone back to laying brick in the streets surrounding the courthouse.

"What's going on?" Tom asked. Hugh could tell by looking at me. Buckskin Charlie figured it out real quick.

"Who are you waiting for? Is there gonna be another shooting?" He asked.

I glanced at them. "Leave it alone, boys. This is a personal matter. Whatever happens, don't mix in."

The door to the Sheriffs' department opened and we could all see Clay Atwater coming up the steps. Tom tried to grab my sleeve, but I shook him off.

Clay reached the top of the steps and he had his hands out away from his body. He wasn't wearing his gun. I was aware that, like me, he could have a hide-out piece on him somewhere, so I was watching him closely. He stopped at the top of the stairs.

He was only about fifteen feet away.

I figured he was unarmed. He had to know I wouldn't shoot an unarmed man. I fully expected him to rush me and beat me to a pulp. I would be nearly defenseless against him. If he decided to fight me barehanded, he could crush me like a bug.

"OK, let's go talk to Yellow Horse" He said.

Mercy can be better than justice, especially when we are the beneficiaries.

DAN ARNOLD

19.

As we walked over to the livery stable he explained that after he calmed down, he realized he had brought all this on himself. He even thanked me for my offer of help. He also explained that he couldn't stand killing. He hated it and wouldn't even kill a rattler. He couldn't imagine killing a man.

I was astonished. I asked him why he carried a gun.

"All lawmen do, don't they?"

Clay never ceased to surprise me with his basic honesty and accurate self-assessment. His pride had temporarily blinded him to his responsibility, but it had not goaded him into a fight. I was all too aware *my* pride had done so. Pride may be the worst sin of all. I apologized for my earlier behavior. I also told him that not all lawmen carried guns. There were other options. It could be his choice, either way.

We said hello to Al, then went to the back of the livery where Yellow Horse had his room.

Yellow Horse was standing in the door to his room. Behind him, I could see his things were on the bed, packed and ready to go.

"John," he nodded "you have my ticket?"

He ignored Clay

"Not yet. Clay would like to say something to you."

Yellow Horse looked at him as if he had just noticed he was there.

Clay looked like he was feeling kind of sick.

"Uh, yeah…you see the thing is…I'm a jackass sometimes…" he trailed off.

Yellow Horse regarded him silently.

"What I mean is…you aren't…uh….." he trailed off again.

Yellow Horse turned to me.

"I will take the train to Denver."

"Yellow Horse, I'm sorry. Really, I acted like an idiot. I shouldn't have said what I said." Clay blurted.

Yellow Horse turned back to face him.

"No?" He raised an eyebrow.

"No, I shouldn't have. I'm sorry I did."

"Yes." Yellow Horse nodded, looking him in the eye.

Clay looked at me, clearly baffled. He had no idea where to go from there.

I did.

"Yes. What?"

Yellow Horse turned to Clay.

"Yes, I accept your apology. Yes, you are an idiot. Yes, if you say it again, I will take your hair."

He turned to me.

"Tell me what you need."

We decided a small party could be prepared and provisioned much more quickly than attempting to put together a larger posse. Even so, by the time we made arrangements and got outfitted for the trip, it was nearly noon.

Clay told us the place where the bank officer was killed was only about a mile above North Fork, but much higher up in the mountains. Because it was pretty much uphill all the way, it would take at least three hours to travel the ten miles to North Fork. Past North Fork the road got narrow and there were many switchbacks. We would need to rest our horses often. It might take nearly another hour to travel the extra mile to the scene of the theft. I wondered if Clay's horse could handle the challenge.

When we rode past Lora's boarding house, she was working in the garden. I stopped to have a word with her, as Yellow Horse and Clay went on.

She and I had been spending some time together. I explained the situation to her, and as I started to remount Dusty, she stopped me and kissed me.

"Be safe out there, and come back to me as soon as you can."

I was more than sufficiently motivated.

I caught up to the others, and as we rode west, I learned that the payroll was mostly in gold and silver coins. The miners only got paid once a month and many didn't like paper money. Usually there was about three thousand dollars in coin and paper. To be more secure, the payroll never went up the mountains on the same day of the week. It sometimes went in a strong box on the stage, sometimes on a freight wagon of one kind or another. The freight wagons were frequently on the road, hauling equipment or supplies in, and the ore back out. The stage went to Flapjack City only once a week. The stage was the preferred method of the bank officer who always traveled with the payroll. This time it had been on a freight wagon. This time there had also been more money than usual.

That was a surprise to me.

"Why was that?

"The snow will come soon, so about this time of year they usually send up three or four months' worth of payroll. They secure it up there in the mining offices," Clay said.

"It isn't even fall yet," I pointed out.

"Not down where we live. We have another six weeks or more before it gets frosty, but up there," he pointed toward the top of the mountains, "where the mines are, you can see the old snow. New snow could fly at any time now. They try to keep the roads open, but heavy snows can close the roads for weeks at a time. And there are rock slides and avalanches. It's too dangerous to try to take the payroll up in the winter."

"Your deputies knew that," Yellow Horse observed.

The search party had found the body of Preston Lewis slumped in the wagon seat, where he had been shot. One deputy had been mounted and one had been driving the team. The deputies and the harness horses were missing. They had abandoned the buckboard wagon, because it was too big to negotiate narrow mountain trails.

It was nearing dusk in the high mountains when we started on their trail. Night comes fast up there, so we wanted to get a sense of where they might be headed. There were few ways they could go, because of the steep mountainsides.

Although the search party had messed up the tracks at the scene of the murder, the thieves trail was obvious from where they left the road. They had headed downhill, along the edge of a narrow creek that ran down into Bear Creek.

Yellow Horse spent some time on foot to become very familiar with the size and shape of the hoof prints their horses were leaving in this soft ground.

"Three men mounted, leading two horses, one is carrying a load." He said.

"That can't be right," Clay said. "There were only two men and they only had three horses."

Yellow horse shook his head. "Five horses, three men."

"Are you sure about that?"

"I could follow this trail in the dark," Yellow Horse replied.

"That's good, we'll need to. They have a day's start on us," I said.

"We can't keep going in the dark. We'll lose their trail and it's dangerous." Clay opined.

Yellow Horse got back on his mount and continued down the trail. I followed him. The Sheriff of Alta Vista County didn't have much choice, he had to follow us.

We crisscrossed the stream wherever the trail led, letting the horses drink occasionally. We were often moving through chest high thickets of Pussy

Willow, working to avoid bogs. Doing that became more important when the sun went down behind the mountains.

At one point we stopped and Yellow Horse got off his horse and studied the ground. He took us up an embankment. We started working our way up the shoulder of a mountain through the spruce and aspen groves, then around and down. It was now fully dark; the only light was that of the moon and stars. The ground here was firm and often rocky. I couldn't see any sign of the trail the thieves had left.

Yellow Horse could.

We had been riding in the dark for hours. We came to an opening in the aspen trees and out into a meadow. The stars above us were spectacular. It was very cold now. I could hear a creek running somewhere.

Dusty pricked his ears forward, something moved at the far edge of the meadow. It could have been an elk, mule deer, or even a moose. It had been that big. Dusty was calm though, and unconcerned. We heard a whinny.

Yellow Horse and I hit the ground holding our reins in one hand and our guns in the other. Clay managed to get down beside us. We waited for a shot that didn't come.

After a minute Yellow Horse motioned he was going to circle around the edge of the meadow. I nodded and took his reins, and he disappeared. The big thing I had glimpsed materialized at the other edge of the meadow. It was a horse. After a few more minutes we heard a whippoorwill call.

That was the "all clear" signal from Yellow Horse.

I stood up and started out into the meadow, Clay was right behind.

We led our horses across the meadow. Yellow Horse met us part way across.

"We will sleep there," he said, pointing back the way we had come.

"What's wrong with over there?" Clay asked, pointing at the edge of the aspen grove Yellow Horse had just come out of. We could hear the creek just beyond the trees.

"Dead men," Yellow Horse said.

Taking the reins from me, he led his horse past me and I followed him. Clay followed us.

After we had secured our horses and unsaddled them. We gathered together to talk.

"They camped over there," Yellow Horse began, "late last night. They had a picket line for the horses and a small fire. They had food and coffee. Two men were killed, while they slept. There are no horses on the picket line now. I saw two in the meadow grazing. I don't know where the other three horses are or where the third man is. I will look again in daylight."

"OK, let's get some sleep." I directed.

"Wait a minute. Where is the mine payroll, Yellow Horse? Did you see any sign of the money?"

Clay was clearly tired and cranky. We all were.

"John and I will look tomorrow."

"I say we go over there now. We can build a fire and have a look around. At least we can have a hot meal."

"No."

Clay was about to argue some more, but I was too tired to listen to it.

"We'll do it in daylight, Clay. We'll just make a mess of any sign that might be over there, if we stumble around in the dark tonight. Besides, do you really want to sleep over there with the dead bodies?"

"No, I'm just saying…"

"We have maybe four hours till first light. We'll sleep now, if we can." I said.

He didn't like it, but he didn't fight it anymore. We chewed on some jerky and cornbread and drank from our canteens, and then we rolled up in our blankets.

When we woke up, just before sunrise, we had frost on our blankets.

We left our horses tied where they were and walked across the meadow in the gathering daylight.

We found the camp exactly as Yellow Horse had described it. There were two dead men wrapped in blankets, lying beside a new fire ring, made of stones from the creek. Both men had been shot in the head. No animals had been chewing on them, yet.

There was cooking gear and a coffee pot on the edge of the fire ring. I could see a picket line stretched between trees about twenty yards away.

We had seen two horses grazing as we crossed the meadow. There was a single pannier, hung high in a tree, over at the edge of the creek. There was also a tarp stretched between trees to form a rain shelter. There were two riding saddles, a pack saddle and some other gear under the tarp.

"I will look around." Yellow Horse said.

I began gathering some of the tinder from the pile of wood at the edge of the fire ring. I started building a fire.

Clay was practically dancing with annoyance and excitement. "What the hell are you doing? We should be looking for the payroll."

"The less we move around right now the better. We'll warm up by the fire and have some coffee. When Yellow Horse gets back, we'll decide how to proceed."

"What about the pannier hanging over there?" He wanted a look in the pack bag that was hanging up in the tree.

"OK, go get it and bring it back here."

He ran over and untied the rope to lower the bag, and then he ran back with it. When he got back he rummaged around in it, but all he found was some bacon, coffee and some canned goods.

"Perfect, we might as well use their supplies." I said, as I lit the fire.

I handed Clay the coffee pot.

"Take this down to the creek and wash it out, then bring it back, full of water."

"Do you plan to sit here and have breakfast, with these dead men lying here?" He asked.

"No, I plan to sit here and have breakfast with you and Yellow Horse. These boys have lost their appetite. After breakfast, we'll probably carry them back to Bear Creek for burial."

Clay actually stood there with his mouth open.

Yellow Horse came back.

"Are they your deputies?"

He indicated the dead men.

I knew that he already knew the answer, as well as I did.

Clay looked at them a bit more closely. He looked pale and drained.

"Yeah, that's Rogers and the other is Glenn."

"I'll go get our horses and water them at the creek. Are you just going to stand there holding the coffee pot?" Yellow Horse asked Clay.

"What? No..." Clay started.

"Come with me then. You can help with the horses and fill the coffee pot." Yellow Horse turned and Clay walked with him across the meadow.

I took the opportunity to have a quick look around. Close to the tarp, I discovered a place where there was an old, much used campfire ring. Under the tarp there was some stacked firewood. The ground under the tarp was smooth and there was a place where spruce bows had been used to form a mattress. The area around the picket line was trampled and littered with manure. Clearly, the camp had been here for weeks.

I was laying bacon out in a frying pan when Yellow Horse and Clay returned to the fire. As we waited for the coffee to heat, we discussed the situation.

"At the scene of the robbery, there was a man waiting for the wagon, one man alone. He was on foot and probably appeared harmless. He had secured two saddle horses down by the creek, tied to some willows. I found where they had been tied. He must have been in cahoots with the guards, because they were expecting him. I don't know who killed the bank man. They took the horses and the payroll from the wagon. The three men rode the saddle horses and led the harness horses, one of which was carrying the mine payroll in panniers on a pack saddle. Once they were sure they weren't being followed, they came to this camp, which had been prepared before the robbery," Yellow Horse began.

He looked over at me, to have me take up the narrative.

"They settled in for the night. When it was time for the third man to take the watch, he shot your thieving deputies while they were sleeping."

I looked back to Yellow Horse, who nodded in agreement and said, "The third man turned the horses loose to graze and get water. When he left here in the dark, the other two saddle horses may have followed him. There are many tracks here. It took me awhile to sort it out."

As I put the bacon pan on the coals, Clay asked the obvious question.

"Do you think maybe the third man took the money out, packed on the two harness horses?"

Yellow Horse shook his head.

"No."

"How can you be sure?"

"They are still here."

Yellow Horse pointed to the two horses now grazing close to each other in the meadow."

I could smell the coffee as it began to boil.

"So, maybe he carried it out on the other two saddle horses."

"Maybe," I said "but I don't think so."

"…Why not?" Clay was frustrated and getting impatient.

The bacon began to hiss and sizzle.

I looked back to Yellow Horse, and raised my eyebrows.

He shook his head. "He wasn't leading the other two horses. They wandered some. They weren't carrying any kind of load, the saddles and bridles are still here, and so is this pannier."

I took some cold water from a canteen and poured it over the boiling coffee grounds, to settle them.

Clay jumped up.

"Why are we just sitting here? We're burning daylight. We have to track down the third man."

"Yes," I said, as I poured coffee into three cups. "We will. First we have to have breakfast and pack up this camp."

I stirred the bacon some.

"You're crazy; we need to get on the trail now!" Clay shouted.

As the morning sun had begun to drive away the chill, the flies had shown up and began to buzz around the dead men.

I used a fork to pull a piece of bacon out of the pan, gently shaking the extra grease off into the pan.

"Clay, settle down. We know what we're doing. We need to eat something, drink some coffee and think for a little bit. Ten minutes won't make a whole lot of difference."

He really didn't have any choice. He was as cold, tired and hungry as we were, and that bacon sure was good. We drank all the coffee and ate all the bacon, using some of our corn bread to sop up the grease.

Sitting by the dead men's fire ring, I gave some thought to what kind of a man would care more about horses, than he did for human beings. The horses had value to him, the people did not.

We often value the wrong things. We can spend our lives working to surround ourselves with things that don't matter. We can sacrifice the things that do matter, to gain those things that don't.

Later, we caught the loose harness horses and packed up what we could. We put the dead men on the pack horses.

We only had that one pannier though.

When we were ready to go, I looked at Yellow Horse, a question in my eyes. He shook his head in response. I shrugged. We mounted up and followed the trail, in the tracks of the killer.

20.

We found one of the saddle horses within about a mile of the camp. We kept following the trail down out of the mountains. At one point it went down into the same valley with North Fork, but veered away from the town. We saw a loose horse in a meadow just below the town, but left it there. It appeared to be at home. Yellow Horse lost the tracks when the rider got back on the road. There had been too much traffic, spoiling the hoof prints. The killer could have taken the road headed down toward Bear Creek, or gone back up into the mountains. Yellow Horse kept looking to see if the rider left the road, but there was no sign of it. He was convinced the rider had gone on to Bear Creek.

We rode back into Bear Creek, a little after noon. We dropped the bodies at the morticians and took the horses to the livery stable. Al agreed to see the harness/pack horses got sent back over to the freight yard.

He took me aside for a moment, to have a word in private.

I gave Dusty a good rub down before I turned him out in a pen. Then I went and had lunch at a certain boardinghouse, with a spectacular view of the creek and mountains.

Later that afternoon, I went to the Sheriff's office to talk to Clay.

"You've done pretty well as Sheriff," I said. "You recovered the stolen horses and the bodies of two of the robbers. When you recover the payroll you will look really good."

"I don't see any hope of that," Clay said. "I have no idea where the payroll went, and those dead men were, my men. I hired them and they stole the payroll. The newspaper will crucify me."

"Well then, you'd better go get the payroll."

He narrowed his eyes at me.

"Are you saying you know where it is?"

I nodded. "I do, and so do you."

"Are you accusing me of something?" He started to bow up.

"Easy, Clay," I held my hands up. "I'm not accusing you of anything. I just mean you will be able to find the payroll, because you already know where it is." I grinned.

He snorted in exasperation.

"Get to the point John. You know I don't have a clue what you're talking about."

So I told him where the mine payroll was hidden.

The *Bear Creek Banner* told the story about two employees of Clay Atwater, the Sheriff of Alta Vista County, stealing the payroll. The paper went on and on, about how outrageous and scandalous it was. They suggested I had probably killed the deputies. They briefly mentioned Sheriff Clay Atwater had retrieved the stolen horses. They did say he had gone back to the camp in the mountains and single-handedly found the bulk of the payroll, in a pannier, buried under a fire ring. The newspaper couldn't tell the story of how he figured it out.

Yellow Horse and I had both noticed the new fire ring, with a border of stones from the creek. We could clearly see the earth had been disturbed, before the new fire ring was built. There was no reason to build a new fire ring so near the more practical and much used, existing fire ring. That new fire ring was there as a marker over the hiding place. The payroll was in the missing pannier, buried beneath it.

Yellow Horse and I had both arrived at that conclusion, when we saw the evidence. Yellow Horse was not willing to tell Clay about it. When we got back to Bear Creek, we went back to the livery stable where Alexander Granville Dorchester III, told me the big bay horse that had belonged to Rawlins, was now in a stall. Yellow Horse picked up the bay horse's feet and nodded. It was the horse we had tracked out of the mountains.

When I had looked in the saddle bags on Rawlins' saddle, I had found several hundred dollars in gold and silver coins.

It was apparent Rawlins had been working with the two men inside Atwater Freight. He was probably thrilled when they got hired as deputies. In preparation for the robbery, he had set up the camp and provisioned it with supplies from North Fork. He used it as his hideout while he waited for the day of the theft. He was probably responsible for the death of the bank officer, as well as killing both of the deputies.

As far as Rawlins had been aware, there was only one person in Bear Creek who knew him by sight. He may have been planning to kill Tom, or maybe he just felt lucky. It was his bad luck that morning at the Bon Ton, to discover I was still in Bear Creek. It was an unfortunate coincidence for him, when I walked out of the Bon Ton, just as he started to step off his horse. He never got the chance to go back for the rest of the money.

I don't believe in luck or coincidence.

Shortly after the first frost of fall, a little girl went missing from her family's farm. Yellow Horse started tracking her, and then he found himself tracking a man. Yellow Horse found the little girl, but she was no longer living. He tracked down the man who had taken the girl.

Later, when I found the man, *he* was no longer living. I found him hanging naked by his ankles from a corner of his front porch roof. He'd been castrated, scalped and left hanging there to bleed out.

Evil for evil - the way Yellow Horse lives his life.

If Yellow Horse hadn't gone to Texas, I would've had to arrest him for murder. Instead, I paid for his train ticket.

Early in the spring Bob Maxwell got drunk, one time too many. When Clay Atwater tried to arrest him, Bob managed to get his gun out of its holster. Clay pulled his own gun quick, and smacked Bob on the head with it. Clay is a great mountain of a man, and he hit Bob too hard, caving in his skull.

It took Bob Maxwell four days to die.

Clay couldn't stand it. He concluded that between the scandals surrounding the payroll theft, his accidentally taking a life, and the conflict of running Atwater Freight, he wasn't cut out to be a lawman.

To some of us, it had always been evident.

Clay Atwater resigned from the office of Sheriff, and the county had a special election. I decided to run for the office.

The shooting of Ed Rawlins, along with newspaper stories suggesting I had killed the two payroll thieves at their camp in the mountains, had made me famous and advanced my reputation as a lawman that killed without hesitation. I didn't like it, but at least I had some name recognition going for me.

My only opponent was Tommy Turner, the sheriff of North Fork. He ran a good campaign with the support of the mine owners, the miners and the colorful citizens of North Fork. I had the support of Atwater Freight, the Courtney's at the Bar C and even the Governor of Colorado.

I won, in a landslide victory.

I was sworn into office in the spring.

Tom took over as the town marshal of Bear Creek. Almost immediately they changed his title to "Chief of Police."

Lora and I realized we had fallen in love. One night, as we were having supper in the Palace, I asked, and she agreed to marry me!

Things were changing fast. There was talk of running lines for the electric lights and the telephone from here to Denver. The telephone, now there's a strange deal. I hear you can talk to someone on the other side of the country, by speaking into a cup mounted on your wall.

The day I was sworn in as Sheriff, I was summoned by the Governor. It wasn't clear what he wanted to see me about, but I hopped the 12:10 train to Denver.

21.

Denver was a busy place. There was the sound of construction everywhere. There were even little railroad tracks set into the brick streets for trolley cars. I knew there were plans in the works to build the State Capital building.

I was met on the platform by a man named Irving McCormick. He was an aide to the Governor.

"Sheriff Sage, I've heard a lot about you. I know you must be wondering why the Governor has sent for you, but he will explain all that to you himself."

The Governor's mansion was just that. It was even bigger than Bill Courtney's house, out at the Bar C. A good deal more refined as well. This house had three stories and was made entirely of granite, cut from the heart of the Rocky Mountains. The entire mansion was equipped with electric lights.

"Congratulations, John. I'm sorry I couldn't swear you in myself. I'm confident you'll do a better job as County Sheriff than Clay Atwater did, but I had more pressing issues."

"Of course, Governor, I completely understand. It wasn't any big deal."

"John, I know you are a man of few words, so I'll get right to the point. Do you know where Capitol City is?" Governor McGhee asked me.

"No, sir, I don't."

"It's southwest of here, up in the highest mountains."

He pointed to a map on the wall.

"It's a heavy mining area. At one point, it was thought the town would be the State Capital instead of Denver, hence the name. To get there from here, you have to take the train to Gunnison and a stage from there to Lake City."

"Are you asking me to go there?"

"Yes, John, I am. My nephew is the newly elected Mayor of Capitol City. I know, it's ironic isn't it?" He grinned. "He's asked me to send a lawman to confront the local authorities. They have established their own little system of justice, and it has nothing to do with the law. I'm sending U.S. Marshal, Maxwell Warren. I want you to go with him."

Now, why on earth would the Governor be sending me off to some God forsaken corner of Colorado, when I had a job to do at home? I thought.

"Yes of course, Governor, but if you don't mind my asking; why me? Maxwell Warren and his deputies can handle whatever the problem is, without my help."

He nodded.

"Yes, they could, John, but this is a big state and sometimes I need to be able to call on local men who can be trusted, to do things for the state without involving federal employees. Will you do this for me?

"Yes sir, I'll be happy to help out."

I met Max Warren later that morning at his office.

"I tried to tell the Governor this wasn't really a matter for the U. S. Marshal's office to address. I don't know that there has been any violation of Federal law. I like to keep out of local conflicts, but he insisted and pointed out I have a duty to help get this new state into compliance with the rest of the Union. He's right about that. I have a mandate to address anything that's a threat to law and order in the region. This just seems kind of petty, and it's a hassle to get there."

"I hope you aren't offended he's sending me along for the ride."

He grinned.

"No, on the contrary, you're getting a reputation for hard-nosed law and order in this state. What did Jasper say he wanted you to do.?"

"He asked me to help you convince the locals of the value of law and order, and to, and I quote; "make damn sure they get the message.""

He chuckled.

"What do you know about Capitol City?"

"Nothing, the Governor pointed to it on a map."

"Well, it's pretty much out back of beyond, way up in the mountains, in Hinsdale County. Lake City, the County Seat, and the only real city in the county, is the supply hub for all of the mining in the region. It's like your town, Bear Creek, in that way. Capitol City is one of several mining towns on the high slopes. A guy by the name of George Lee pretty much built the whole town. Hundreds of people live up there. Its remote and rugged country and they live a hard scrabble life. Most of the townsfolk are miners and their families. You know what the rest are likely to be, in a boom town like that. There is a sheriff in Lake City, but he has little support in the mining towns. We'll get him to take us up to Capitol City."

"Isn't Lake City the place where Alfred Packer killed and ate his fellow prospectors, before the town was built?"

Max nodded.

"Yep, they put him on trial and convicted him there again, just a few years ago."

Two days later, Max Warren and I arrived in Lake City. It was a pleasant and fairly prosperous town, built on the banks of the Lake Fork of the Gunnison River. Along with Don Talbot, the Hinsdale County Sheriff, we took a stage from Lake City up into the higher mountains. Capitol City was built at about 11,000 feet above sea level. At this elevation it was still early spring, with great patches of snow still on the ground. The road was steep and muddy, but there was considerable traffic. This county, reminded me of Alta Vista, which was where I really wanted to be. I had just been elected Sheriff, but here I was, on the opposite side of the state, running an errand for the Governor.

I knew Max Warren didn't need me. He could have brought his deputies, or Don could have brought his. This was a test of some sort. I hate tests. On another level, I figured this was some kind of political favor and I had to do it. I might need to get re-elected, at some point

As we stepped off the stage, we could see a noisy little knot of people in front of the black smith's shop. Evidently, our arrival coincided with a party.

It turned out it was a necktie party. A mob was in the process of hanging a man.

I think Max and I both fired at the same time. We had each pulled our guns and fired in the air, to announce our presence. The three of us immediately spread out around the edge of the mob.

"I'm United States Marshal, Maxwell Warren, that man over there is Hinsdale County Sheriff, Don Talbot, and this man is Sheriff John Everett Sage. Who's in charge here?"

The mob kind of shifted around, with people looking at each other. Finally, a man with a bowler hat, and an enormous, bushy mustache spoke up.

"We're the Citizen's Action Committee. This nigger has committed murder, and we're hanging him."

"Not today you're not," I said.

"If this man has been accused of a crime, he will stand trial in a court of law," Max said.

The mob was made up of about a dozen rough looking men. Several of them were armed. They were taking stock of the situation. I was hoping three lawmen with guns drawn had to be pretty intimidating. Fortunately, none of them looked like they wanted to argue the point, except the spokesman.

"He's had all the trial he's gonna get. String him up, boys!" He yelled.

The spokesman was standing closest to me, so I walked right up to him and planted the barrel of my Colt up under his chin. The mob froze. The sound of me cocking my.45 was surprising loud in the clear, high mountain air.

"You're under arrest for disturbing the peace, inciting to riot, and attempted murder. Now, if you're feeling lucky, we'll have *your* trial right here. I'll be the judge, and this six-shooter Colt, will be the jury. That's all the trial you're gonna get. Is that OK with you?"

His eyes were about to pop out of his head. Standing this close, I could smell the whiskey on his breath.

"You men disperse; go on about your business. This is over," Don said.

That was it. The crowd broke up, with a little grumbling. I didn't let my man go. I kept my gun under his chin. As I looked him in the eye, I could see him sobering up.

The badly beaten, black man was still standing on the crate, with his hands tied behind his back, the noose around his neck.

Several new people started to gather around. These were the local shopkeepers, clerks and visitors.

Max went over and cut the ropes, so the black man could hop down off the crate.

"Thank you, suh. Ah surely do thank you," he said.

I holstered my gun and put my manacles on my prisoner.

Don raised a hand toward the people gathering around.

"There's nothing to see here, folks."

One of the men who had just arrived spoke up.

"I'm Mark McGhee, the Mayor. I'm sure glad to see you here. I guess the Governor must've sent you."

Max made the introductions. We learned my prisoner was named Frank Loughner. He was the self-proclaimed leader of the Citizens Action Committee. He owned a local saloon, popular with the rougher element in town. Clearly he enjoyed the product he purveyed.

The black man was Ed Jackson. He owned the blacksmith shop.

"Mayor Mcghee, is there somewhere we can go to sort this out," Max asked.

We went to the Mayor's office, which was just a room behind his dry goods store.

In the end, we determined Ed Jackson had killed a man named Earnest "Earnie" Myers. Myers (a member of the Citizen's Action Committee) had refused to pay his bill, saying it would be a cold day in hell, before he would pay a black man to serve him. When Jackson had grabbed him by the shirt collar, Myers had grabbed a pair of tongs and proceeded to beat Jackson with it. Jackson had managed to shove Myers away from himself, causing Myers to fall back against the anvil, striking his head on the sharp end. He died as result of the head injury. There were several witnesses to the incident. When the word reached Loughner's saloon, he had stormed out with his "Committee" to punish the Negro.

"Loughner has been the main actor in this 'Citizens Action Committee'." Mayor McGhee said, "They've all but taken over the town. We had a town marshal, but they scared him off. They've been the only law around here since last fall."

"I was up here when they cleared the road right after the first snow flew, back in August. Nobody said anything to me about this," Don said.

"Our marshal hadn't thrown in the towel yet. Besides, its eleven miles down to Lake City and eleven miles back up here. It takes more than half a day to get up here. There's damn little travel at all when the snow flies. This is a big county, and you're often gone. We need some real law, right here in this town."

"This town has got to make that happen. The good citizens need to stand together and back whatever lawman you get. I'll see to it one of my deputies moves up here, but you have to band together and ensure that justice is served. Otherwise, this town won't survive," Don said.

"I agree completely. Mr. Lee tried to build a real town. They called it Galena City. I'm the Mayor of Capitol City. It's chaotic up here. There are too many people trying to make money any way they can, there are crooked organizations and the population is constantly changing with the miners and drifters coming and going. We're divided up into factions. Right now we just need some law enforcement." Mark McGhee replied.

"Don is right. He'll provide a good deputy. You'll have a local lawman, but the town has to decide how it wants to live. To grow and be healthy, you'll have to have stability. As long as a town is only about people making money, any way they can, open to prostitution, gambling, and vice, there will be no stability or safety for anyone," Max said.

Don stayed on in Capitol City, while Max and I took the prisoners down to Lake City. Don came down the next day and arranged to have one of his deputies move up to Capitol City. Max and I stayed on a few days, for the trials.

Loughner was convicted of disturbing the peace. The other charges were dropped. He was fined $50.00, and released

Ed Jackson was found innocent of the murder of Ernie Myers, by reason of self-defense. Everyone had their day in court. The law was enforced, but justice was only partly served.

Mr. Jackson told us he was going to sell out and move on to a different town. He believed he couldn't live safely in Capitol City.

I hate injustice.

We do what we can, but life is not fair. In the end there is only so much a lawman can do.

Some of us have to try harder.

DAN ARNOLD

22.

On the ride back to Denver, Max told me what I had already been suspecting.

"John, I like you and I think you have the right to know the reason the Governor sent you and me off on this little side show."

"I figured he wanted you to assess my attitudes and abilities as a lawman."

"That's it exactly. You have a reputation as a lawman that gets things done with a gun. I expect it's the way you had to do things as a Texas Ranger, but the times are changing and the rule of law must prevail. The job of the lawman is to see to it justice is done according to the law. Bringing law and order into tough and lawless places takes more than just a man with a gun."

I nodded in agreement and answered, "There are still places out here where the only law is whoever has the most muscle, guts, or guns, but the times *are* changing. I've had to be the law in some rawboned towns, but I've also tried to change with the times. I look forward to more peaceful times. The whole country is becoming more civilized and that's good for everybody."

"Well, the Governor's primary concern was finding out what kind of man you really are. He recognizes there is a limited supply of truly reliable lawmen. "

"That's what I try to be."

He grinned.

"Yep, me too."

When I got back to the Governor's mansion, I was shown to my own room, by a liveried servant!

There's something to be said for who you know. I thought.

"Supper will be served in the main dining room, promptly at nine. You will want to dress appropriately," the servant said, with a sniff.

Supper at nine! I was usually ready to go to bed by then.

What did he mean by "appropriately"?

I was wearing my best suit. The servant had looked at me with some disdain. Did he expect me to show up wearing velvet short pants and high stockings, like he had on?

Fortunately, after I was settled into my room, I met Irving McCormick coming up the stairs. He was carrying a bag with a hanger sticking out of the top of it.

"Mr. Sage, the Governor asked me to pick this up for you. We dress for dinner, and formal wear is expected. The Governor realized you probably were not prepared for the occasion, as uh… you've been traveling and you hadn't been informed."

He looked relieved, to have come up with a clever lie. He probably could tell, just by looking at me, that I didn't own any "formal" wear.

Later, when I had dressed for dinner, I looked at myself in the mirror. I looked like any other "swell" in a white tie, waist coat and dinner jacket. I was glad I didn't have to wear some sort of silly hat.

Dinner was a very formal affair. We were seated at a huge table with fancy place cards, to let us know where we belonged.

The table was set with china, crystal and silver. Liveried servants brought the food, and I'll tell you it was quite a feast!

At first, I felt as out of place as a toad in a china tea cup.

The people around me were the most elegant I had ever seen, especially the ladies. These were some of the most powerful and influential people in Colorado, but I soon learned nearly all of them had started with nothing. Very few of them had any more education than I did.

The gentlemen had "adjourned to the smoking room" after dinner, for brandy, cigars and business discussion. This house had more rooms than most hotels I've been in. There was a library, a sitting room, (I suppose a standing room too, somewhere) and a sun room. There was even a billiards room. All of the ladies were in the Parlor.

The men here in the smoking room, had been introduced to me at dinner. These men were cattle barons, timber barons, rail road tycoons and captains of industry or masters of political persuasion. They were among the richest and most influential men in the state. There were a couple of mine owners in the group.

"Here's the thing John, there are some problems up in your neck of the woods that have to be handled properly. For instance, right there in Alta

Vista County there are some specific issues to address.

I've been aware that in the past, some of the mining owners were reluctant to see any real law and order, up there in Flap Jack City. Some of them were making money from every angle available, even owning gambling houses and what not. Times are changing and some practical business changes need to be made as well.

I know the mine owners didn't support your bid for Sheriff of Alta Vista County. I hope you are aware that *I* was supportive and I'm thrilled to have a real lawman in Alta Vista County."

I nodded. I was a bit embarrassed to be having this conversation in front of the other men in the room.

"I appreciate that, sir. I hope to earn your endorsement."

Governor McGhee chuckled, and a couple of other men in the room held up their glasses.

"John, please call me Jasper. My friends all do. I'm well aware of your credentials, as is every man in this room."

"Yes sir, I mean thank you, uh…Jasper."

He nodded, with a twinkle in his eye,

"Now then, let's get down to brass tacks. I asked you here to address a couple of issues which are sensitive and could have political implications. Do you follow me?"

"No sir, I'm not sure I do, Governor."

"Jasper," he reminded me.

"Yes, sir, I mean…Jasper. The thing is, I have no idea what you're talking about."

He looked around the room. Some of the other men were amused at my answer, some appeared impatient, even annoyed.

"Gentlemen, you'll have to excuse Sheriff Sage. He isn't your typical political animal."

He looked at me.

"John, What I mean is, the things we're about to discuss should never be discussed outside this room. There is a very real chance the decisions we make here this evening could affect my political ambitions, and yours, if you have any."

"No sir, I don't have any political ambitions, but I'll be glad to discuss anything with you and you can count on my discretion."

Governor McGhee looked around the room again and slapped me on the shoulder.

"Good man, John. Let's sit down."

When we were all seated, Governor McGhee resumed the conversation.

"First, I need you to look into a situation in Chaparral County. That's the county just to the east of Alta Vista County. I have reason to believe there is a land grab going on out there. Some of the big ranches have started claiming land that does not belong to them, in order to prevent newcomers from establishing homesteads. More and more people are coming out here to settle. Some of the men who first got here and built their ranches from nothing, fighting Indians and the elements at great risk and peril, won't tolerate newcomers. They're used to having things their way and using whatever means necessary to get more for themselves and keep what they get. It's a powder keg. I believe the situation is dire and there is a possibility of serious violation of State and Federal law.

We're a real part of the United States now and we need to start moving toward the 20th Century. Having lawlessness and people establishing their own control over large areas of our State, cannot be tolerated. I would like to be able to call on you, from time to time, to deal with some of the worst problems we're facing. Do you follow me?"

I thought about that.

"Sir, I'm just a lawman. I haven't done much else, for a long time. I have duties and responsibilities within Alta Vista County. I'll see law and order enforced in my county, everywhere in my county. That includes North Fork and Flap Jack City. I don't have any authority outside my county. You must know other good lawmen in the other counties. If not, you have access to the United States Marshal, and the U.S. Army. I'm not a hired gun," I concluded.

He nodded.

"I appreciate your position. I'm not asking you to hire out as a gunman. I have a number of resources in private practice, like the Pinkerton Agency and others, for that sort of thing. I've already arranged to have a private detective look into a rustling problem in Chaparral County. I need a man I can count on to represent the law, and represent this administration.

The County Sheriff over there is not someone I can count on. I believe he's too closely tied to the people conducting the land grab. The goal is to enforce the rule of law.

You're right, there are other good lawmen, all over the state, but it's a very big state and there is corruption and vice in some areas as yet untouched by real law. Chaparral County is one of those places. If you'll help me up there, and look into the situation, I'll promise you the full support of this office and all of the men in this room."

"In that case, yes sir. I'm your man."

"Good, I knew I could count on you. We're all familiar with your history."

"Yeah, well, don't believe everything you read in the papers."

The room erupted into laughter. After all, each of these men had been the subject of newspaper stories. A couple of them were probably even newspaper publishers.

DAN ARNOLD

23.

The Union Pacific train from Denver to Cheyenne made its usual stop at Bear Creek.

It was the second time I had arrived by train, but it was the first time I arrived as the County Sheriff of Alta Vista County.

It was also the first time I had ever been met at a railroad depot by a woman.

She was wearing a dress made of light blue satin with long sleeves. There was some sort of black lacey trim on the collar, cuffs, and as a border near the bottom hem. The dress appeared to be draped over many layers of petticoats. Apparently, bustles were going out of style, but clearly, corsets were not! She had on a hat of matching color and style, with a couple of black plumes, set at an angle on her head. She was easily the most beautiful woman in Bear Creek, probably in all of Colorado, maybe even the whole world.

She was Lora O'Malley, my new fiancée!

"Oh, John, thank God you're home!" Lora cried, as she rushed into my arms. I dropped my gear on the platform. I knew it was unseemly, perhaps even vulgar, but I kissed her right there in front of everyone at the station.

"I missed you so, darling," she whispered in my ear.

I held her at arm's length and looked into her deep brown eyes.

"I couldn't stay away from you for one more minute," I winked.

I gathered up my saddle bags and my valise and we walked down to where the buggy was parked. As I was putting my gear in the buggy, Hugh Lomax came hurrying toward us.

"'Evening, Mrs. O'Malley," he rasped. "John, I hate to bother you the minute you get off the train, but you need to know, William Courtney has been shot."

"What…when?"

I had too many questions whirling through my mind.

"Today, John. He was shot this morning. It was out at the Bar C. Somebody with a rifle."

"Was he killed?"

"No, but he may not live. Doc Johnson was out there all day. He says the bullet broke a rib and punctured a lung. He was able to remove the bullet, but he fears there may be complications. He gathered up some more supplies and went back out to the ranch."

"How did this happen, was it an accident?"

"Apparently it was deliberate. Glen Corbet, the foreman out there, says the shooter fired from a hideout on the top of a hill, as Mr. Courtney rode by. Corbet says he found Mr. Courtney shortly after hearing the shot. After he got him back to the ranch house, he sent some cowboys to bring back Mr. Courtney's horse and see what they could find. They found the hiding place and…this."

He was holding a spent .44-40 cartridge.

"Well that's common enough. I have a Winchester in this caliber. We have three of them in the rack in the Sheriff's office. It could've been a hunter."

"No John. It wasn't accidental. The shot was fired from a distance of only about sixty five yards, in semi-open country, and this shell was deliberately left sitting upright on a rock."

That worried me some. A single shell left on display could be a signature. A way of saying "I was here." It was highly unlikely anyone would mistake a man on horseback as a game animal, especially at a range of only a few hundred feet.

"Still, maybe some idiot…"

"John, the whole place is fenced in barbed wire."

Yeah, I knew that.

I told Hugh I would ride out to the Bar C the next morning.

That night, as I was lying in bed in one of the bunks at the Courthouse, I was thinking about the shooting.

The Bar C was completely fenced with barbed wire. Nearly 65,000 acres, surrounded by barbed wire. At one time, and not that long ago, I would have been surprised by that. Now, all the open range was nearly gone. The railroads had been fenced with thousands of miles of barbed wire. This was partly to keep wildlife and livestock off the tracks, but mostly it was to delineate railroad property. Most of the larger farms and many of the smaller ones were fenced to prevent livestock from getting into the crops. Ranchers fenced their property to contain their herds and improve feeding and breeding practices. In most of the country the open range was gone, forever. I hated that.

There was no way a hunter or anyone else could have wandered onto the Bar C. The shooter would have had to get through the wire to gain access, or have been on the ranch already. The hidden blind indicated some planning. The shell left on display was a signature. Someone had planned to kill Bill Courtney, and had celebrated the shooting afterwards.

The world is not a safe place, I thought. Life is uncertain. Building fences doesn't make you safer.

Law enforcement is a calling. It's about being willing to serve the public as a protector of the innocent and enforcer of the law. The law represents the codified moral beliefs of the people. Ever since God sent the Ten Commandments, people have had written record of the definition of sin, and crime. Sin is the violation of God's law. Crime is the violation of man's law. Man's laws are based on God's laws.

I was not going to allow anyone to go around bushwhacking my friends, or any citizen of my county.

People ask how a Christian can be willing to be in an occupation which might require the use of violence. Jesus never used violence against anyone. He advocated turning the other cheek. He taught forgiveness and gave His life as a sacrifice for others. He didn't enforce the Law of God, He fulfilled it. He overcame the law of sin and death through self-sacrifice.

Some say when Jesus plaited a whip, overthrew the money changers tables, and drove the sacrificial livestock out of the Temple courtyard, putting an end to corrupt commerce; He demonstrated righteous anger and just punishment. The fact is He didn't hurt anyone, not then or ever.

The Bible says we are to do justice, love mercy, and walk humbly with God.

Justice requires both law enforcement and mercy enforcement.

Who would not be willing to protect the innocent? Who would not protect their own loved ones? Who would not defend themselves from an attacker? Who would not want to see the guilty punished? Who would not desire mercy when they have failed?

Jesus was and is, perfect.

I'm not perfect. I'm a work in progress.

Progress has been slow.

The next morning I walked to the Livery stable to saddle up Dusty.

We trotted east on Omaha Street, across the tracks and out through the east side of town. We crossed the bridge over Bear Creek, and continued on out to the Bar C, the home of William and Annabelle Courtney, and their daughter Lacey.

I stopped Dusty at the top of a hill and looked down on the ranch headquarters. As always, it was a beautiful sight, marred only by the presence of several armed men.

Bear Creek, lined with giant cottonwoods, wandered along below a bluff. On this side of the creek down by the stone bunkhouse, there were a couple of men with rifles standing out in the open.

On the other side of the stone bridge that spanned the creek, I could see two more men with rifles, standing on the porch of the big house.

Glen Corbet met me as I rode close to the bunkhouse.

"Howdy John, I'm glad you're here," he said.

I stepped down from the saddle and shook his hand.

"Glen, can you tell me what happened?"

He looked down at the ground, his hat brim hiding his face.

"We were out to the west pastures, rounding up the mamma cows with new calves, for branding and culling. Bill was on his way out to the roundup. We heard a shot. At first we didn't think much of it, but I decided to go check it out. I thought maybe somebody was sending a signal of some kind."

Glen was still looking at the ground. When he looked up at me, meeting my eye, he looked like hell.

"I found Bill lying on the ground with his horse grazing nearby. Bill was kind of squirming and gasping," he choked. "I could tell right away he'd been shot. His shirt was soaked with blood. I jumped off my horse and ran to him. He couldn't talk. He tried to say something, but he couldn't get air."

Glen took a deep breath.

"I don't even know how I got him up on my horse and brought him back here. I sent a rider to Bear Creek to get the doctor. Doc Johnson has been in there all yesterday and all last night," he concluded.

"Tell me what you think happened."

"I sent a couple of the boys back out to the place where I found him, to bring in his horse. They found a hidey hole on the top of a hill, with a single rifle shell set on a rock. Somebody shot him from hiding. I pulled all the men back here. Your deputy, the old guy, came out here. The deputy told us he thought it was a deliberate ambush. That's all I know, John."

I handed him Dusty's bridle reins.

"I'm going up to the house," I said.

Glen nodded.

I walked across the stone bridge over the creek and up the hill, to the big house.

I nodded at the men on the porch, and turned the bell crank by the enormous front door. After a few moments it was opened by Fred, in his tuxedo.

"Sheriff Sage, we were not expecting you," he said. "I'm so glad you're here, do come in."

I stepped into the foyer. Fred, the butler, left me there, as he walked over to the big double doors and knocked. I heard some sort of answer from within. As I now knew was his habit, he slid the doors open just enough to allow his entry, then turned and closed them behind himself.

"Sheriff Sage, I'm sure glad to see you," Doctor Johnson said, as he came out into the foyer.

He ushered me into the sitting room through the double doors, closing them behind us.

I loved this room.

"Let's have a seat, Sheriff Sage," Doc Johnson said, with a motion toward the furniture.

When we were seated, Fred once again appeared from somewhere to offer refreshments.

"Would either of you gentlemen care for tea or perhaps some coffee?" he inquired.

We both declined.

"Bill seems to be stable for now," Doc Johnson began, without preamble. "He was unconscious when I got here yesterday. He still is. I've been giving him laudanum, to keep him under. I got the bullet out, but he had lost a lot of blood. He has a collapsed lung. It's possible that it will become functional again, now that I've sealed the wound. I am worried about infection though."

"Was the bullet a 44-40 round?

Doctor Johnson nodded.

"I'd say so."

"Will he live Doc?"

"I don't know, Sheriff. It could go either way. His color is much better and he doesn't have a fever, yet. If he gets pneumonia…We'll just have to wait and see. It's in God's hands, now"

We heard the doors slide open.

"Hello, Sheriff Sage," said Lacey Courtney.

Doctor Johnson and I both rose to our feet.

"Mom is upstairs with Dad. She won't be joining us. She asked me to speak with you."

"I'm going to go check on him," Doctor Johnson said.

He excused himself and left us alone.

"Lacey, do you have any idea who might have wanted to do something like this."

"No, Sheriff, I don't. Mom told me to ask you to find whoever did this. I know you will."

"Yes ma'am. First, I'm going to have to get some kind of a lead. Are you sure you don't know anyone with a grudge against your dad?"

She shook her head.

"Dad handles all the business. Mom and I don't have any idea why this happened." She choked up, tears welling in her eyes.

I opened my arms and she dropped her face against my shoulder. I held her for a moment, as she cried.

Shortly she straightened up, dabbing at her eyes with her handkerchief.

"I'm sorry, Sheriff. We Courtney's don't break down in adversity. I don't know what came over me. Please forgive me"

"Of course, Lacey. Do you think Glen might have some idea about your dad's contacts and business associates?"

"Oh, yes! He might at that. He and Dad are very close."

I saw her blush. It dawned on me that she always blushed, whenever Glen was part of the equation.

I suspected she and Glen might be very close as well.

DAN ARNOLD

24.

When I walked back down to the bunkhouse, I found Glen holding two horses. He was waiting for me with Dusty and his own horse, saddled and ready to go. I appreciated his anticipating my next move. I noted he was wearing a handgun and had his rifle in the scabbard.

"I'll take you over to where Bill was shot."

"Thanks, Glen," I said, as I tightened the cinch on Dusty.

We mounted and headed west along the edge of the creek. As we rode, I asked Glen if he had any idea who might have had a grudge against Bill Courtney.

"We've had some trouble over in Chaparral County, nothing to kill anybody over though."

"What kind of trouble?"

"We've got a little over a section of land, along both sides of the creek over there. That area is home to the Thorndyke Ranch."

"Is that the same Thorndyke, as the town is named for?" I interrupted.

"Yep, the Thorndyke's have the biggest ranch in Chaparral County. There is pretty much nothing over there in Chaparral County except ranches and farms. It's virtually still all open range. There are no clear boundaries for the Thorndyke spread. That's the cause of the conflict. Old man Thorndyke resents our land being in 'his' county and he wants it for himself. He also wants the access to that part of the creek. When we fenced our land it cut his herds off from the water along that part of the creek. Mr. Thorndyke claims it was a deliberate move to cripple his operation in the western part of the county."

"Was it?"

"Hell, no! We fenced our entire ranch. It just so happens, part of our ranch is in 'his' county. Mr. Thorndyke tried to buy it for pennies on the dollar. Bill told him he wasn't interested in selling. The next day our wire was torn down and our cattle scattered. Our cowboys were turned back when they went to go gather the cows. They said they were told they were trespassing on Thorndyke land and they better stay clear."

"What did you do?"

"Bill said to let things cool off for a little while. He went out to see Joe Holden, the Sheriff of Chaparral County. The Sheriff told Bill he would look into it. Bill told him he expected our cattle to be returned, or he would file a rustling charge against whoever had the cattle."

"Were they returned?"

"No. Bill thinks they were probably driven to Kansas and sold."

"That's rustling. In Texas we consider it a hanging offense."

"Yep, here too, but we couldn't prove it happened that way. The Sheriff of Chaparral County won't do anything, so Bill said to just write it off."

We rode along in silence for a moment.

"It was only about fifty head, but it hurt us. Bill said he didn't want to get crossways with the Thorndykes. In the old days, we used to do our roundups together, back when there weren't any fences between here and Canada. This was all open range. I miss those days," he said, wistfully.

I nodded In agreement.

"Yeah. Me, too."

After a while, we pulled up where Bill had fallen. The signs were all messed up from too many horses having been over this ground. I studied the surrounding hills and spotted the best place for an ambush shooting.

I pointed it out to Glen.

"Is that the place?"

I don't know. When I found Bill, I wasn't really looking around. Seems about right though. Jose and Junior found the spot, later, when they brought Bill's horse back."

I got off Dusty and handed the reins to Glen.

"You stay here and I'll go have a look," I said.

I worked my way around the edge of the hill until I found the two sets of tracks left by the Bar C cowboys. I followed them up to the spot they had found. Sure enough, the ground had been smoothed out and the brush chopped and crushed down to give a clear sight picture of the ground below. There was a rock placed to make an excellent rest for the rifle. I expected the shell had been left carefully placed on that rock. I eased down and crawled up into a shooting position. It was perfect.

I went back down to Glen.

"Yeah, that was the bushwhacker's shooting spot. I could see you, but I'll bet you didn't see me, even though you knew where to look."

He shook his head.

"The thing that bothers me is how the bushwhacker knew Bill would be riding through here."

Glen shook his head again.

"I don't know either, except this would be the best route to get to the roundup. We all rode through here, back and forth from the ranch headquarters the last couple of days, before the shooting."

I thought about that.

"Yeah, you know this is the best route, but the shooter would have had to scout around, watching and figuring it out. Then he had to find the best place to shoot from. This was no spur of the moment thing. He lay up there waiting and watching for Bill. This was planned by a professional."

"Who would do a thing like that?" Glen asked.

"I don't know, but I plan to find out. Glen, I have to see your rifle."

"What for, oh, do you think I did this?"

"No, Glen, but I have to check it anyway."

He pulled his rifle out of the scabbard and handed it to me. It was a .30/30, not the rifle that had been used to shoot Bill.

"You're in the clear, Glen. Sorry, but I had to know."

"Yeah, I reckon you know what you're doing. What'll you do now?"

"I'm going to try to track the shooter back out of here."

"I'm going with you," he said.

"No. I need to do this alone. If he's watching his back trail, he might shoot one or both of us. The Bar C needs you alive. I think maybe Lacey does too."

Glen blushed red as a beet.

"You can't go after him alone. He might shoot you," he said.

I shook my head.

"No, alone I won't be distracted. I know what to watch for. I've done this before. Besides, the shooter probably high tailed it out of here, before you or your cowboys could catch him."

I could see he didn't like it. He nodded though.

"Alright, what do you want me to do?"

"Go back to the headquarters and keep your eyes open. You were smart to pull your cowhands in close. Ya'll have to protect the home place."

"I'm no gun hand, none of us are," he said.

"I hope it won't come to that. This looks bad though. Somebody wants to see the Bar C damaged or even shut down. I intend to find out who, and why."

I swung up into the saddle, and with a wave, I headed back toward the shooters hill.

DAN ARNOLD

25.

It didn't take me long to get on the trail of the bushwhacker. There was little he could have done to disguise his tracks on this range land. That worried me because he would know how easy he was to trail. He would be expecting to be tracked.

I sure missed Yellow Horse. He was the best tracker I had ever seen. He would know far better than I, what to expect and how to prepare for it. He could think like the man or animal he tracked. I could read trail sign, but that was about all.

The trail I was following turned east. It skirted around behind the Bar C headquarters and went down into Bear Creek. I expected to lose it there, but I found it again fairly quickly on the opposite bank. It wandered to the south, where I found a section of the barbed wire fence had been cut. The tracks went up onto the road and headed due east. I followed them as best I could, but there had been too much horse and wagon traffic on the road, since the day before. Most of the time all I could be sure of was the tracks I was following never left the road. It bothered me to think the rider could have just turned his horse around and gone back west. I wouldn't have any way of knowing. I'm not that good at tracking.

There was nothing else I could do, so I kept going east.

After about two hours, I came to the little town of Waller. Here, I knew I had lost the tracks for good.

Waller was nothing special. It was a stage stop and rest point for freight haulers. It served the few farms and small ranches in the area with the essential supplies and little else, other than the saloon. Everything available in Waller came from or through Bear Creek.

They had a one room school house and a town sheriff.

Recently, Waller had been abandoned when the Sioux and Cheyenne had attempted to fight off the white invaders. Now that the threat of renegade Indian raids was pretty much over, it had been reclaimed. I had heard some talk that there was a medicine man up in the Dakotas who was getting the Indians up that way all excited again. He had some weird religious thing going on. It was called the Ghost Dance.

Waller had another distinction. It was the last town in the eastern part of Alta Vista County. In fact the county line was right on the east side of town.

I got off Dusty at the hitching post right in front of the sheriff's office. I try not to ever tie a horse by the bridle reins, so I just draped them over the rail. I was curious to see if Dusty would stand there.

I went inside.

The office was dark and empty.

It took me the better part of half an hour to find the sheriff. I met several of the local citizens before I finally went into the saloon.

I was concerned my quarry might be in there, so as I came inside, I stepped immediately to my right to clear the doorway. I didn't want to be silhouetted in the light from the doorway and blind to whoever was inside. As my eyes adjusted to the dim light I could see this place was a dump. It was dark and plain. It stank of tobacco smoke and stale booze. There were no stools or rail at the bar. There were several tables with chairs and I was surprised to see that many were occupied. The bar tender was not to be seen, so I went up to the bar and leaned back against it, facing the room.

A chair grated against the floor and a man stood up from one of the tables. He had his thin hair plastered over the top of his head with some kind of hair grease. The dirty apron around his waist suggested he was probably the bartender.

"Yeah, what'll it be mister," he said as he approached. He looked startled when he saw my badge.

"Howdy. I'm John Everett Sage, the Sheriff of Alta Vista County," I said, smiling

"That's nothing to me, mister. What do you want?"

"I see you have a sheriff's office, so I was wondering if you might know where the town sheriff is."

"I'm the sheriff," a voice called from one of the tables. There were four men sitting there.

I waited but nobody moved. I walked over to the table. It was apparent they were deep into a poker game. There was a pile of silver coins and three gold coins in the pot, with some paper money. Each man had his cards breasted.

I started over.

"I'm John Sage…"

"Yeah I know who you are. What do you want with me?" The speaker was sitting a little to my right, He had his left hand on top of the table, holding his cards, but his right hand was somewhere out of sight. That's bad form in a card game. I took a step to my left, putting a seated card player between us.

The sheriff of Waller smiled and brought his right hand up onto the table top. He was wearing a black leather vest over a pale blue shirt. There was a tin star pinned to the vest.

"You're a careful fella." He said. "I can respect that. What do you want with me?"

I was watching him and the whole room.

"There's been a shooting out at the Bar C. I'm looking for the man who did it."

"Did somebody get killed?"

"That isn't the point. I believe the shooter came here."

It was dead still in there. Nobody was moving or speaking. I had the full attention of everyone in the saloon.

"Yeah? Well, this is a busy place, lots of traffic passing through. When did this shooting happen?"

"Sheriff, this is a matter I don't care to discuss here. Can we go to your office?"

"No. As you can see, I'm busy at the moment." He looked back around the table. "Whose deal is it?" he asked.

"Just to make this clear, I'm asking for your cooperation in the investigation of a crime."

"No problem, Mr. Sage, you go on and investigate. I'm giving you my best cooperation, unless or until you cause trouble. Then we'll see what happens," he chuckled, and the other players joined him in the hilarity.

I waited for the laughter to stop.

"I don't believe I got your name, Sheriff," I said.

"My name is Jack Sloan. What's that to you?"

"I just wanted to know who to address the 'thank you' note to."

Nobody laughed.

"You know, Sheriff Sage, you're a long way from Bear Creek. Out here we don't need you coming around and bothering folks. You go on back to the big city and there won't be any fuss. You leave the law enforcement in Waller to me. Deal the cards, Hanson," he addressed the man to his right.

"Waller is in Alta Vista County. I have jurisdiction here."

Sloan took a deep breath and blew it out slowly.

"Sage, you're not welcome here. I don't give a rat's ass about Alta Vista County. That's just some lines somebody drew on a map. Now, you git!" he spat.

Clearly Jack Sloan was used to scaring people. I knew there wasn't much he could do. He was sitting down, with his hands on the table, where I could see them.

I figured he was bluffing, but if he moved a hand…

"I'll leave when I'm ready. If you're feeling lucky you go ahead and try to push me. I'm standing right here…I'll call your bluff. Let's see what you've got."

"Hold on now, everybody just calm down. I'm stuck in the middle here and I aint looking to get shot," said the man seated in front of me. "Sheriff Sage, I believe we may have gotten off on the wrong foot. I'm real nervous having you stand behind me like that."

"Who are you?" I asked. I was still trying to watch Sloan and everyone else in the room. All I could see of this guy was the top of his head and his hands on the table.

"I'm Spencer Wilson. This is my place and I'm the Mayor of Waller."

"Yes sir, Mr. Wilson, we did get off on the wrong foot. Call off your dog."

I looked Sloan in the eye. He didn't like it, but he didn't move a hair.

"Jack, let it go. I don't want any trouble with the Sheriff here."

"OK, Mr. Mayor." Sloan sneered, "Whatever you say." He relaxed in his chair.

"Can I stand up?" Mayor Wilson asked.

"Certainly," I said. I stepped away from the table out into the center of the room, watching, always watching.

Mayor Wilson pushed his chair back from the table, and walked toward me. He was a fat man wearing a blue shirt with no jacket or vest, over tan pants. He had some leather suspenders holding his pants up, while his belly tried to push them down. I could see he wasn't armed. He extended his hand. I hesitated because in some situations it isn't a good idea to tie up your gun hand. He smiled and nodded, indicating he understood my reluctance to shake hands.

"Seriously, Sheriff, we don't want any trouble. Hell, I voted for you myself," he smiled again.

"OK. Thanks for the vote. I don't suppose you can offer any help with my investigation?"

"No. Not really. Jack's right, we have people passing through here all the time. This town is just a place to stop, on the way to somewhere else."

"Maybe somebody saw my man yesterday morning. Maybe he stopped here"

"Might be, but unless he was wearing a clown suit, I doubt anyone would have noticed him."

I could see it was a dead end. I couldn't even be sure the shooter had come this way. I thanked the Mayor and made a careful exit.

I was glad to find Dusty, half dozing, exactly where I had left him.

DAN ARNOLD

26.

"I can't believe I haven't gotten one positive response to any of my telegrams. I guess I'm going to have to advertise for deputies," I said.

It had been nearly a month since I had sent telegrams to nearly everybody I knew who might be available. I had sent them as soon as I knew I had won the election.

"Well that's not unusual John. I've done it myself," Hugh rasped. "The hard part is interviewing the candidates," he chuckled.

His chuckle ended in a cough. Hugh's health was in question. He was probably too old for this job, and he had aged even more over the last year. He had given me my very first law enforcement job more than twenty years ago, in Arkansas. I hadn't sent for him because of his physical abilities, but because of his experience. Six terms as a County Sheriff, was a hard won education. I knew he was far wiser than I could ever hope to be.

After my fruitless search for the man who shot Bill Courtney, the day before, I needed to address some of the issues with my office. I had been gone to the other side of the state, on the Governor's errand for more than a week. I'd left immediately after I was sworn in. This morning I was starting only my second full day on the job as Sheriff of Alta Vista County.

"OK. I'll do that, but I don't like the idea of hiring strangers or people with no experience."

"Oh, really? I seem to remember hiring you, when all you had done was drive cattle. I think it worked out pretty well," Hugh rasped, grinning.

We heard someone coming down the stairs from the courthouse above. A moment later, '"Buckskin" Charlie Owens walked into the office. Now that I was the County Sheriff, he had come along as my only other sheriff's deputy.

Before Buckskin Charlie could say a word, Hugh pointed at him and rasped;

"People's exhibit number two, your Honor. I rest my case."

I laughed.

"OK, I said I would do it and I will."

"Do what?" Buckskin Charlie asked, looking perplexed.

"I'm going to advertise for deputies, so y'all don't have to work twelve hour shifts."

He snorted.

"That'll be the day. If there were ten deputies, you'd still have us all working twelve hour shifts. You are a heartless and relentless SOB," he grinned. "I know because I read it in today's newspaper."

I saw he was carrying a copy of the Bear Creek Banner. He tossed it on my desk.

I read the headline.

"RELENTLESS MAN HUNTER TO PURSUE SUSPECTED ASSASSIN."

I read on.

"John Everett Sage, the celebrated Sheriff of Alta Vista County (best known for his cold blooded and heartless treatment of miscreants), has pledged to personally hunt down and bring to justice, the man who shot noted rancher and philanthropist, William Courtney. This reporter has learned that the ruthless man hunter, Sheriff Sage, has taken up pursuit of the subject only yesterday. No word at this time as to the outcome, but we anticipate bloodshed."

I think I probably said something colorful and inappropriate.

"Yeah, I figured you'd feel that way," laughed Buckskin Charlie.

"The thing is, I don't have a clue where to go from here," I sighed.

"I think you do, John," Hugh rasped.

"The Thorndykes?"

"Yep. You told us the Bar C has had trouble with them. That's where I'd start."

"I don't have any jurisdiction in Chaparral County," I pointed out.

"Chaparral County has a new Sheriff, too. He's just been the County Sherriff over there for a few months. You could check in with him, as a courtesy, and kind of get a feel for the lay of the land."

"Hmmmm, I hadn't thought of that. The governor has asked me to look into it. I've been trying to think of a good cover story. That's actually a pretty good idea."

"Surprise, surprise!" Hugh rasped, raising his eye brows.

Buckskin Charlie laughed again.

I had promised to take Lora to supper at the Palace. This was kind of a big deal, because Lora ran a boarding house. As I said, she is a highly appreciated cook. Consuela would be cooking and serving the food at the boarding house tonight.

The Palace Saloon was a gemstone, set in granite and brick. It was no ordinary or typical saloon. It was a landmark and a destination. I had heard people came all the way from Denver and Cheyenne, just to visit the Palace of Bear Creek.

To be sure, alcohol was available at the Palace, just as one might expect from a saloon. Every imaginable whiskey, wine, champagne, and liquor known to man could be found in the Palace Saloon. They even had COLD beer. I knew that for a fact. I was told the bartenders there could make any kind of cocktail. The Palace was by no means a typical saloon. It was very different in other ways as well.

In most of the frontier saloons I had been in, women were not allowed, unless they were employees. Most saloons either didn't serve food, or it was basic, greasy fare.

The Palace was cosmopolitan and refined. The clientele was mostly ordinary folks who had a lot of new money. They were attempting to appear and become more sophisticated. When the Palace had begun serving a full lunch and dinner menu, a few months earlier, they'd become even more popular. Most folks didn't know what I knew. The Palace had stolen the chef from the Bon Ton Café. In no time at all, the Palace had become the finest restaurant on the Front Range. They even had electric lights, powered by batteries. They got those from Cheyenne, by train. Everybody who was anybody visited the Palace Saloon.

On my earliest visits to the Palace I had always felt as out of place as a skunk at a picnic. Dining with Lora made me feel like the Grand Duke of... somewhere or other. With her on my arm, I knew I was the envy of every man in the room. For us locals, it was second only to church, as a place to meet friends and socialize. Also, like at church, when dining at the Palace, we dressed in our Sunday best and tried to mind our manners.

For this and other reasons, the Palace was the place I had chosen when I proposed to Lora.

DAN ARNOLD

27.

Lora and I had just been seated at the Palace. The waiter had come to take our drink order.

"I'll have a …Why, hello, Bob," I interrupted myself in mid order. "Excuse us a minute," I said to the waiter, as I stood up.

The man who had been walking by our table stopped and studied me for a moment.

"As I live and breathe, if it isn't John Everett Sage! You're a long way from home. What brings you to Bear Creek, Colorado, and who is this vision of loveliness?

We shook hands.

"Bob Logan, may I present my fiancée, Lora O'Malley. Lora this is Bob Logan, a man I know from Texas."

I didn't mention his nick name, "Bloody Bob" a moniker he had earned in his line of work. Bob is a gun hand for hire. He prefers to be called a range detective or private investigator. He had worked for the Pinkerton agency, prior to going into private practice.

"Enchante, mademoiselle," Bob said.

He took Lora's offered hand and kissed it. I was glad she was wearing gloves.

A giant loomed up beside us. It was Clay Atwater, the owner of Atwater Freight and former Sheriff of Alta Vista County.

"Good evening, John, Mrs. O'Malley." he said, eyeing Bob."

"Hello, Clay. Bob Logan, meet Clay Atwater. Clay is the owner of Atwater Freight."

They shook hands.

"Would you gentlemen care to join us?" Lora offered, to my annoyance. I wanted her all to myself.

"Can't," said Clay. "I got business with them fellers over yonder. John, a couple of my teamsters were in the saloon over in Waller, yesterday. They said you made Jack Sloan back down. That true?"

Clay is not a sophisticate.

"Uhhh...no. Not really. He and I had a little misunderstanding and the Mayor intervened."

"Not what I heard. Nobody ever made him crawfish before. See ya later. You folks have a nice meal. Nice to meet ya," he added as an afterthought, nodding at Bob.

Clay wandered off to his business dinner.

"I, on the other hand, will be delighted to join you," Bob said.

When he saw my face he amended his statement.

"...Just for a drink, perhaps."

He pulled out one of the extra chairs and sat down, looking smug.

I sat down again as well.

"You know, Bob; we have a city ordinance against the carrying of handguns inside the city limits," I said, while signaling the waiter.

Bob was carrying his Colt .45 in a cross draw holster, the same way I do, for the same reason. I knew he also had a hideout gun on him somewhere.

"I noticed you aren't bothered by such trivialities," he replied.

"Good evening, Sheriff. We are delighted to have you with us this evening. May I suggest a wine?" The maitre de asked. "Bring a bottle of the Cabernet Sauvignon '85 to the table," he said to the waiter. "Compliments of the house," he said to me, with a little bow.

Bob was watching all this with a wry expression. He sat with his fingertips together.

"Why, John...I had no idea."

I opened my jacket and showed him my gold badge where it was pinned to my vest.

"Are you planning to relieve me of my firearm?"

I shook my head.

"No, Bob. That's a matter for the police. I'm the County Sheriff. I could take it from you, but we both know how complicated that might get."

I was aware of the way Lora was watching us.

"That's a relief. I might need it to defend this ladies honor against such a disarming gentleman as you," he smiled.

I bowed.

"Besides, I am not the only other person in this establishment who is armed."

"Probably not."

"Most certainly not. Do you see the man sitting alone over there?" he indicated with his eyes.

"I do."

"Do you know who he is?"

"I don't."

"He's Tom Horn. He works for the Pinkerton Agency, my line of work. You might say he's the competition."

The waiter arrived with the wine bottle. For some reason, he showed me the label. When he uncorked it, he tried to hand me the cork. I shook my head and he set the bottle down with a thump, and walked away. When the waiter left, I swear he seemed annoyed.

"Tom Horn, huh? I've heard the name somewhere."

"I should smile you have. He's a famous rodeo bronc fighter, and they say he helped capture Geronimo."

"I thought he was down in Arizona. You have some business with him?"

"No, Sheriff, none at all. As I mentioned, he's quite good at riding rough stock. I expect he's here for the rodeo. Do you see the couple over there?"

I nodded.

"You can be sure that gentleman is armed. You probably know him."

I shook my head.

"That's Wyatt Earp and the attractive lady with him, is his wife, Josie."

"Why are *you* here, Bob?"

He looked over at Lora.

"May I pour you a glass of wine?"

She smiled and extended her glass. Bob poured wine for all of us. I didn't want wine. I wanted a cold beer.

The orchestra started playing on the stage at the end of the room.

"Bob, I asked you what your business is, here in Bear Creek."

"Oh, yes of course, John. Sorry. I have no business in Bear Creek. By the way, if you really did have a run in with Jack Sloan, you are lucky to have survived it. I think there's paper on him. I believe he is wanted for a murder in Idaho. Jack Sloan is not his real name; he goes by a number of aliases…"

"Bob…"

"All right, no need to be tiresome. I am here at the request of a friend of the Governor." He said, picking up a menu.

I raised my eyebrows.

"It seems you have a rustling problem in the area and the Governor has asked me to look into it, on behalf of this rancher, and others. He asked me to come here more than a week ago, but until today I was tied up elsewhere. I arrived here on the train about an hour ago."

"Tell me who it is, Bob. Who hired you?"

I could see Lora was anxious and tense.

Bob sighed and put down the menu. He put his finger tips together again.

"You can be very bothersome and stubborn when you put your mind to it, John. I honestly don't know what this lady sees in you."

I looked him in the eye.

He sighed again

"OK, I'm supposed to work for a man named William Courtney, owner of the Bar C Ranch. Do you know him?"

I thought about that. Bob was, for all intents and purposes, a gun thug. Why had Bill Courtney hired a gun thug? I had been gone to Capitol City at the time. The Bar C only had a handful of cowboys and none of them were skilled at dealing with desperados. They had been turned back when they had gone to retrieve the lost cattle in Chaparral County. What was Bill Courtney thinking?

"Of course we know Bill and his wife, Annabelle…" Lora started.

"Bill Courtney was shot on his ranch, the day before yesterday," I interrupted.

"What? Does the Governor know?" Bob sputtered.

"I expect he does. It's been in all the papers."

"Who did it? Was he killed?"

"Bill was ambushed. He is gravely wounded. We don't know who did it, or why…yet."

Bob considered the new information for a moment.

"This changes things. I'll have to contact the Governor. Can Mr. Courtney still direct his affairs? He was to be my meal ticket, if you follow my meaning."

I told Bob as much as I wanted him to know. Then, I offered him a job.

"Thank you, John. It means a lot to me that you would consider me for such a position. You understand of course, I'll have to consider my options. I have become accustomed to my freedom and a certain amount of luxury, afforded me by the significant income from my business ventures,"

"I expect I know better, Bob. You do make good money, *when* you get hired and *if* you don't get killed. Between jobs you have to conserve or starve.

How often do you find yourself on the wrong side of the law?"

Bob frowned. He looked over at Lora.

"I see how he was able to talk you into marrying him. He's all charm and kindness."

Lora laughed.

"Come see me in the morning at my office in the courthouse. We'll talk about all this some more. I'm done talking business tonight." I looked at Lora.

"Ah, yes of course. Well then, if you will excuse me." Bob stood up and bowed to Lora.

"Until we meet again, mon chere…" He turned and left.

"Oh, my! He is quite the ladies' man, isn't he?" Lora asked.

"Don't be deceived. He's a very dangerous man."

She smiled sadly.

"Yes, he reminds me of you."

DAN ARNOLD

28.

Bob Logan wandered into my office in mid-morning. I figured that was early for him.

I introduced him to Buckskin Charlie. They had never met.

"John, I wired the Governor first thing this morning. It took a couple of hours for him to get back to me, but he indicated I should defer to your judgment. I need to be lawful in my participation. I might consider your offer, under certain conditions." Bob said.

"What did you have in mind?"

"I need to have the freedom to take an occasional job away from Alta Vista County."

"I think we can arrange that."

"I might need to operate under cover. It would be best if I didn't identify myself as a deputy...no badge. If I operate outside this county the badge won't mean anything anyway."

I thought about it. There could be advantages to having a plainclothes detective. There had been a couple of times when I didn't show the badge, until I had a handle on the situation. On occasion, I had passed myself off as an outlaw, to get close to wanted men.

"It might work. Though if you are going to be on the County payroll, some people outside this office are going to know you're a deputy. You'll need to have a badge, but you don't have to wear it."

"That shouldn't be a problem."

"This is the deal breaker though. If you work for me, you do what I say, when I say. I'm the boss. That is non-negotiable."

"I understand. You have to be able to trust me."

I nodded.

"Can you handle that?"

He held out his hand

"I can, if you can."

We shook on it.

"Good," he said, "this way I will be able to see more of Lora."

He winked.

I said something colorful, but not at all inappropriate.

I filled him in on the circumstances surrounding the theft of the cattle from the Bar C. We discussed what our approach needed to be.

"The Governor told me there have been a lot of settlers moving onto any available land and homesteading, all over the state. These are mostly farmers and small ranchers. That's a good thing for the State. County land offices are recording deeds left and right as well. Every new landowner is another tax payer." Bob said.

"Yep. We have it happening right here in this building. We also have real estate offices opening. Some of the original homesteaders have land to sell and there are people practically standing in line to buy it," Buckskin Charlie added.

"Everything used to be open range land and there was more than enough land for everybody. The Indians objected to us taking it from them, of course, because it was their ancestral homeland. We've all seen what's happened to them. I've had occasion to kill a few myself, Indians I mean, just trying to keep my hair. Still, not long ago if you could take the land and hold it against Indians and renegades, it was yours. Now there is more demand and less land available."

"That's exactly the issue in this case. The Thorndykes claim land they don't have rightful title to. They've tried to steal that section from the Courtney ranch. Add to that the fact some of the settlers have helped themselves to cattle without brands, cattle that may have belonged to the big ranches, and it all adds up to bad news. Worse, some of those 'settlers' really are rustlers. They steal cattle and change the brands as a way of life.

The big ranches have formed a Stockman's Association. The Thorndykes hold the reins, and control too much of the country. That's why the Governor wanted me to look into the Courtney's claim." Bob concluded.

"Alright then, it seems to me all of this is interconnected. There's a good chance Bill Courtney was shot because he wouldn't stand by and let the Thorndykes steal his land or his cattle. We don't know who shot him, but we may know why."

Both Bob and Buckskin Charlie nodded.

"The problem is, the shooting took place in Alta Vista County, but the trail leads to Chaparral County. I'll go to Joe Holden, the Sheriff of Chaparral County, in my official capacity and request his help."

"Good luck with that," Bob said.

I raised my eyebrows.

"Why do you say that?"

"Joe Holden works for whoever pays him. He's the County Sheriff, and the Thorndykes own the county. He knows which side his bread is buttered on. Therein lays the rub." Bob observed.

"Do you know Joe Holden?"

"No, but I know of him. He and I are in the same line of work, or we were until he put on the badge. He was a killer for hire."

"I would remind you that you've put on the badge, yourself," I said.

"Right, so I have."

"But Holden doesn't know that." I pointed out.

A wolfish grin slowly spread across Bob's face.

It was nearly sixty miles to the town of Thorndyke, the county seat of Chaparral County. It would take a full two days to get there by stagecoach. The stage stopped for the night at Waller and had stops for mail delivery and passenger comfort. Riding across country would shave a few miles off and some hours as well.

We decided in the morning, Bob and I would ride out together, but enter the town separately.

That afternoon Glen Corbet came into the office. He looked very worried.

"Howdy, Glen, how's Bill doing?"

"He's awake and able to eat and drink a little. Doc says he thinks he'll pull through. He's weak as a kitten and sleeps a lot. He wants to see you."

"I'm going to be gone for a few days, I'm leaving at daylight, but I have to go right past the Bar C on the way. Can I stop by in the morning?"

"I expect that will be fine. I have some bad news though."

"OK…?"

"There's been another shooting, this time a man was killed."

"When and where?"

"It was this morning. It happened on that section of land over east of the main ranch, in Chaparral county."

"Who was shot?"

"A surveyor, there were two men working over there the last couple of days. Before he was shot, Bill wanted to get the boundaries clarified with metes and bounds descriptions as well as the section, township and range descriptions. He wants to be certain we know exactly where the lines are before we rebuild the fence. He'll have the survey filed of record, in the land records of both Chaparral County and Alta Vista County."

"That's expensive, but a really good idea. Any idea as to who the shooter might be?"

He shook his head.

"John, the thing is, it looks like it could be the same shooter. I know you told me to keep the boys close to the headquarters, but we have a lot of cattle and a lot of fence. We have to get some things done. I send out one pair of riders at a time. Donny and Jim were over on the east side when they heard the shot. I'll say this, they didn't run away. They pulled their rifles and high tailed it toward the sound of gunfire. They found the other surveyor hiding under the survey wagon. He told them where he thought the shot came from. Donny and Jim eased up there and found the same set up as before. They also found this."

He held up a single 44-40 shell case.

"It was sitting straight up on a rock."

I didn't like it at all. The first thought I had was that Glen was automatically a suspect. Both shootings were on the Bar C. It could mean someone from the Bar C was the shooter. Glen had been the one to find Bill after he was shot. Then again, Glen had been with the others by the branding fire, when Bill was shot. Had he been at the headquarters when the second shooting happened? What about Donny and Jim, or Jose and Junior. Actually, all I had to go on was what Glen had told me. And, there was the set of tracks I had followed.

I reminded myself that at this stage in an investigation it was important not to draw any conclusions, but to continue to gather information.

"How long was it from the time they heard the shot, until they found the rifle shell?"

"I don't know. I didn't think to ask them that."

"OK. I'll want to talk to them in the morning."

"We'll be watching for you," He said, as he turned to the door. He stopped.

"Sorry, John, under the circumstances, that didn't sound right."

I shook my head.

"No, it didn't."

29.

A couple of hours after daybreak Bob and I rode onto the Bar C. I introduced Bob to Glen, but didn't mention why we were traveling together. I didn't have to.

"Aren't you the… uh…range detective, Bill said the Governor had recommended?" Glen asked, tactfully.

Bob looked at me and raised his eyebrows.

"Glen, when we talked a couple of days ago. You didn't mention Bill had hired a gun hand. Why is that?"

Glen looked away.

"Ah… John, I didn't know whether Bill had actually done it, or not. It was at least a couple of weeks ago when we talked about it, and nobody ever showed up." He shrugged and studied the ground.

I could understand his not having said anything. Hiring a gunman wasn't the sort of thing people talked about.

"Let's go talk to Bill, I said. "Then, I want to talk to those cowboys."

"Hang on a minute," Glen said. "Mrs. Courtney and Lacey don't know anything about this. Bill wouldn't want them to know he had hired a…

"…Bob, my name is Bob, Glen. Don't worry; we won't reveal the true nature of my occupation. The usual explanation is that I am assisting in the investigation of some reported criminal activity.

Nothing further need be said." He smiled a mirthless smile. "Besides, technically Mr. Courtney hasn't hired me. We haven't even met, yet."

Glen looked relieved.

Up at the big house, Fred the butler answered the door with his usual aplomb, and also as usual, he left us standing in the foyer. Today he went upstairs. He returned directly, followed shortly by Annabelle Courtney.

After the introductions were made, Annabelle informed us Bill was awake and would see me. She suggested the other gentlemen should wait in the sitting room. She took me up the stairs and into their bedroom. It was sumptuously appointed.

Bill was lying in a giant canopy bed. The heavy curtains had been opened and light flooded the room. There was a large upholstered chair drawn up right next to the bed.

Annabelle went and leaned over the bed; she spoke quietly with Bill for a moment, and then beckoned me forward.

"I'll leave you alone for a few minutes, while I see to the comfort of our guests. John, he's very weak and can't talk long. Please be brief." She chewed on her lip a little. "Ring this bell if you need anything." She left the room, closing the door quietly.

"Sit down, John," Bill croaked. He attempted to clear his throat, but it was little more than a weak cough. I could see the effort was torturous. He lay flat in the bed with his head on a pillow. The covers were pulled up over his chest, but his arms were on top of the bed clothes. After a moment he regained his composure.

"Bill, don't talk, just listen for a moment. If you disagree with anything I say, just shake your head. I'll ask some questions and you can just nod 'yes' or 'no'. OK?"

He looked at me and smiled weakly. He nodded.

"You've had some trouble with the Thorndyke outfit. They tore down your fence on the quarter section of the Bar C that's over in Chaparral County. Yes?"

He nodded again.

"They stole the cattle that had been over there?"

He pondered for a moment then gave his head a little shake. "I don't know," he breathed.

"Ok, I understand. You don't know for sure what happened to the cattle."

He nodded.

"When your cowboys went out to try to retrieve the cattle, the Thorndyke crew stopped them and accused them of trespassing."

He nodded.

"You were concerned the situation was getting out of hand. You were afraid your cowboys might get into a shooting war with the Thorndyks."

He nodded again.

"I'll bet you were mostly concerned for Glen, because he and Lacey are getting serious?"

He smiled weakly and winked, nodding.

"So, you contacted the Governor. He recommended you hire a range detective."

Bill looked startled. "John, I didn't know what to do…" He coughed again. It tore him up. He grimaced in pain and started sweating. His hands gripped the bed clothes.

"It's not a problem, Bill. I know Bob Logan, he's here now, and we're working together."

After a moment he began to relax. "Thank God," he croaked.

There was a quiet knock on the door and Annabelle came in.

"I'm sorry, John. I'll have to ask you to stop now. He needs to rest."

"Yes ma'am. Don't worry, Bill; we'll get this thing figured out." I reached out and gripped his arm.

"John, thank you," he said, his clearest words yet.

You're welcome. I'm just doing my job. You get some rest. I'll see you again soon."

When I walked into the sitting room, I found Bob, Glen and Lacey sitting and having coffee.

I noted that Glen and Lacey were sitting together on a couch.

"May I offer you some coffee, Sheriff?" Fred enquired.

"You bet, Fred! Thank you."

I sat down and caught Bob's eye. He raised his eyebrows. I nodded.

I noticed that Glen had observed this exchange.

After I drank some coffee and engaged in some brief small talk, Glen, Bob and I, walked back down the hill to talk to the cowboys, Donny and Jim. They said they figured it was probably less than thirty minutes from the time they heard the shot, until they found the place from which the shot had been fired.

By that time, the shooter, riding fast, could have been two or three miles away.

They told us how to find the place.

Bob and I mounted up and pointed our ponies to the east.

.

30.

"That Lacey Courtney is, to phrase it in the parlance of the working cowboy, 'one cute filly'," Bob observed.

"She's spoken for, Bob."

"I don't believe that is the case."

"She and Glen are sweet on each other."

"Indeed, I observed that. However, there is no ring on her finger, and 'There's many a slip between cup and lip'. I expect she is available, and she was not indifferent to my charm." He grinned

"Few women are, Bob, but it's not a good idea for you to mix in."

"Au contrare, mon ami. She is beautiful, single, available and quite rich. I think it is a very good idea, 'Fortune favors the bold'," he added.

I didn't like it, but it was none of my business.

When we eventually found the site of the shooting, there was no doubt it had been the same shooter. If the single flat rock, used as a combination rifle rest and display shelf, were not enough evidence, the tracks of the shooter's horse were. I remembered their size, shape and irregularities. I'd spent some time following them, just a couple of days before.

I was tired of always being at least a full day behind the assassin.

We tracked him back out to the road, but again he could have gone either east or west. If he went east, he would eventually come to Thorndyke. If he went west, he would come to Waller first, then on to Bear Creek. Waller was just a couple of miles from this spot on the road.

"Here's where we part company, Bob. You go on to Thorndyke. I'll go into Waller and have another look around. I'll meet you in Thorndyke."

"Wait a minute. I don't think we should split up here, John. If you have another run in with Jack Slade, you'll need me to back your play," Bob said, earnestly.

"You might have a point, but I don't intend to have a run in with him, yet. If he *is* wanted, I'll have to arrest him eventually, but today won't be the day. I have bigger fish to fry. You said he uses aliases?"

Bob nodded.

"He goes by John Sloan, Jim Sloan, and of course, Jack Sloan. Jack Slade is his real name. You'll find wanted posters for Jack Slade, AKA Jim Sloan, out of Idaho. He's probably wanted elsewhere too."

"And you know all this, how? Is he also in the same line of work as you?"

Bob smiled slightly, with kind of a faraway look in his eyes.

"No John. He is just a name on a list of wanted criminals. There is a reward associated with his being found and brought to justice, dead or alive."

"Dead or alive! Are you saying you hunt men for the bounty?"

Bob sighed.

"I do whatever comes my way, to make a living. You were quite correct on that point."

I thought about that.

"It's none of my business. The plan stays the same. We split up and go in to Thorndyke separately, me wearing the badge, and you under cover. You go on east from here, and I'll go into Waller."

He reluctantly agreed.

A moment later, we were headed in opposite directions, on the same road.

Just before I got to Waller, I rode past a huge two story house. It had a covered porch all the way around it. It reminded me of Lora's house. It turned out it was a boarding house of sorts, as well. There was a sign hanging above the front steps that said "Mrs. Poole's Boarding House." There were a couple of buckboard wagons tied out front and five saddle horses. Off to the side were a couple of freight wagons.

"That's an unusually busy place." I thought.

I noticed there were people out on the porch. A couple of those people were women who appeared to be…in their underwear!

I figured it out quick.

I dismounted and started examining the saddle horses. I was hoping to identify the one who had left its tracks at the murder scene. As I was checking the feet of the last horse, a man came hurrying down the front steps.

"Get the hell away from my horse, mister."

I recognized the voice.

I straightened up.

"Howdy, Sheriff Sloan," I said.

He jerked to a stop.

"What are you doing here?"

"Well, it appears to be a popular establishment."

"Don't matter, you aint welcome here."

"I believe everyone is welcome to come…and go, as they please, unless of course this is your place."

He shook his head.

"No, it belongs to Mayor Wilson."

"I guess I'm not surprised."

"What were you doing with my horse?"

"I thought maybe I knew your horse, but after we shook hands, not so much. I'm disappointed. He isn't the horse I thought he was."

He scowled.

"You'd better just be passing through. You got no jurisdiction here. This is Chaparral County."

"Right you are. I'm actually on my way to Thorndyke. I just need to go into Waller for a minute. I'll be going now."

"Damned right you will!" He yelled loudly, clearly for the benefit of the people on the porch.

I swung up into the saddle.

"You get the hell away from here, and don't come back!" He screamed.

I fixed my eyes on his.

"Oh, I'll be coming back. Sooner or later, I'll be coming for you, Slade."

He froze. For about one second he thought about reaching for his gun. He changed his mind and spun away, nearly running, as he headed for the house.

I gave a little wave as I rode away.

DAN ARNOLD

31.

I found nothing of interest in Waller. Mayor Wilson wasn't in the saloon, and it only took me a few minutes to look over the few saddle horses tied in front of the saloon.

When I went back past the "Boarding House," I noticed Jack Slade's horse was gone. He hadn't come into Waller. I wondered where he was.

Shortly later, as Dusty and I were headed east, trotting down the road, headed for Thorndyke. The road passed through a narrow defile between two rocky hills. I was fully alert and scanning the hillsides, when I heard a rifle shot at the exact second I saw a flash and puff of smoke.

I was surprised to realize I had been shot.

The road was very hard when I landed on it, but the pain associated with the impact indicated I was still alive. I was pleased to discover I could move my legs and body. The pain of the gunshot wound itself hadn't fully arrived yet.

After a moment, I became aware there was nothing between me and the shooter except Dusty. He was standing stock still in the middle of the road, looking down at me.

I could see my rifle in the scabbard hanging on the saddle, right there! It was just a few feet away.

I knew that if Dusty didn't move, the rifleman above me would either shoot him, to get a shot at me, or move to where he had a clear shot. Either way, my horse and I were sitting ducks.

I figured I had one chance to save Dusty, and myself.

I leapt up and ran out from behind Dusty, then stopped and reversed direction.

A bullet struck the road, right where I had been a split second ago.

As I ran past Dusty, I grabbed my rifle out of the scabbard and dove behind a pile of rocks at the edge of the road. Another bullet hit those rocks, ricocheting away.

Now, I had good cover and the opportunity to fight back.

Dusty continued to stand in the road, looking over at me hiding behind the rocks, like I had lost my mind.

I took inventory.

My whole left side was on fire. My left arm was getting very stiff and didn't want to work. On that side, my shirt and vest were saturated with blood. I was surprised there wasn't even more blood. As I examined the damage, I saw how blessed I was. The bullet had torn through part of the bicep on my left arm and grazed along a rib on my left side, passing through the thick muscle behind my arm pit.

I was hurt, but if I got treatment soon, possibly not fatally.

I needed to get medical attention, and I couldn't do that with a killer in the rocks above me.

I had lost my hat, there was sweat in my eyes and I wasn't thinking very clearly.

I knew exactly the spot from which the shots had come. I couldn't clearly see up there without exposing myself. I crawled painfully a few feet. I peered through a narrow gap between the rocks. He was only about sixty yards above me, but at that range, the other rifleman couldn't see me through the crack. I eased my rifle forward and sighted in on the spot where the shots had come from.

I fired three shots in rapid succession and raced across the road. With my back against a boulder, I put three new shells from my gun belt into my Winchester. Somewhere behind me I heard the other man climbing over the rocks, just a few yards above.

I ducked out from behind my cover and saw a figure move out of sight, over the top of the hill. Very weak now, I raced up the hill as best I could. From the top of the hill, I saw the man jump on his horse.

I shot the horse. It was the best I could do under the circumstances.

The horse pitched forward, flinging the man to the ground. I kept my rifle on him as I eased down the hill toward him. He was up on his feet in a hurry, so I shot him. The first shot dropped him; the next two bullets were just to be sure he stayed down.

When I staggered down through the rocks to where he lay, I recognized the shooter. It was Jack

Slade. He and his horse were both dead. I picked up his rifle and ejected a shell. I was disappointed to see it was a 30-30 round, and not a 44-40.

I left the bodies of horse and man, lying under the sun, and struggled back over the hill to where Dusty still stood in the middle of the road. With all that shooting, he had never spooked or jumped.

Somehow, I managed to get up on Dusty. I was so very weak and tired I needed to rest from the effort. I wasn't able to think clearly. I just sat there.

From somewhere off to the east I heard a horse coming fast. For a moment I thought I heard Bob talking to me. I was dimly aware we were moving and he was helping me stay in the saddle. Then I passed out.

For some hours after that, things swam in and out of focus. At one point I was aware of riding in a wagon.

I woke up in a feather bed. I was all bandaged up and could barely move. I was incredibly thirsty. I had no idea where I was. The room was filled with light and smelled vaguely of sweat and cedar. Still, it was a very nice room.

The door opened and in walked Annabelle Courtney and Doctor Johnson. Doc Johnson smiled. Annabelle looked drawn and worried.

"Well, well," Doc Johnson said. "It's good to see you back among the living. I expect he'll be ready to eat something," he said to Annabelle Courtney.

She rang a bell.

Fred, the butler, appeared almost instantly.

"Fred, would you please bring the Sheriff some of that good soup?"

"Indeed. May I say it is good to see you doing so well, Sheriff," Fred said.

"Thank you, Fred."

I was surprised I could speak, my mouth was so dry.

I tried to sit up. Everything, everywhere, hurt.

Doctor Johnson helped me up into a sitting position and sort of held me like that as Annabelle put some pillows behind me. I felt a little better.

Doctor Johnson poured some water from a pitcher into a cup, and handed it to me.

I drank, marveling at how good the water was, and at the strength in my right arm.

"How did I get here?"

"Mr. Logan brought you here in the back of a buckboard." Annabelle answered.

"When?"

"It was late yesterday afternoon. I had been here checking on Bill. I was just leaving when he drove up," Doc Johnson said.

"I don't remember much."

"That's the laudanum Sheriff. I gave you enough to knock you out, while I stitched you up. You slept all night."

"I think I killed Jack Slade."

"You did," Bob said, from the doorway. "I'm on my way to go collect his body now."

"Hey, Bob. I guess I owe you my life. Where did you get a wagon?"

"Yeah, about that, I'm afraid I stole the horse and wagon from a whore…uh...boarding house, over near Waller."

Annabelle nodded. "Mrs. Poole's, everybody around here knows the place," she blushed.

"Anyway, I stole the horse and wagon and brought you here. It was just luck that the doctor was still here."

"I don't believe in luck."

"OK. I stole it and now I'm going to use it to go retrieve Slade's body."

"Where's Dusty?"

"He's here. I tied our horses to the back of the wagon and brought them along. You stayed on him, till we got to the, uh…"

"Mrs. Poole's," Annabelle offered.

"I'll go with you," I started to try to swing my legs off the bed. I instantly realized two things. The first was it hurt too much and my head was pounding. The second was that I was naked under the sheets.

"No," Doc Johnson said. "You're in no shape to be going anywhere, at the moment. I sewed up the bullet gash through your arm and both holes through your back. If you try to move around much, you could tear them open. Bob here, bandaged you up enough to stop the bleeding, but you lost a lot of blood. I had to clean the wounds and sew you up. You'll need some time to recover."

"Swell," I said, "how long?"

"We'll see. If all goes well you can probably walk some, later today. You won't have much use of that left arm for a couple of days, though."

This called for a change of plans.

"Bob, you might do better to take Sloan's body to the Sheriff of Chaparral County, the county in which he was killed. I believe you said he was a wanted man." I suggested.

Bob was quiet for a moment.

"Yes, I think I follow your line of thought. I have some credentials as a bounty hunter. My bringing his body in for the reward would sort of support my bona fide. Would it not?"

"...Exactly."

"But, surely you understand, if I am credited with his demise, I would have lawful claim to the reward money."

"That can't be helped."

Bob beamed. "Right then, I'll be off."

"I'll see you in Thorndyke." I called.

The doorway was empty.

Fred showed up with a tray, on which were a bowl of soup a spoon, some fresh bread, and a napkin.

It was the best soup I had ever eaten in my life. It made me want a steak.

Later, Annabelle came back into the room with a suit of clothes.

"I understand your suit coat, vest and shirt were ruined. You and Bill are about the same size. He has kind of outgrown this suit, though. He told me he wants you to have it."

Other than the formal wear the governor had gifted me with, it was a far nicer suit than I had ever owned. I planned to get married in the suit the governor gave me.

"Fred will help you get dressed whenever you're ready. Your other garments have been washed and are now dry."

I knew she was referring to my formerly blood soaked union suit and my socks. I remembered my left boot had started to fill with blood.

With Fred's help, I was walking before lunchtime.

32.

Unknown to me, Lora had arrived at the Bar C. She found me being helped down the stairs by Fred.

By the time Bob had hauled me to the Bar C, all shot up, it was late in the day. It was nearly dark, when Doc Johnson had gotten me put back together, too late to send word into town. I had been out of it, and the others had not been thinking of Lora at that point. Annabelle sent Glen to fetch Lora first thing in the morning, just before I woke up. Lora had dropped everything, and Glen had driven her carriage out to the Bar C.

From my elevated position on the stairs, I could see how beautiful she was, and how angry she was.

As Fred helped me down the stairs, Lora was pacing in the foyer. No running up the stairs to relieve Fred. No calling my name and rushing to embrace me…none of that.

I could see Fred was nearly as frightened as I was.

When we reached the bottom of the stairs, she let me have it.

"Oh! You idiot! How could you do this to me? John, you told me you were going to visit with the Sheriff of Chaparral County."

She was quite loud, it echoed in the huge room.

We were at the bottom of the stairs. I wished I was back in bed.

Fred, seeing the storm warnings, abandoned me.

"If you folks will excuse me…"

He ran away, the coward.

"Glen told me, you and that Bob person, are looking for a killer." Lora hissed.

Glen chose that moment to open the front door. He looked back and forth between us.

"I'll wait by the carriage," he said, quickly closing the door again.

We were alone, at last.

"Well, what do you have to say for yourself?" She crossed her arms and tapped her foot.

"Uh…I don't feel too well."

I was down there at the bottom of the stairs, with my new suit coat draped over my left arm, that arm being in a sling, and I was leaning back against the elaborately carved newel post. It was only the post that was holding me upright.

"Oh, John!" She came forward and put her face against my chest and started crying!

I held her as best I could, with my right arm.

After a little while, she looked up at me, with a somewhat more concerned expression.

"How bad is it?"

"Oh, it's nothing serious. The bullet didn't hit anything vital, Lora, I'm just a little stove up. I don't exactly feel like dancing, but I'll dance with you," I grinned.

"You could have been killed!" She snapped, suddenly angry again.

"Glen told me you killed the other man," Now, she was sad.

I was having a hard time keeping up.

Fortunately, Annabelle Courtney came to my rescue.

"Lora, I'm so pleased you're here. We're having a problem with John here. He's being obstinate and uncooperative. The doctor told him to take it easy, but he is willfully disobedient. Perhaps you can put him in his place."

I felt like a naughty six year old, in more ways than one.

"Hello, Annabelle. Thank you so much, for all you've done," Lora said. "I assure you he won't be any further bother to you today."

"Won't you stay for lunch, Lora? It's a long drive back into town."

"Now hold on a minute. I'm right here. Y'all can speak to me, instead of about me, and who said anything about me going back into town?" I tried.

"Oh, Annabelle, I'm so sorry for his rudeness and general lack of manners. Yes, thank you, we would be delighted to stay for lunch. Tell me, how is Bill doing?"

The two ladies walked out of the foyer chatting together, leaving me to totter along behind them, as best I could.

At lunch, we were joined by Lacey and Glen. I was informed that I would be riding back into Bear Creek, with Lora in her carriage. One of the Bar C cowboys, Junior, would be our driver.

"Glen, thanks for bringing Lora out here," I said the words, but I knew he understood I was being partly facetious.

"I'm sorry you had to spend the whole morning driving back and forth between here and Bear Creek."

"No problem, John. Unlike you, I just do as I'm told," He said, smugly.

I saw Annabelle and Lacey look at each other meaningfully.

After lunch, I was unceremoniously escorted to Lora's carriage by Glen and Lora. I was glad to see Dusty, tied behind the carriage, next to Junior's saddle horse. I took a moment to pat and rub on Dusty some, and then Glen helped me get up into the carriage. On the ride into town, the sun was beating down on my face. I sorely missed my hat, which was probably now blowing aimlessly down the road, somewhere to the east.

When we got to Bear Creek, we dropped Dusty off at Al's livery stable. I didn't even get to get out of the carriage. Junior did it all. Then he drove us to Lora's boarding house. I had protested this, of course. I pointed out that I was a grown man and I could take care of myself. That statement earned me the silent treatment for most of the ride between the Bar C and Bear Creek. Lora would only look at me, to see if I was still alive.

At Lora's, Junior helped Lora out of the carriage first, then he helped me. I felt useless, watching Junior drive the team to the carriage house, to unharness the horses and turn them out in the pasture. I was almost too weak and tired, to care.

"The first order of business is to get you a bath," Lora said, when we were inside.

I was past complaining. In fact, a bath was a really good idea.

There was one problem though; where was I going to take this bath? To my surprise, Lora had a bath room. A whole room, set aside for bathing, right next to her bedroom. It had a cast iron bath tub in it. Previously, I had been impressed that Lora had running water in the house. She had a cistern capturing rain water from the roof of the house and porch. This was piped indoors and fed by gravity flow for drinking water. She also had a windmill that pumped water from the creek, up the hill into a storage tank and then into the kitchen. She had water available, indoors, year round, rain or shine!

But that wasn't the marvel. The marvel was she didn't have to haul hot water from the kitchen to her bathtub; she had a dedicated pipe for heated water.

In the kitchen was a huge copper pot sitting on its own little stove. It was there solely for boiling water. That water could be drained out of the pot through a spigot on the front, or through a pipe in the side. The pipe carried hot water into the bathroom, and outside to the laundry room on the back porch.

When she had heated enough water for the bath she filled the tub by turning the valve in the kitchen, then turning the valve on the faucet of the bathtub. That bathtub had hot and cold running water!

"You know, my guests are not permitted to use this bathroom. They have to use the one upstairs and they have to haul their own hot water from the kitchen. It appears to me, even though you 'are a grown man and able to take care of yourself', that might be just a little too much work for you to do, in your present condition. Can you even pull your boots on?"

I had known my previous statement was going to come back to haunt me.

I sighed and shook my head. I couldn't pull my boots on. Fred had helped me do that.

"Can you take them off?"

"Maybe, but it will probably take a while."

She narrowed her eyes at me.

"Fine, you do that. I'll be back to check on you in a little while." She breezed out of the bathroom.

I was very proud of myself. Eventually, by pushing with the opposite foot, and using just my right hand, I was able to get both boots off. It was a difficult struggle.

I was sitting on the edge of the tub, panting and sweating from the effort, when Lora came back into the bathroom, with a clean towel and washcloth.

"Can you get dressed by yourself?"

"No."

I could see this was going to be a problem. It was bad enough Fred had to help me get dressed. Now Lora would have to do it.

"Can you get undressed by yourself?"

Her snotty attitude was beginning to annoy me.

"Look Lora, if I take my time and exercise a little caution, I can get myself undressed and into the tub. I'm sorry I got shot, but I'm about done in. I don't have enough energy left, to both bathe and fight with you."

"We're not fighting, John. We're just establishing the facts. Something you seem to struggle with."

She turned and left the bathroom again.

I was able to shed my jacket and vest with very little trouble. Fred had helped me get my shirt on. When I tried to take it off, I discovered it was amazingly difficult. I had to grasp my right shirt cuff in my left hand and pull my right arm out of the sleeve. Holding the shirt cuff didn't require me to move my left arm. But holding on to the cuff caused my bicep to flex a little, and it was no fun. I was able to gently pull the left sleeve down my arm, but I had to straighten the arm to do it. It was painful, but I was pleased I could do it.

"The rest ought to be pretty simple," I thought.

I dropped my pants and stepped out of them, but when I tried to get out of my union suit, I discovered it fit me more tightly than my shirt had. Even though I got the buttons undone, I was bound up in my underwear. I was in trouble.

Just then, Lora walked back in!

She took one look at my red face and started laughing.

It's a wonder how quickly we can go from strength and independence to weakness and dependence. It's humbling. We walk in our pride and dignity every day, but it's an empty vapor.

I was clearly embarrassed to be caught in my drawers, but I was out of options.

"When you stop laughing, would you please help me with this…" I gestured at my predicament.

"Of course, John, thank you for asking."

She held my right sleeve so I could pull my arm out and then she gently helped me peal the left sleeve off.

"Somebody did a good job of sewing up the tears in these long johns," she observed

This was the first time she had ever seen me bare-chested. She was immediately drawn to the bandages. She removed those and examined the wounds.

"Doc Johnson did a good job of stitching you up, too. These should heal nicely if we keep them clean. You've still got some dried blood on you and…oh, John, you've been hurt before!"

She was examining my scars.

"Thank you, baby, I've got it from here," I said.

"Oh, don't be silly. I'll help you finish getting undressed and into the tub."

"Uh…I can manage it."

Just like that, I knew I had made her angry again.

"You are such a prude. Do you think I haven't seen a man naked before? Who do you think you are? We're engaged to be married and…I don't know if that's such a good idea anymore."

"What? Oh, baby, I'm sorry I got shot. I'm sorry I didn't tell you what Bob and I are doing…"

"Shut up! Don't you say another word to me!" She turned and stormed out.

I stood there with the top of my drawers hanging around my waist, feeling helpless. I didn't know where to go or what to do.

Eventually, I got in the tub.

I could hear bustling around in the kitchen. I knew she was working on getting supper ready for her guests.

The difference between the sexes often causes conflict and miscommunication, equal to that between nations which speak different languages from each other.

Men and women are so different we are strangers and aliens to each other.

Thank God. That's part of what makes it all so much fun!

While I was soaking in the tub, taking care not to get water into my bullet wounds, I realized what was wrong.

Lora was afraid.

My being shot had frightened her. She had already lost one husband, and I had nearly gotten myself killed before we were even married. She was having trouble communicating that to me, possibly to herself, as well.

In the same way hitting your thumb with a hammer makes you angry, the emotional pain was causing her to feel angry. Anger is the natural aggressive response to a real or perceived threat. It's a survival instinct.

There was a knock on the door. I quickly put the washcloth in a strategic location.

Lora came in, carrying a robe. She hung it on a hook on the back of the door and started picking up my clothes.

"John I don't know if I can marry you. I can't stand the thought you might leave for work one morning and never come back."

"I know baby. I understand. You've lost one husband and you can't imagine going through the pain and loss again."

She came over and sat on the edge of the tub. I offered her my right hand and she took it.

"That's exactly the point. No, I can't go through that again. I know you John. You won't change. What you do is dangerous. What you do isn't just a job, it's who you are. The funny thing is I love you, partly because of that. I love you just the way you are. I'm confused. I need some time."

"OK. Nothing has changed for me. I'll marry you tomorrow, if you'll have me. You take all the time you need though. We can work through this. I love you and I want you to be my wife."

Later she brought me my supper on a tray, so I wouldn't have to dress and join her boarders having dinner in the dining room.

33.

I spent the night in Lora's bed. She slept somewhere else.

In the morning, she helped me get dressed. I had a little better flexibility, but I was much sorer. After breakfast in the dining room with the other guests at Lora's table, I walked up the hill into downtown Bear Creek.

When I got to my office in the courthouse, I had a surprise.

Walter Edward Burnside had arrived.

He didn't like to be called Walter, Walt, or Eddy. His friends call him Ed.

Ed is a young guy who had been a deputy to some very good men in a couple of towns in Texas. I had gotten to know him some when I had been a Texas Ranger.

He had left Texas to become a railroad detective, but when he found out what the railroad wanted him to do, he became dissatisfied with his employers, and they with him.

After Ed got my telegram, it had taken him two weeks to get to Bear Creek, because he wouldn't ride the railroad.

Here was a ready-made young deputy I could trust. I introduced him to Hugh and Buckskin Charlie.

"John, you look pretty stove up. What happened to your arm?" Ed asked, eyeing my sling. The others were equally curious.

I told them the story.

"Boys, here's the situation. The town of Waller now has no sheriff. The man who had the job was an outlaw, on the run. Jack Slade was hiding in plain sight, under an assumed name. His body has probably turned up in Thorndyke, by now.

Waller needs some sort of law enforcement, and I don't intend to let it continue as a den of cut throats. I propose to put one of you in the town, in your official capacity as a Deputy Sheriff of Alta Vista County. You would look after the town and the surrounding farms and ranches. You'll be answerable to the County Sheriff." I pointed at myself.

"Waller is barely in Alta Vista County, it's at the eastern extreme of the county. The Omaha road runs right through the middle of the town, so there's a lot of traffic through there. It's a stop over town, for freighters and the stage line. I expect there'll be conflict over issues associated with the county line. There may be problems with the local mayor because he owns the only saloon and 'Mrs. Pool's Boarding House', a house of ill repute, just over the county line in Chaparral County." I concluded.

I let them think about all that for a moment.

"I'm open to suggestions, so let's discuss it."

Hugh was the first one to speak up.

"I'm not sure you can pull that off, John. Politically, because it will involve a budget change, you'll have to get approval from the County Commissioners. You would have to arrange for an office and housing for the deputy. You can't prevent the town from hiring another sheriff. Also, we're still understaffed here. If you send one of us over there, there'll only be two of us here to run the jail and do whatever else needs to be done. We have three prisoners in here now, so you and Bob are the only ones who aren't completely tied to the jail." He looked worse than I felt.

We all thought about what he had said.

Buckskin Charlie spoke up next.

"John, we don't have any presence up at the mines in Flap Jack City, or even in North Fork. At some point we're going to have to spread out from Bear Creek into the surrounding communities, but we aren't ready yet. As it is now, the ore shipments and the payroll for the mines are being guarded by privately hired men. It ought to be done by this department."

I couldn't argue with any of those points. The governor had specifically asked me to address some of those issues, so I knew I could count on his support, but it would take some time and money to get them done.

"You're right, boys. We'll get the ball rolling, but it'll take some time to get there, and we'll be rolling it up-hill, all the way. In the mean-time, here's the way I want to organize the Sheriff's department.

When I was a Ranger we had rank. I was a sergeant in the Rangers. We'll do the same thing here. I'm the Sheriff; Hugh will be a captain and

Chief Deputy. Buckskin Charlie is a lieutenant and you, my young friend, are a sergeant," I indicated Ed. "Bob will be a lieutenant as well. New recruits will just be deputies. This will establish the pay grades and provide incentive for promotion. New recruits will start working in the jail and be trained by the Chief Deputy."

I looked at Hugh.

He nodded. I could see he was pleased with my thinking.

"Hugh, I'll write up those advertisements we talked about. We'll run ads in several newspapers and have some handbills printed up. We'll get some new recruits. How many do you think we'll need?"

"To man the jail, we'll need at least three men. That's one man for each eight hour shift. We have that now, but we'll need to be able to send deputies wherever they're needed, whenever they are needed. There are some patrol responsibilities we should start right away. That's one way to address the problem with Waller, North Fork and the others. When they know a Deputy Sheriff will be coming through every now and then, it should put them on alert to clean up their towns."

"I like it. So how many do we need to hire right away?"

"Could we have four? With those of us already on the payroll, that will make a total of nine."

"No, I don't think the current budget will accommodate that many. It's a big county but it seems like every department is demanding more money or more staff. Hire three. I can sell that to the commissioners. They know we need more men."

Hugh coughed and cleared his throat.

"I was hoping for one!"

"If you get enough good quality candidates, Tom needs deputies too, and his budget is set by the city. I got them to authorize three new deputies, before I took the job as town Marshal. Now that he's the Chief of Police, I guess the new hires will be called 'police officers' I saw that in Chicago."

"Now we're getting somewhere!"

"I still need to go out to Thorndyke. The bushwhacker who shot Bill Courtney is still around, somewhere, and the issue with the cattle theft has to be resolved. Bob is over there waiting for me now."

"I reckon you probably got the shooter, when you killed Jack Slade," Buckskin Charlie said.

"No, Slade was just a coward. He knew I would be coming for him eventually, and he just didn't want to face me straight up. He was riding a different horse, he was firing a different rifle, and he wasn't as good of a shot as the other man. He fired at me three times, and he still couldn't kill me. For sure he knew about the other shootings, or at least Bill's being shot. He probably read about it in the Bear Creek Banner. He probably figured to get away with killing me, because my shooting would be chocked up as just another victim of the polecat we're searching for."

"John, you're not in any shape to be chasing a killer." Hugh rasped.

"I'm getting a little stronger every day, Hugh. If I leave tomorrow, I won't even get to Thorndyke for two days. I'll take it easy and I'll be fine."

To prove the point, I took the sling off. I kept my arm partially bent though, because it hurt too bad to straighten it out. I knew I wouldn't be able to lift anything with it, not even my saddle. I would have to get Al to saddle Dusty for me.

That afternoon I walked over to the office of the Bear Creek Banner. I wrote out an advertisement for deputies, and had a handbill laid out for printing.

I met with Alexander Granville Dorchester III, at his place of business, the livery stable. Al told me he would be happy to have Dusty saddled and ready to go at daybreak. He'd be sure to have a full canteen and three days' worth of travel rations tucked into my saddle bags. From there, I wandered over to the general store and bought a new hat.

I figured I was better off on the road. The situation with Lora was precarious. "Absence makes the heart grow fonder," or so they say. Besides, a couple or three days of riding to Thorndyke would give me some time to heal and toughen up.

That's my motto.

"Get tough or die."

34.

It was a little after eight o'clock in the morning by the time I got to the livery stable. It had taken me awhile to drag myself out of bed. Then, it took me a long time to get dressed. I was so proud. I dressed myself! Dusty wasn't impressed; he'd been standing around saddled and waiting for about two hours.

I was stronger by the time I got to Thorndyke. It only took me the better of three days to make the two day ride. The first morning on the trail, my breathing was labored and I sweated through half an hour, just to recover from grooming and saddling Dusty. He was patient, but he looked at me a couple of times, like he didn't know who I was.

When I finally did get to Thorndyke, I was nearly back to normal. It still hurt to work my left side, but I could do it. There was a painful pulling on the stitches, but I was able to do all the things I normally did. Things like pulling on my boots.

The last day and a half of riding, from the moment I left Alta Vista County, I had been on the Thorndyke Ranch. I wasn't even sure when, or where, it had happened.

I wasn't impressed with the county seat of Chaparral County. In the beginning, this town had been the original Thorndyke ranch headquarters. There had been little or no attention to detail when the older buildings were built. Nearly all of the buildings were built of wood. It had gradually become a good sized and reasonably civilized town, an oasis on the plains. Thorndyke did have a courthouse. It was a single story wooden building, right next to a dry goods store. I could tell some effort was being made to gentrify the place, but it still had the look and feel of a company town.

Everyone who worked at the Thorndyke Ranch in the early days had to buy everything they needed from the company store. They spent their hard earned wages buying the essentials at exorbitant prices, from the only store available, which was owned by their employer. The High Times Saloon was owned by the Thorndykes, as was the one across the street, The Diamond T Saloon.

The Thorndyke brand was a diamond with a T in it. It was called the Diamond T. It was on display, all over town. I found the livery stable and arranged for Dusty's board.

It appeared to me as if the Thorndike's owned just about everything in the town. I had been told it also included the County Sheriff.

The Sheriff's office was right across the single main street from the courthouse. Like the Marshal's office in Bear Creek, it was a stand-alone building. Unlike the Marshal's office in Bear Creek, it was made entirely of wood. It had a wide porch on the front with two windows facing the street. There were a couple of benches on the porch, but no one sat on them.

I went inside.

"Can I help you?"

The man asking the question was seated behind a desk, on the other side of a low partition. The partition was like a railing you might find on a staircase or around a porch.

"Thank you, yes. I'm John Everett Sage, the County Sheriff of Alta Vista County. I'm here to see Sheriff Holden."

"I see. Do you have an appointment?"

"No."

He rocked back in his chair. He made a show of considering how to respond.

I liked it. I liked the railing, and the deputy right out front. It was a good set up. It made me want to get a railing for our office. I wondered where you could hire a jackass like this guy.

He rocked forward.

"Please wait here. I'll see if he has time for you."

He stood up and stretched. Then he moseyed over to a door behind his desk and knocked.

There was a vague reply, and he went inside closing the door behind him.

I thought pleasant thoughts about butterflies and bunnies

After a moment, the door opened and another man came out, with somewhat more energy than the man who went in.

He came right over to the rail and opened a gate in it.

"Sheriff Sage, I'm so glad to meet you. Please come in. I'm Joe Holden."

We shook hands.

The other man came wandering out.

"John Sage, meet Curt Watson, my deputy."

We shook hands.

When we were seated inside Joe Holden's office, we got down to brass tacks.

"I've heard of you, Sheriff Sage. I read the story about how you shot down that Rawlins fella, in a stand up gunfight in the street, when you were still the town marshal of Bear Creek."

"You can't believe everything you read in the papers."

Curt Watson snorted.

Joe Holden nodded and gave me an appraising look.

"What brings you to Thorndyke?"

"I'd kind of like to talk to you about that in private."

"Whatever you want to talk about, I don't have any secrets I need to keep from Curt here. After all, he is my deputy." He gave me an odd look.

"Well, it might be I have some secrets *I* need to keep. Meaning no offense to you, Deputy Watson," I added, looking over at Curt.

"I don't know you, mister, but I already don't like you," Curt sneered.

"OK, Curt. That'll be all. Go back to your desk."

When Curt had left the room, closing the door behind him, Holden leaned forward over his desk. He spoke loudly enough so Deputy Watson could hear.

"Make it quick, Sheriff Sage."

He held up a hand to stop me from saying anything.

"Look, I apologize for his behavior. This is just part of the cross I bear. What can I do for you?" he asked quietly.

"I need to ask you some questions about the trouble between the Thorndike's at the Diamond T and Mr. Courtney's Bar C."

He nodded. "Yeah, that's what I was afraid of."

"Why?"

"Mr. Courtney came in here and talked to me about three weeks ago. He said he thought the Diamond T boys had run off his cattle. He wanted for me and him to go out there and look for them. I wouldn't do it. He told me if his missing cattle were not returned, he would file a rustling charge against whoever had them cows. I guess this visit means he thinks he knows who stole his cattle and he has filed charges in Alta Vista County."

"Actually, no, he told me he doesn't know for sure who stole the cattle. He's not looking for trouble. I just want to get a better idea of what's going on."

Joe Holden managed to look both relieved and very tense at the same time.

"I'll tell you what's going on. All hell is about to break loose." He gave me a pointed look.

"…In what way?"

"We've got settlers moving into the county and the big ranches like the Diamond T don't want them here. The Diamond T is not really any bigger than the Bar C; I'd say sixty five thousand acres or so, but the Thorndykes are controlling twice that.

They've put together this 'Stockman's Association', which is really just them and a couple of other big ranches, trying to gain total control of every inch of this county. Right now if a single cow goes missing from a herd grazing on any land controlled by the Stockman's Association, they call it rustling and they're putting together a list of suspected 'rustlers'. If someone finds their name on that list, they'd better skedaddle, or face the consequences."

"What 'consequences'?"

"There have been two people shot."

It took me a moment to realize he might be referring to two people I had not heard about.

"Who was shot, and where did these shootings happen?"

"The first one was about two weeks ago. His name was Joe Clancy. He showed up just a few months ago and settled over to the south east, by Needle Rock. He was found shot, lying just outside his own outhouse. His name was the first one on the list. The second one was just yesterday. Rusty Jones, he and his family have been here for years. They have a small ranch of just a couple hundred acres, a few miles outside town, on the north side. They raise horses mostly. His name showed up on the list just recently. It seems somebody claims to have seen him changing a brand with a running iron. He was shot from ambush. I guess the message is, if you are not welcome here in this county, for any reason, you're gonna get dead."

"Tell me about the ambush, and I'll tell you a couple of things you might find interesting. You do know Bill Courtney was shot don't you?"

"I read it in the papers, I understand he's recovering. A surveyor who was working on his ranch was also shot, right?"

I nodded.

"…And killed."

"Do you think there might be a connection?"

"Tell me what you know about how the men over here were shot."

He told me both men were bushwhacked from about seventy yards with a rifle. At the scene of each shooting they had found a single 44-40 shell casing, sitting upright on a rock.

"What did you learn about the theft of the Courtney cattle?"

"Nothing, they had been gone for days by the time I learned of the theft from Mr. Courtney."

"Did you ask the Thorndykes if they had any information?"

"No, you'll have to do that yourself." He stood up and called for Deputy Watson.

"Why is that?" I asked as Curt Watson charged into the room.

"Because I'm the Sheriff of Chaparral County, that means I do what Mr. Thorndyke wants me to do."

I was startled by the sudden change in his attitude. Was this simple theater for the benefit of his deputy, or a shift in personality? I stood up as well.

"I see then. I'll take it up with Mr. Thorndyke. I guess I'll be in town for a while. Perhaps you could give me directions to the hotel?"

"Certainly, Curt, show the Sheriff where the hotel is and tell him where he can find Mr. Thorndyke. Nice to meet you, Sheriff Sage," he dismissed us.

Out on the street in front of the Sheriff's office, I repeated my request for directions.

"We got a couple of places you could stay. How long you gonna be here?" Deputy Watson asked.

"Gee, I'm not sure. I need to meet with Mr. Thorndyke."

"Which one?"

"Excuse me?"

"Which Mr. Thorndyke do ya need to meet with?"

"Well, I'm not sure. How many are there?"

"Six, old man Thorndyke and his five sons."

"OK. Which one does Sheriff Holden answer to?"

"All of um," he laughed. "What kinda room you want?"

"That's not important to me."

"Well, it's important to me," he laughed again. "You can get a room with or without a woman. Which one you want?"

"Do you have an ordinary hotel?"

"Course, two blocks down, on the right."

"Thank you, now how do I go about finding the senior Mr. Thorndyke?"

"You mean old man Thorndyke?"

"Yep"

"Hell, that's easy. Just look for the biggest house on the highest hill."

He was chuckling to himself as he walked away.

DAN ARNOLD

35.

To my surprise, the hotel was called the Paradise Hotel and Saloon. I was surprised that it wasn't called the Diamond T or Thorndyke. This saloon made three I knew of, within just a couple of blocks of each other. The good thing was the hotel entrance was separate from the saloon entrance, although there was a hallway connecting them. The bad thing was that the hotel occupied the second floor above the saloon, and it was one noisy saloon.

I decided to go in search of Bob. I went downstairs and into the saloon to get some supper. The place was filled with cigar and cigarette smoke. The piano player was asking to be shot, because what he lacked in talent he made up for in volume. Since he was so loud, all the men in the place were yelling at each other, by way of conversation.

There was no sign of Bob, but I had a pretty decent ham sandwich with a mug of warm beer. I stood at the bar with one foot on the brass rail, while I ate.

Since I had no idea where Bob might be, I decided to go saloon hopping.

I found him playing faro in the second place I looked, the High Times Saloon.

Posted on a sign board right beside the front door was a handbill. It stated:

"RUSTLING of livestock is a crime PUNISHABLE BY DEATH. The following people are hereby notified to leave the county."

There was a list of nine names. Two had been crossed off.

This High Times Saloon was a reasonably clean and well-polished place. The clientele was typical of this type of saloon. There were drovers and cowboys, local business types, some I suspected were travelers and some who looked to be the kind who pretty much lived in saloons. There were two attractions here. One was the girls. Some were dancing in scanty costumes, on the stage that ran down the side of the place, and some were making an attempt at seducing the customers. There was a little band playing banjo, fiddle, piano and guitar. They were pretty good, and they made me feel like dancing a little myself.

The other attraction was the gambling.

Nearly every table had a faro, stud, or draw poker game going.

Watching over it all was a man sitting up on a high chair with a shotgun across his lap. He was wearing a tin star.

I ordered a beer and wandered around as if I were interested in getting in a game. There were others doing the same and some were just staggering around, one man was pawing at the girls.

When I came to the table where Bob was playing, I didn't recognize him right at first. He hadn't shaved since I last saw him and he had his hat pulled low. There was a cigar stuck in the side of his mouth. He wore no jacket, vest, or tie and his shirt was partly unbuttoned. There was a girl sitting in his lap, rubbing his chest. He didn't appear to be losing, at either game.

It took two trips by that table before he noticed me. We made eye contact, and then I headed back over to the bar and got another beer.

I was pretty sure nobody in the place had any idea who I was.

After a little while Bob came over to the bar and ordered a beer. I turned to face the room and he continued to face the back of the bar.

"What brings you here?" he joked.

"I'm looking for the guy who stole a horse and buckboard from Mrs. Poole's."

"I know exactly where it is. I'll meet you at the livery stable at eight o'clock tomorrow morning," Bob said, as he walked away, headed back to his games.

We were standing behind the livery stable the next morning, talking.

"It worked out just as you had envisioned it would, John. When I arrived here with Jack Slade's body in the buckboard, I checked in with Joe Holden to collect the reward. Sure enough, he's heard of me. He wired for the money, and I received the full reward yesterday. As far as he or anybody else knows, I'm just another bounty hunter gambling with my blood money, which is rightfully yours if you want it. I may have been uh...temporarily divested of a small portion of it, due to the vagaries and inexact nature of games of chance."

I shook my head.

"You've been here for a couple of days, what's going on? Is it true the Thorndyke's have been stealing land?"

"The situation here is worse than I thought. The day I got here, I sent a letter to Hugh Lomax asking him to send a telegram to the U.S. Marshal in Denver. I didn't think I could trust the local telegraph office. It appears the people in key positions in this town are all in the Thorndyke's pocket, one way or another. Sheriff Holden works for Herman Thorndyke, so he's no help, as far as law enforcement goes.

The Thorndyke's are attempting to make all of Chaparral County into their own private kingdom. Herman Thorndyke has organized a "Stockman's Association." If you support the Thorndyke's, you're a member, and they'll leave you alone. If you oppose the Thorndyke's plan, you're an enemy. They eliminate their enemies. Most of the small ranchers and farmers are struggling just to survive. The Thorndyke's are forcing them out and stealing their land.

The Stockman's Association has hired a regulator. They've over played their hand and the small ranchers and settlers are going to fight back. They've formed a vigilante committee," Bob stated.

"Wait a minute, what is a regulator?"

Bob looked away.

"A regulator is a man like me, John. He's a range detective. Typically we investigate rustling and help eliminate it, by whatever means necessary. Whoever the Stockman's Association has hired, he's killing the people on their list of suspected rustlers. It's actually just a list of people they want eliminated."

"Yeah, that's what Joe Holden told me. Do you have any idea who this regulator might be?"

He shook his head.

"What exactly is this vigilante committee planning to do?"

"I don't know, but once people start choosing up sides, there's going to be a range war, for sure. That's why I sent for the U.S. Marshal. We also need to get word out to the Governor. This is a powder keg, and it's about to blow up."

What do you know about the Thorndyke's?"

"I've seen the whole family. Herman Thorndyke, the father, and two of the sons live here in town. The oldest son, Henry, lives out on the ranch headquarters. He runs the ranch these days. I don't know for sure where Howard lives. He's the youngest and just returned home from college, back east. He seems to be fond of the ladies, if you take my meaning."

"I'm going to go meet Mr. Thorndyke senior. I want you to try to find out the names of everyone in the Stockman's Association."

"That will be easy enough. Why do you want to know?"

"I'm going to tell them all, the Governor and the U.S. Marshal know who they are, and what they've done."

"I don't think that's a good idea..." Bob started.

"You know Bob; this is the second time you've balked when I gave you specific instructions. How did you find me so fast when I got shot? You must have still been close to the area where I left you. I told you to come directly here."

"Well, I didn't like the idea of you facing Slade alone. I decided to follow you, to be there as back up, just in the event you needed me. I saw you talking to Slade at Mrs. Poole's Boarding House. When you rode over the hill into Waller, I watched the town from the top of the hill. I could see there were only a few saddle horses in the town, so I figured you wouldn't be there for long. I turned around and headed this way. I was probably only a little over a mile or so ahead of you, when the shooting started. It took me several minutes to get back to you. When I got there, you were sitting on your horse in the middle of the road, as if you were waiting for me. You informed me, rather casually, that you had killed Slade."

"How can I trust you, if you won't follow orders?"

He stared at me for a moment.

"Would you rather trust me with your life, or just to follow your orders?"

I thought about that. He was right.

"Fair enough, you did save my life. I'm sorry I put it that way. I probably should have listened to you, but I do need you to follow my lead as well. Why shouldn't I brace the Stockman's Association?"

"They're pretending they don't know who the killer is, even though he works for them. They'll probably be willing to do just about anything to protect themselves."

"We might be able to use that to our advantage. Right now, we can't predict where the killer will strike next, except at the people on that list. We can't watch everyone on their list, but we could watch just one person."

"Indeed we could, but which one?"

"I was thinking maybe me, or…you."

"I understand your reasoning, John. If we can get them to send the regulator after one of us, we could try to take him. The problem is it would be far too easy to get killed, and very difficult to set the trap. Also, we may not have time to set up something like that. There were nine names on the list; two have been killed and four have fled. There are actually only three names left on that list now. It would be better to try and watch them."

"I'll bet those three people have taken steps to protect themselves."

"I've heard they are in armed camps, and more than one has hired gun help. It's going to be a full blown range war."

"I'm focused on catching this bushwhacking regulator. The members of the Stockman's Association know who it is, and the most prominent member of that group is Herman Thorndyke. I'm going to see him. Where does he live?"

DAN ARNOLD

36.

When I got to the Thorndyke house, I was amused to see they didn't seem to have a butler. Mr. Thorndyke answered the door himself, in his shirt sleeves. Herman Thorndyke, the "old man", wasn't much older than me, which meant his sons would be in their twenties. We were sitting in his office in his home. It really was the biggest house on the highest hill, in the town of Thorndyke. However, it was the original two story wood sided ranch house that had been built to raise a family in tough times. It was practical, not pretty.

"Mr. Thorndyke, you and Bill Courtney used to be friends. His foreman Glen, tells me before they fenced the Bar C, you used to run your cattle together on the same range. What happened to change that friendship?"

"Until Sheriff Holden told me you would be coming by, I wasn't aware that we were no longer friends. I've done nothing to offend Bill Courtney. What's his complaint?"

"That was a bald faced lie," I thought.

"He has a section of land along the creek over in this county y'all used to run cattle on. He fenced it and he believes y'all tore down his fence and someone stole his cattle."

"That's ridiculous. I had nothing to do with any of that. I've been busy organizing a Stockman's Association, to combat this very type of thing. So many people have been moving in here and helping themselves to our land and cattle, something has to be done. Bill wouldn't join us. He may change his mind now. How many cattle has he lost?"

"He lost about fifty head."

"Fifty head! Why, that's not rustling, its outright theft. It would take an organized crew to steal that many head. I haven't heard of a cattle theft like that, in many years."

"When the cowboys from the Bar C came looking for the herd, your cowboys stopped them and turned them back."

"That's a damned lie! We would be happy to assist in the recovery of Bill's stock. My son Henry runs the ranch these days. You could ask him about it."

"I'm headed out there, to do just that, later today."

Herman Thorndyke's attitude changed when he heard me say those words.

"You have no jurisdiction in this county. The crime you describe occurred here in Chaparral County, I suggest you mind you own damned business. We have a fine lawman in Sheriff Joe Holden. He can investigate the theft. You should go on back where you came from."

"Bill Courtney was shot in Alta Vista County. I tracked the shooter here."

It was close enough to the truth. The evidence certainly led here.

"Are you suggesting we had something to do with it?"

"No, I'm merely pointing out that I'm in pursuit of a criminal who has committed crimes in my county. It is my business. I will be happy to cooperate with Sheriff Holden, but I'll continue to investigate, as I see fit."

"We'll see about that." He was actually gloating.

"You would be unwise to try to stop me. I know you and your Stockman's Association have hired a killer. I intend to find him. You are on the brink of an all-out range war in this county. Additionally, the Governor is aware of my investigation and Maxwell Warren, the United States Marshal in Denver, has been sent for."

That rocked him.

"Now see here, this is outrageous," he spluttered. "We've done no such thing. You can't prove any of that.

"I can and I will. You've gone too far. It's time to pay the piper."

I walked out of his office and his big house on the hill.

I didn't have any trouble getting directions out to the new Diamond T headquarters. Everyone in town seemed to know where it was. I know, because I spent some time wandering around town, asking questions and telling people I was going out there. The ranch headquarters was just down the road, only a few miles outside the town. Bob already knew where it was.

I walked to the livery stable and saddled Dusty. I spent more time than I usually did grooming him and talking to him.

I wasn't looking forward to what I was about to do.

I checked my Colt and my Winchester. I led Dusty outside, tightened the cinch, mounted up and headed out of town.

It was a pretty day, but it was starting to get hot. As I rode down the road, I studied the country side. I could see for miles in any direction. I knew pretty much everything I saw was considered Thorndyke land.

People tend to think of the Great Plains as being flat and featureless. There are actually very few parts of the plains that are featureless. In most places there are rolling hills, arroyos, rock outcroppings and even the occasional mesa. It tends to be very dry country, prone to violent storms. A dry gully can become a roaring stream in a flash flood, washing away everything in its path. Trees can be very scarce. You could ride twenty or thirty miles and never see even one tree.

Yellow Horse and I had first come into this country, more than twenty years ago, driving a trail herd up from Texas. Back then, there had been times when the only shade we could find was in the shadow of our own horses. You could ride all day, and never see a tree.

Here the country was dry and brushy. The road was a nearly straight line and the ground was rolling, not at all flat. From the top of any little rise, I could look back and see the town, but occasionally

I would be in a low place and the view was blocked by the heavy brush and rugged terrain. In this arid setting, I knew the Thorndyke Ranch headquarters would be near a river or creek.

Eventually, I came to a dry wash. This was one of those gullies prone to being churned to pieces in a flash flood. Where the road went through, it slanted down and away, off toward a creek somewhere farther to the north. The road dipped down into the wash, and up the other side.

I stopped as I approached the wash.

This was the only suitable place for an ambush I had seen since leaving the town of Thorndyke. I studied the ground and the surrounding area for a moment, and then I asked Dusty to walk on. I was sweating profusely now.

We proceeded through the wash and up the other side, without incident. I caught a little breeze, up on the high ground. I shivered. About ten minutes later I was looking down a long slope at the new Diamond T headquarters, about a half a mile away.

I could see why they had chosen the spot. A stream meandered through this little valley and wrapped around a small piece of higher ground, on three sides. The ranch buildings were on that little rise, surrounded by massive cottonwood trees and smaller willows.

It was an ideal location. There was water and good grass in abundance. I was aware it used to belong to another, smaller ranch. That family had been bought out or driven out by the Thorndykes. It was an example of the changing times.

Twenty years ago, all this land had belonged to no one, except maybe the Indians, or the United States of America, depending on who you asked.

As I approached the ranch buildings, I passed several pens. Some had horses in them, but most were empty, waiting for a time when they would be used to gather and sort the stock. There was the usual assortment of outbuildings and barns. I could smell good things being cooked in the cook shack and I could hear the ringing sound of a blacksmith, hammering away on something. Over by one barn, a couple of ranch hands were throwing hay out of a wagon. There were two men watching a third man saddle a bronc in the breaking pen.

I had expected to find a bunch of hired guns here, but this was about as normal a scene as I had ever observed.

The two men at the breaking pen noticed me and came walking over, as I stepped down off Dusty.

"Howdy, mister, what can we do for you?" the smaller of the two men asked.

"Howdy, I'm John Everett Sage, the Sheriff of Alta Vista County. I'm here looking to meet with Mr. Thorndyke."

"…Which one?"

"I was given to understand Henry Thorndyke, lives here."

"Oh, yeah he does. I only asked because all five of the brothers were here earlier this morning. They've been gone all day since."

"Do you know where they went?"

"No, I have no idea. Sometimes they ride out together and don't come back for days. I'm Bud, the foreman here. Is there anything I can do to help you?"

"Yes, Bud, thank you. When Henry does come back, will you tell him I was here and I'll be waiting to meet him in Thorndyke?"

"Sure, who did you say you are again?"

I mounted back up on Dusty.

"I'm the Sheriff of Alta Vista County, John Everett Sage."

I turned Dusty and rode back out the way I had come in.

As I approached the dry wash from this direction I continued to be vigilant, but I could see nothing threatening. Never the less, at the moment I reached the near edge, I slapped spurs to Dusty. He leaped forward into the wash and galloped up the other side, with me stretched low over his neck.

The sound of his hooves hitting the rocky road surface hadn't masked the sound of the rifle shot.

I pulled him to a stop and leapt off. I grabbed my rifle. There was the sound of someone sliding down into the wash from somewhere farther up. I crouched and sighted down my rifle barrel at the opening in the brush where the road came up out of the wash. I could hear running feet coming down the wash toward the road. I put my finger on the trigger, just as the figure appeared in the gap. He jerked and fell, as another rifle shot rang out. I stayed where I was, ready to fire.

"John, it's me. Can you hear me?"

I whistled a whippoorwill call. Then I realized Bob wouldn't know what it meant.

"Yeah, Bob, I'm OK."

I stood up and approached the fallen man, keeping my rifle on him.

When I reached him, he was face down and completely still. His rifle lay near him. I could see a bullet wound in the back of his left shoulder.

He nearly surprised me when he rolled over, with his pistol coming up in his right hand. I kicked it out of his hand and smashed him in the head with my rifle stock.

Bob emerged from the brush, carrying the rifle he had used to shoot the man.

"Is he dead?"

"No, fortunately he's not dead, yet. Let's see what we can do to keep him alive."

I picked up his rifle and gently jacked open the breach. The shell that popped up was in .44-40 caliber.

We examined his wound. The bullet had hit him under his collar bone near the breast bone and exited through his left shoulder. He was bleeding profusely, suggesting his heart was still strong and indicating there was extensive damage to a big artery or vessel somewhere in his chest or shoulder. The worst bleeding was at the exit wound. I slapped my scarf on the chest wound and rolled him face down, applying strong downward pressure on the exit wound, and indirectly to the chest wound. He moaned a little at the pain. In this way, by keeping pressure on the wounds, I was able to stop the worst of the bleeding. When he became conscious, I asked him if Thorndyke had sent him to kill me. He nodded his head.

Bob left and retrieved the shooter's horse from where it was tied out of sight, farther up the wash. I had recognized the fresh tracks when I rode through here, the first time. On the way up the wash he found a single 44-40 shell lying where the shooter had jacked it out, as he was heading for the road. Bob also found the bushwhackers hiding place. There was a flat rock which the shooter had used for a rifle rest. It was that fixed and prone firing position that had caused him to miss his shot at me. I had counted on his not being able to adjust quickly enough at a fast moving target.

"I can't believe it worked. I'm sorry he got a shot off at you. When I got here, I decided to go down the wash, and when he showed up, he went *up* the wash. I couldn't see where he set up. When you rode through here from town, I thought he just might try to kill you. I figured he hadn't had time to really get set up yet, but I nearly fired a warning shot, anyway."

"I'm glad you didn't, he would've gotten away."

"It was horrible waiting here, not knowing for sure where he was. I couldn't move. If I had, he would have known I was here."

"It worked out nearly perfectly."

"No, John, it didn't. He got a shot at you and I didn't even know for sure where he was."

"The point is we've got him. When you could, you took the shot you had. There won't be any more

of his signature killings. We'll get him to finger the
Stockman's Association in a court of law,
eventually he'll hang. I call that a good days work."

37.

We brought the wounded assassin back into the town of Thorndyke, in the same stolen buckboard Bob had used to save my life. He drove it out of Thorndyke a couple of hours or so ahead of me. We figured nobody would notice another buckboard headed out toward the Diamond T. Bob had driven it across the wash and then hidden it out in the brush on the other side. He worked his way to a good spot down in the wash and waited for the shooter to show up. The plan was that Bob would find the best spot for an ambush, wait for the bushwhacker to show up, and then ambush the assassin. He was supposed to shoot the bushwhacker before he could get a shot at me, but things seldom go entirely as planned.

You should have seen the look on Deputy Watson's face when I told him we were taking over the county jail. He told us we would be real sorry when Sheriff Holden got back. He annoyed me so much, after I gave him instructions to fetch the doctor, I threw him headlong out the front door, to land rather unceremoniously in the street, No wonder he didn't like me.

I guess I was just feeling cranky.

I knew it wouldn't be long before real trouble showed up. So, I decided it might be fun to add further complications. After we got our prisoner settled, I went to see Mr. Thorndyke.

Imagine my surprise at finding Deputy Watson at the Thorndyke manor! When I walked into Mr. Thorndyke's office, Curt Watson was in the process of telling Thorndyke about our theft of his jail.

"Hello Curt, I thought I told you to go fetch the doctor."

He tried to grab his gun, so I smacked him over the head with mine. He crumpled in a heap. I took his gun away from him.

Thorndyke reached into a desk drawer, but froze when he heard me cock my Colt, which he could see was now leveled at his head.

"I have your hired gun locked up in the county jail. Since you're the one who hired him, I'm arresting you for conspiracy to commit murder."

Thorndyke scowled, but he raised both his hands, high.

Curt stirred and looked up at me. There was blood streaming down his face and getting in his eyes. I had torn his scalp with my gun barrel. Scalp wounds bleed a lot, but they heal quickly. He would need some stitches though.

"I'll bet you'll go to the doctor now, Curt. Get up and do what I told you to do the first time."

He did.

The walk through town from the Thorndyke mansion to the Sheriff's office was something I never want to do again. I didn't restrain Thorndyke, I simply kept my Colt jammed in the small of his back and tried to look casual. My .45 has a soft trigger pull, so I told him the truth.

"If you make any sudden move, I'll blow a hole through you my fist would fit in. Hell, you'll be lucky if I don't shoot you accidently."

I was half afraid I *would* shoot him by accident, but I had a hard time caring.

Herman Thorndyke was locked in a cell, when the doctor showed up.

The ride in the wagon had been hard on our assassin, and our makeshift bandage had failed to prevent further bleeding.

The doctor informed us that if he survived, the man should not be moved again for some time. Because there would be considerably more blood loss, there was a good chance he would die as the doctor was working on him. I wondered how much the two bit bushwhacker was suffering, from the taste of his-own medicine.

"Do the best you can, Doc. He just needs to live long enough to stand trial for murder. I don't suppose it will matter much, but which side are you on in this mess?" I asked.

"I've known the Thorndykes since the boys were little. I liked them a lot better back then. This land and power grab is bad for everyone. This community has become dangerously divided. It's probably just the beginning of the real bloodshed. I don't need the business. I hope it won't come down to more killing. Though whatever happens, I don't see you surviving this," he added.

"…How's that?"

"When the Thorndyke boys find out you have their father locked up, they'll tear this jail down around your ears. They're wild and dangerous. They think they own the world."

"Clearly, we would appreciate your discretion on that point, doctor. Perhaps you could help us delay the impending conflict, by not mentioning this situation to anyone." Bob suggested.

"I'm not your problem. That stinking rat, Curt Watson, now, he may run straight to them. I told him if he wanted to stay alive he'd better get out of town. He's too stupid to scare easily, but you managed to get the job done. He took off like a cat with its tail on fire."

We left him to his work. I had some planning and some praying to do.

"We have sufficient provisions, we can hold this building for some time," Bob said.

"We can't hold it for very long, if there are very many trying to get in. There are two doors to defend, and only two of us. We could hold off the Thorndyke boys, but if they bring enough help, they could either overwhelm us, or burn us out."

"They won't try to burn us out if they want their father alive. He's our 'ace in the hole'. So long as we have him; they will have to proceed with caution. I'm glad you arrested him. How long do you think we have to prepare before they lay siege to the jail?"

"I don't know, a couple of hours, maybe a day or more. It will take a while for the Thorndyke boys to find out we have him, and some time to get here, from wherever they are. Unless...."

"Bob raised his eyebrows at me.

"Unless what?"

"I left word with the foreman at the Diamond T, to have Henry Thorndyke come see me here in town. If they came back to the ranch headquarters today, they could be here at any time."

The doctor came back into the office.

"Well, I've done all I can do for him. It could go either way. I've seen men shot a dozen times survive, and I've seen men die from a simple cut. If he does recover, he'll be crippled in that left shoulder. There was a lot of tissue damage; the bullet pretty much blew his left shoulder blade to pieces. I cleaned out all the bone fragments I could find. I think I have the bleeding stopped, but I don't know how much blood supply he has to his left arm. I might have to take it off."

"It won't matter much, Doc, he'll probably hang anyway," I said.

"You want him to live long enough to testify, don't you?"

"Yes sir, I do. Assuming we all live long enough to get him to court."

"I've thought about that. I could say something to one or two people I know. Some folks here are ready to hang Mr. Thorntdyke, right now. They could form a posse in no time."

"Thank you, but it would be vastly better from our perspective if you were to remain silent on the matter altogether, Doctor…?" Bob wanted his name.

"My name's Ralston, I'm Doctor, Dennis Ralston."

"He's right Doc. We want to keep a lid on this for as long we can. We believe help is on the way. Can the operator at the telegraph office be trusted to keep his mouth shut?"

"It depends on the message. He'il tell somebody something."

I looked at Bob

He nodded.

Our finished telegram was addressed to the Governor, by way of an aide. It read:

"Urgent <STOP>Thorndyke<STOP> Send aid<STOP> as discussed<STOP>

It was signed JES & BL.

Doctor Ralston promised to personally see it was sent, immediately.

"If anyone asks what it means, I'll tell them I'm sending for some special medicine to fight sickness and infection, and by golly, that's the truth," the doctor said.

He rushed off to send the telegram.

38.

The next morning there was a loud knock on the front door. We were as ready as we were going to get.

"Who's there?" Bob called. He was down behind the desk with a ten gauge shotgun leveled at the door. I was covering the back door. Both doors were locked and blocked.

"Buckskin Charlie Owens and Walter Edward Burnside, deputies from Alta Vista County," was the reply.

We were shocked! Why were they here? How had they gotten here so quickly?

Talk about an answer to prayer.

Bob took down the bar and threw open the door.

They were as surprised to see us, as we were to see them.

"When Hugh got Bob's letter, he figured you were riding into a meat grinder. He sent us to back you up. We rode straight through. We didn't know where you might be, so we came here first. What's going on?" Buckskin Charlie asked.

We filled them in.

"I don't like leaving Hugh alone in Bear Creek," I said.

"Oh you don't need to worry about that. He has his pick of help."

"…How's that?"

"Those handbills and newspaper ads brought men out of the woodwork. Before we left, there were six guys who showed up applying to be deputies. Hugh was going to put them all on duty under his supervision and test them to see who could make it on the payroll. Nobody gets a badge, except the men he hires. The others just get room and board at the courthouse, till he makes his picks. Tom gets the leftovers"

Things were looking up. The additional manpower was a huge asset for Hugh. Having these men show up to help us was an answer to prayer. We made plans to take advantage of it.

At about ten o'clock that morning I was sitting on a bench on the porch of the Sheriff's office, enjoying a cup of coffee before the day got really hot. I had a ten gauge shotgun handy and when I saw five riders approaching, I picked it up and walked over to the top of the stairs. Standing there put me about level with the riders.

"Morning, boys" I said with a smile.

They had spread out side by side facing the porch.

The older man looked like he might be pushing thirty. He had on a leather vest with some extra fancy silver Concho buttons. It seemed a little odd, because he was also wearing a celluloid collar and a tie. The others all wore wool vests. They had shunned collars, ties and jackets, as the day was starting to heat up. The youngest appeared to be a man of about twenty years old, or so.

I figured the man with the fancy vest was probably Henry Thorndyke. He spoke up.

"Howdy, mister, we're here to see Joe Holden."

I decided to go with the Deputy Watson act.

"I see. Do you have an appointment?"

They looked at each other and shifted around on their horses a little. The youngest one snickered.

"No. We don't need an appointment. You go inside and tell him Henry Thorndyke and his brothers are here."

I made a show of thinking about it and then I shook my head.

"He's not seeing visitors today. You might try coming back tomorrow."

"Who the hell do you think you are," Henry asked.

I smiled again.

"I'm John Everett Sage, the Sheriff of Alta Vista County."

They looked back and forth at each other for a moment.

Henry addressed me.

"My foreman said you'd come by the headquarters, looking for me. What are you doing here?"

"Here in town, here on the porch, or here at the Sheriff's office?"

He was getting very angry now.

"Mister, I'm tired of talking to you. Bring Sheriff Holden out here, right now!"

He started to get off his horse.

"Stop, you stay right where you are." I lifted the muzzle of the ten gauge.

He froze for a second and then eased back into his saddle.

Before he could say something stupid, I got right to the point.

"I'm in charge here now. I've arrested your father on five charges of conspiracy to commit murder. We have him locked up inside."

They looked back and forth at each other, again.

"Mister, do you really think you can stop us from taking you down," Henry asked.

I cocked both barrels of the ten gauge, aimed it straight at his face, and whistled.

"It's up to you, Henry," I said.

From across the street, there was the sound of rifles cocking. The Thorndyke's looked back over their shoulders. Buckskin Charlie and Ed were standing on each side of the roof of the courthouse. They had their rifles up and aimed at the Thorndyke boys. They were only about twenty yards away.

"If you decide to try to take me down, Henry, I'll blow your head clean off. My men across the street will kill your brothers. You might get me, but either way, you'll be dead, in about one second."

They looked at each other again.

"We'll come back here with more men and guns, and we'll see who kills who," Henry said.

"Did I mention we have your dad locked up inside. We can kill him whenever we feel like it. If you come back here and try to bust him out, he'll die and most or all of you, will die in the fight.

What ya'll want to do now is leave. Go somewhere else and spend a little time thinking about that."

He sat right where he was, and thought about it, for a moment.

"I guess we'll see you around. You've got yourself all boxed in here. You can't leave town. You'll never get him to trial in this county. The judge will throw out the charges."

He turned his horse, his brothers turning to follow him. As they rode by me, the youngest, Homer Thorndyke, grinned at me.

"In the meantime, maybe we'll pay a little visit to your family," he smirked.

DAN ARNOLD

39.

As the Thorndyke's rode away, I felt weak in the knees. I eased the hammers down on the ten gauge. My hands were shaking.

Buckskin Charlie and Ed climbed down the ladder on the side of the courthouse and came running over.

"Well, that went according to plan. I still say we should've locked them up with their father. We'll have problems with them, sooner or later," Buckskin Charlie said.

"We don't have anything to charge them with. We can't lock them up to prevent a crime. I don't even have jurisdiction in this county. At this point I'm not sure what our standing is. I'm afraid Henry Thorndyke is right. We'll never see Herman Thorndyke face a jury in this county. Even if he does, that jury will be handpicked by the prosecutor and his defense attorney. I'll bet Thorndyke owns every official in this town."

We went back into the office. Bob was there, with his shotgun.

"I was covering you from the window," he said. "They could see me, but you couldn't."

"Thanks boys. That was very good work. I'm sorry I got y'all into this mess."

"Heck, Sheriff, it just comes with the job," Ed said.

I thought about it. Ed was right. A career in law enforcement put you in harm's way. I knew Lora was struggling with exactly that issue. Each of these men had families somewhere. Every day they wondered if they would ever see their loved one's again.

I was also thinking about Homer Thorndyke's threat. Maybe I was better off not having anyone in my life. My whole family was in California and few people here even knew who my family was. They were safe enough.

On the other hand, Lora was here and she was vulnerable.

I was responsible for her safety. What if someone went after her, because of me?

Then I remembered the scripture:

"...For I have not given you a spirit of fear, but of peace, love, and a sound mind."

There was nothing good that could come from *imagining* all the horrible things which *could* happen. A man has to deal with the things that *are* happening. No point in worrying.

We trust God for the future, and *"a very present help in time of need."* I have to live my life with confidence, not in fear of imaginary issues.

Help came that afternoon. U.S. Marshal, Maxwell Warren and two deputies came to the jail. They had departed Denver by train to Bear Creek, the day they got the telegram from Hugh Lomax. I explained the situation to them. We discussed the possibility of moving the men to Alta Vista County.

"John, as County Sheriff of Alta Vista County, you have every right to arrest them for the shooting of William Courtney. The other murders will be additional charges. They should stand trial in Alta Vista County. The security in Bear Creek would be much better, and the Thorndyke boys would have to travel all the way there, if they want to cause any trouble. They wouldn't find many friends when they got to Bear Creek, either. Those reasons are precisely why your prisoners would get a fair trial in Alta Vista County. Nobody really knows them there," Marshal Warren concluded.

"It's a two day ride to get to Bear Creek. The Thorndyke's could try to take their dad from us, somewhere along the road," Ed said.

Max shook his head.

"Not likely, son, there are seven of us lawmen altogether. If they were stupid enough to attack us, we could handle them, and Mr. Thorndyke might be killed in the process."

"OK, that settles it then, we'll take them to Bear Creek just as soon as our wounded man can travel," I said.

"When will that be?" Max asked.

"The doc will be along to see him most anytime now, we'll find out then."

Joe Holden had improved a lot over the last couple of days. He was sitting up in his cell and able to eat and drink. He had no shirt because the doctor had cut it off, and the doctor came and changed his bandages every day. Holden couldn't have put on a shirt if he wanted to. He sat wrapped in a blanket.

"Can he travel, Doc?"

"I expect he can, in a stage or on a wagon, if you take it easy on the road. He needs to protect that shoulder. His left arm should stay completely immovable. Even if the shoulder heals, I don't think he'll ever have full use of the arm again. It may still have to come off. I don't like the color in his hand," he said, as he gathered up his things and put them in his bag. "I'll be off. You be careful out there."

Holden hadn't said much to us since we had gotten him back to the jail. The ride in the wagon had nearly done him in. Out there in the brush that day, when he had tried to kill me, he had admitted to shooting Bill and the others. He admitted he did the shootings at the direction of Herman Thorndyke.

"You're as tough as they say you are," he mumbled.

"Excuse me, I didn't catch that."

"I said you're one tough hombre. You knew I was laying for you and you rode right into the ambush. The fella who shot me, did he kill Jack Slade the same way?"

"No, he didn't kill Slade. I did. Why do you ask?"

"I never even knew he was there."

"The men you killed never knew you were there, either."

"No, I guess they didn't," he smiled and closed his eyes.

The ride back to Bear Creek was uneventful.

After we got our prisoners settled, Hugh wanted to introduce me to the men who had turned up looking to become deputies.

"Hugh, can we do this tomorrow morning? I need to go get my stitches out. Then I need three things, a bath, a good meal and a good night's sleep."

He nodded.

"Sure we can, John. In fact, I'm glad to see you're learning to take care of yourself," he rasped, with a grin.

I walked down to Lora's house.

I stood on the porch, with my hat in my hand, waiting for her to come to the door.

"John! I'm so glad your back. Please come in."

We sat in her parlor. The boarders didn't seem to be around. It wouldn't be supper time for a couple of hours.

"So, tell me all about your trip to Thorndyke. Did you get any helpful information from the Sheriff there?"

Talk about a loaded question!

"Yes, it turns out he was the man who shot Bill and three other men. Bill was the only survivor. How's he doing, by the way?"

"What? Did you say the Chaparral County Sheriff did the shootings?"

"Um, yes, he's locked up in our jail now, along with Mr. Thorndyke. How's Bill?"

"Damn it, John, trying to get information out of you is like pulling teeth."

"Sorry, I'm trying to tell you the story."

"I think you had better start at the beginning."

"OK, I will, but first, how's Bill doing?"

"Oh! He's doing much better. The doctor thinks he'll make a full recovery."

"There's another question I need to ask you."

"What is it?"

"I need to know where we stand. You and I…"

She reiterated her concerns and fears.

We talked about fear and how it can keep us from freedom to experience all that God has for us. Faith and fear cannot be in the same place at the same time. They don't mix any better than oil and water. You either live in one, or you live in the other.

I reminded her that life is uncertain. Each day is a gift from God and comes with no promise for another. She agreed.

"…but, John, can you at least promise me you will be more careful?"

"Um, yeah…I mean, I try to be careful now. I try to think things through, and I pray for wisdom. I'm only human though and I fail sometimes. Thank God for grace and mercy."

She was thoughtful for a moment.

"OK, ask me again," she said.

"Ask you what again?"

"John!" she slapped me on my sore arm. "Ask me again…"

I swear, I can be dumber than a post sometimes.
Then it dawned on me!

"Lora, will you marry me?"

She flew into my arms.

"Yes, oh yes, I will marry you. I'm sorry I have been so scared."

I know you're wondering what happened next. You'll have to use your imagination!

Eventually, Lora used some embroidery scissors and some tweezers to remove my stitches. Then I got that bath and a really good meal.

I had told Hugh, I needed three things.

You know, two out of three, aint bad.

DAN ARNOLD

40.

The trials didn't go as planned, but then again, they often don't.

The first trial was Joe Holden's. His attorney and the prosecutor wanted a show trial. He had already confessed to doing all four of the shootings, and attempting to shoot me, but at his arraignment hearing, Joe Holden pled "not guilty". So, we went to trial.

"Sheriff Sage and his deputy, Bob Logan, have testified you were hired by Herman Thorndyke, President of the Chaparral County Stockman's Association. They testified you told them this, after you were shot by Bob Logan, a well-known gunman. Did you tell them you were hired by the Stockman's Association?" Holden's defense attorney asked.

"Objection, Your Honor. The defense is attempting character assault on the deputy," the prosecutor said.

"Not at all, Your Honor, Deputy Logan has a history of gun violence, as does our Sheriff. They have both shot and killed several men. This is well-known and published information."

"The objection is sustained. The reputations of the Sheriff and his deputy are not pertinent to this trial. The jury is advised to overlook the defense's remarks about Deputy Logan and Sheriff Sage. Let the record reflect that. Further, I would advise you,

Counselor Smith, to restrict your questioning to the issue at hand."

"Yes, Your Honor. Let me rephrase my question."

He paused for dramatic effect.

Mr. Holden, after you were shot by Deputy Logan, and you were lying on the road, badly wounded, did you tell Sheriff Sage and Deputy Logan you had committed these crimes, on the orders of Herman Thorndyke?"

Joe Holden was very calm.

"Not that I recall. I was hurt bad. Sheriff Sage was pressing down on my bullet wound, real hard. I might have said anything to get him to stop."

"Now hold on..." I started.

The judge banged his gavel.

"Silence in the court! I will not have outbursts from anyone. Is that clear? Proceed with your questioning, Counselor Smith."

"Thank you, Your Honor. Now then, Mr. Holden, if I understood you correctly, you stated the Sheriff was torturing you..."

"Objection, Your Honor. The defense is putting words in the defendant's mouth."

"Sustained, the jury is advised to overlook the defense's statement regarding the treatment of the prisoner. Let the record so show it. Further I would advise you, Counselor, to be very careful with your handling of the witness."

"Very well, Your Honor, I will rephrase the question."

He walked back and forth in front of the bench, and then turned to Holden.

"Did you tell Sheriff Sage that Mr. Thorndyke ordered you to kill those people?"

"No, I don't recall ever doing that"

"No further questions, your honor?"

"The prosecutor may cross examine," Judge Tucker said.

"Mr. Holden, do you still admit you attempted to shoot and kill Sheriff Sage?"

"Yes, and I would've done it too, if Sage wasn't so damned quick, but the other feller, Bob Logan, shot me first."

"Do you still admit you shot Mr. Courtney?"

"Yes"

"Did you shoot and kill the surveyor on Mr. Courtney's ranch."

"Yes."

"Did you shoot and kill the other two men in Chaparral County?"

"Yes."

"But, you have entered a plea of 'Not Guilty'. Why is that?"

"I'm not guilty."

"How is that possible, sir? You have stated clearly you *are* responsible for those killings. Are you, or are you not, guilty of those shootings?"

"Oh, I shot those fellas all right, but I'm not guilty."

There was a stir in the courtroom, people murmured to one another.

"Order, order in the court!" Judge Tucker banged his gavel.

The prosecutor looked perplexed for a moment.

"Are you suggesting you shot them with your rifle, from a concealed position, all four of those men being unarmed at the time. You shot them, killing them…in self-defense?"

"No. I wasn't defending myself. They never even knew I was there," Holden smiled.

"Are you 'Not Guilty' by virtue of the fact you were *ordered* to shoot them, by someone else?"

Holden shook his head.

"Nah, I shot them because they were a problem. I shot and killed them, because I could. It's what I do. I'm very good at what I do."

The courtroom stirred a little. The jury looked on, intent with concentration.

"Let me be perfectly clear. Are you admitting you personally planned to murder each of those men? You scouted the best location to shoot them from? You hid and waited until you had a clear shot at them, and then you did, in fact, shoot them?"

"Yes."

"Why would you do such a thing, unless you were hired by Mr. Thorndyke?"

"I object, Your Honor! Mr. Thorndyke is not on trial here."

"Sustained, the prosecution is reminded to ask questions and not lead the witness. Mr. Thorndyke's name is to be stricken from the record. The jury is advised to disregard the statement."

"Your Honor, I am merely trying to determine why Mr. Holden committed these crimes. Let me rephrase the question."

"Mr. Holden, why did you shoot and kill at least three men and attempt to kill, both Mr. Courtney and the Sheriff?"

Holden smiled again.

"I told you, because they were a problem. It made them become my targets. It's what I do, I kill people. I'm very, very good at what I do. But, I'm not guilty. I have no guilt about it, at all."

The courtroom stirred again.

"No further questions, Your Honor. The prosecution rests."

The jury was only out for about fifteen minutes. They came back with a "Guilty" verdict. One week later, we hung Joe Holden from a gallows built on the courthouse square. The city was crowded with spectators. Joe Holden had become famous and even granted interviews to the newspapers. A photograph of him, smiling, inside his jail cell, had appeared on the front page of the Bear Creek Banner.

Herman Thorndyke never even had a trial. When Joe Holden recanted his story and refused to implicate Mr. Thorndyke, the Grand Jury returned a "No Bill." The charges were dropped, and I was forced to release him.

The telegram we had sent the Governor was supposed to convince him to send the U.S. Army into Chaparral County, to preserve the peace. Bureaucracy, time and distance had delayed the Army from moving in.

When Joe Holden was executed, the Thorndyke's understood the Stockman's Association had dodged a bullet. His conviction left them without an enforcer, and there were still three names on the list of people to be eliminated. The Thorndyke boys took it upon themselves to solve the problem.

One morning, right at daybreak, they snuck up on one of the small ranches which had armed itself in defense against the killings. Just as one of the men in the barricaded house stepped out to get some water from the well, they attacked, laying down a hail of bullets. He was killed instantly. The others inside the house, returned fire and a pitched gun battle erupted.

It turned into a siege, until the Thorndyke boys sent a burning wagon load of hay down the hill, into the house.

As the occupants of the burning house staggered out of the smoke and flames, The Thorndyke boys shot them down, one by one. In all, four men, two women and a small child were killed.

That was too much for the vigilante committee. They burned down Herman Thorndyke's house, with him and one of his sons, Horace Thorndyke, inside it. They were both killed. The fire raced from building to building, nearly engulfing the town. Even the courthouse was burned and all the property records were destroyed. The Army finally intervened and restored order.

The remaining four Thorndyke boys disappeared.

41.

For their part in the violence, now known as the Chaparral County War, the four Thorndyke brothers were wanted men. They had killed seven people, two of whom were women, and one, a small child. The Diamond T was still owned by the Thorndyke's, but now that they were outlawed, they couldn't go home to their ranch. The State of Colorado was expected to seize the property and holdings. Bud, the foreman ran the place. It had been whittled back down to its original size, and the neighbors, including the Bar C, were putting up barbed wire to mark the boundaries.

Henry, Howard, Harvey, and Homer Thorndyke, were outlaws on the run, but they were not without resources. The other members of the now defunct Chaparral County Stockman's Association considered them heroes. Upon the death of their father, they had inherited quite a bit of money, still in the Bank of Thorndyke, in which the four of them were now the majority stockholders. The bank was one of the few buildings that had not burned, as it was one of the few buildings in the town of Thorndyke built of brick, rather than wood. Because of their wealth, and for as long as the ranch continued to make a profit, they would not be desperate for money.

They had time on their hands and hearts full of hatred.

Since the Thorndyke's had gone on the run, a couple of the men who had been in the vigilante committee had been murdered. There was no way to know for certain, but everyone believed, the Thorndyke's had done those killings.

Bob made it a personal priority to catch the Thorndyke boys.

I had too much going on in my own county, to worry about them.

"Bob, it's not our problem. I have no interest in trying to hunt them down. That's a matter for the new Chaparral County Sheriff to deal with."

He scowled.

"I'm told they ride right into town and walk into the bank just as if they own it, which they do. The new Sheriff doesn't even try to arrest them. They have the support of too many powerful people. And then, there's the fact they're armed and dangerous."

"Again, it's not our problem. I'm trying to get this department organized. I intend to establish regular patrols of the roads and little towns throughout Alta Vista County. I need my deputies out there earning a paycheck."

Bob thought about my comment for about one second.

"John, sooner or later the Thorndykes will come after you. You should get them first, at a time and place of your choosing. Don't let them bushwhack you when you least expect it."

Bob always thinks in terms of violent action. He thinks like a hired killer, because it is what he was. Maybe, what he still is.

"I don't have time to waste chasing them all over the country. I hear they own a saloon in Cheyenne. Maybe that's where they are, Or Chicago, or Denver or Salt Lake. I've heard they attacked and killed a Mormon drover, over that way."

Bob nodded.

"Yeah, I heard that too, but they do still manage to show up in Thorndyke, every few weeks."

Eventually, Bob got too restless. When he heard the Thorndyke boys had shown up in Chaparral County again, he came to see me.

"You do remember the terms of our agreement, right?"

I nodded.

"What specifically are you referring to?"

"Well, you agreed I could take some time off occasionally, so I can work a job away from Alta Vista County. I want to do that. I want to go after the Thorndykes, on my own. They are worth one thousand dollars, each. I would find the additional financial resources to be of suitable motivation, even if they weren't such terrible miscreants."

I thought about my answer.

If I said "no" he could just quit and go do it anyway. He is a man hunter and predatory by nature. As long he was still technically my deputy, he might show some restraint.

"OK, but keep in mind they're wanted *alive.* There's no reward if they're dead. You check in with Wilfred McCoy, the new Sheriff over there. Don't step on his authority, or do anything that might undermine his position in Chaparral County."

Bob nodded.

"Fair enough, John, but I don't expect he'll be much help. He strikes me as being entirely too diligent in his endeavors toward keeping the peace."

"That's his job, Bob. Wilfred McCoy is a peace officer, and a good one. Try to respect that. They've had enough bloodshed in Chaparral County."

It was Saturday morning. I was having breakfast in the Bon Ton, with Tom and Becky.

"I'm supposed to be levying more fines and citations, to offset my department's expenses. The politics going on in this town is getting so complicated, it's just plain silly. Shoot, even though they changed my title to "Chief of Police", everybody stills calls me 'Marshal'. I'm the same man, doing the same job. I haven't changed, the town has. It's getting ridiculous, John. I have to be careful about saying or doing anything that might have a political implication. I could lose my job if, and/or, when we have a change in the political party currently governing this town."

"I know, Tom, you're hired by the Mayor and the City Council, and I'm elected by the people. Our political affiliations can make us or break us."

"I had no idea what hoops my dad was forced to jump through, beyond law enforcement, how complicated it gets, trying to keep the local business people happy," Becky said.

"That's only a part of it. You know the new hotel and saloon being built over near the rodeo grounds? The two men who are behind it came to me and tried to bribe me into letting them have open gambling and 'working girls'."

I saw Becky blush.

"They offered me one thousand dollars, per year, just to turn a blind eye. That's equal to my entire yearly salary!"

"Ya'll know it's a pretty common practice. The temptation can be overwhelming. In some places, the police are hardly more than organized criminals. I'm about to crack down on some of that, up at North Fork. Tommy Turner is the Sheriff, yet he owns and operates a bar and brothel. There are several up there. They have gambling in the saloons and casinos, as well. The miners are getting robbed seven ways from Sunday. None of it is legal in this state. I need to get some real law and order up into the mountains. I promised the governor I would. I'll start with North Fork."

When I arrived at the office, Hugh wasn't in his usual place, behind the desk. He hadn't missed a day of work since he came to Colorado. He had still been asleep when I left the bunk room down the hall, where he and I lived these days. A couple of the deputies stayed there as well. It was like the barracks where I lived with D Company of the Texas Rangers.

I walked down the hall to check on him, and found that he had checked out.

He'd died peacefully in his sleep.

Alta Vista County Chief Sheriff's Deputy, Hugh Lomax, died the way he had lived his life…On the job.

I wasn't good company for Lora that evening.

"Hugh was a really good man, John. I guess he was like a father to you."

"No, Lora, it was Kergi Alexiev Borostoya, who was a father to me. Hugh was more of a mentor. I looked up to him for his character and his commitment to excellence. He was the single most dedicated lawman I ever met."

Lora nodded.

"You're like him in that way."

"Am I? I get flustered with all the political stuff. Hugh just took it in stride. He believed everyone deserved to be treated the same way, with dignity. He didn't judge people for what they did; he left it to the courts. He told me once he found something likeable in every man he ever arrested. He couldn't be bought and he wouldn't bend to the whims of petty politicians. I swear he liked criminals better than he liked politicians, and he was a pretty good politician himself."

Lora laughed.

"You're more like him than you know."

It's funny how things work out. Life isn't what we want it to be, and it isn't what we try to make it. Life is the gift of God and each day is a journey. The Bible says, "Trust in God with all your heart and don't rely on your own intellect, in everything you do, acknowledge Him, and He will direct your paths." That means He will show us which trail we should take. We still get to choose the trail we take and enjoy the consequences of the choices we make. On occasion, because we are only flawed human beings, we will make a bad choice and ride down the wrong trail. The key is to learn from our mistakes and get back on the trail we should be following.

One day, I caught the 12:10 to Denver and then another train to San Francisco. That train was so fast, at times we were traveling nearly one mile, in one minute!

From San Francisco, I took a Wells Fargo stage to Monterey and then down to Carmel, where I rented a horse. I rode the horse down the California coastline, beside the Pacific Ocean, until I saw, circled in a stand of Coastal Cyprus trees, some familiar wagons.

Well, that about covers it. I've found a place where I can make a difference. I have a job to do and friends to help me. Lora and I'll be married, as soon as I get back to Bear Creek. Did I tell you Tom and Becky are expecting a baby?

As I look at the faces around me, lit by lamplight and the campfire, I see my son Nick with his new wife Rachel. I see my mother Sasha, with Katya and Matthew. And I see all of you, my family and my friends… my people.

Enough talk. Let's have some music!

****

BEAR CREEK

Turn the page for an excerpt from:

SAGE COUNTRY
Book Two
ALTA VISTA
©
DAN ARNOLD

SAGE COUNTRY
BOOK TWO

ALTA VISTA
©
DAN ARNOLD

Bob and I both had our guns on Sheriff Tommy Turner, as he walked into the room with his hands held high.

"Don't shoot me, please don't shoot. I've come to help," Tommy said.

"Too late, get a mop." Bob said.

"Yeah, you've made a hell of a mess," Tommy observed.

"Tommy, go get a doctor!" I spat.

"We ain't got one. The nearest thing to a doctor we had was the bartender here, but I see you've killed him, too."

I knew I hadn't. I looked at Bob, who shook his head. He hadn't shot the bartender either. It must've been Wes or a loose shot fired by someone else. I looked at the man as he lay sprawled on the floor at the end of the bar. He had a sawed off double-barreled shotgun in his left hand.

"It was me. I shot that man," Wes groaned. He was awake again.

"Damned good thing you did—if he had opened up on us with that thing, one or more of us would be dead for sure," Bob said.

Wes shook his head weakly.

"Tommy, we need some help in here. Where can we get help for the wounded?" I asked.

"There's a woman over at Aphrodite's Bower. She was a nurse in the war. I hear she's pretty good with wounds," Tommy said.

"Well, go fetch her, NOW!" I yelled.

He took off at a run.

I looked at my watch.

It was just now eight forty five.

***

Shortly later, Mrs. Poole and Nancy came bustling into the building in the company of Max.

"Wes, I hear you've managed to get yourself shot again!" Mrs. Poole exclaimed. "Nancy, please have a look at him, while I see to the Sheriff here."

She looked first at my neck wound and indicated it wasn't serious but needed cleaning. She'd just begun to undo the makeshift bandage on my leg when Nancy interrupted.

"We need to get this man to the house quickly, Emma. He needs more help than I can give here. He has a bullet in him that has to come out."

"Ah'll take him, Miz Emma," Max volunteered.

"Thank you, Max. Please hurry," Mrs. Poole said.

Max scooped Wes up off the floor and cradled him in his arms like a baby. He and Nancy hurried out the door.

2

Mrs. Poole surveyed the room looking for other injured people. She confirmed everyone still on the floor was indeed dead. She asked Bob if he was hurt. He just shook his head.

"I don't know how even one of you could have survived this," she said sadly.

"I never wanted it to go this way. I intended to make an arrest of just two people, and it turned into a blood bath," I said.

"Well, all I can say is when you say you're going to clean up a town; you manage to take out most of the trash yourself."

"Not like this. Why did everybody start shooting?" I asked.

"I guess there were several men in here who didn't want to be arrested this evening. You killed Martin Pogue. He was sitting at the table with the Thorndykes. He couldn't afford to be arrested. He faced hanging for sure. He just lost his head," Bob said.

"This place was a den of low life criminals, cutthroats, and thieves. A pity you didn't get Ian McGregger while you were at it. Can you walk, Sheriff?" Mrs. Poole asked me.

I nodded.

"I can hobble pretty well."

"Bob, you'd better help him up. We're going to the house to get you all patched up."

"Okay, Emma," Bob replied

It dawned on me they knew each other.

"How do you two know each other?" I asked, stupidly.

They both just stared at me.

I limped over and picked up my John Browning designed Winchester shotgun from where I'd dropped it. I reloaded it with shells from my jacket pocket.

Then we headed out.

***

Outside, the street was crowded with onlookers and some who had escaped the carnage. People had come running as soon as the shooting stopped. Some were standing on the porch of the Gold Dust. Others had swarmed out of the Oxbow.

There were horrified looks on the faces of some. Others nodded their respects.

There was no sign of Homer Thorndyke.

Bob and I were in no mood for trouble, and people sensed it. They moved aside and let us be on our way.

I managed to limp around the corner, but before we had gone very far, I had to lean on Bob. Mrs. Poole hurried on ahead of us.

A note from the author

Thank you for reading Bear Creek. I would love to hear from you. You can contact me at my website ~ www.danielbanks-books.com or follow me on Goodreads~ https://www.goodreads.com/author/show/10798086.Daniel_Roland_Banks
I certainly hope you had as much fun reading this book as I had writing it. If you liked it please tell a friend - or better yet, tell the world by writing a book review on the book's page on Amazon, or on Goodreads.com.

Even a few short sentences are helpful. As an independently published author, I don't have a marketing department behind me. I only have you, the reader.

So please spread the word!

How do you write a review? It's easy.

Did you like the book? What was your favorite thing about it? Did you learn anything new or interesting? Would you like to read another book by this author? Go to the Amazon or Goodreads link, click on the "write a customer review" button and type in your review.

And, to make it a little more fun, **when you write a review, e-mail me** and I'll return a note and an excerpt from one of my works in progress, maybe even a free e-book.

Thanks again.

Dan

Books by Dan Arnold
Daniel Roland Banks

Contemporary Detective

Horse Training Non-fiction

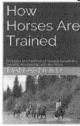

Westerns

About the Author

I've led a colorful life, fueling my imagination for telling stories set in the American West.

I was born in Bakersfield, California and abandoned by my parents in Seattle, Washington. After living in the foster care system for some years, I was eventually adopted. I've lived in Idaho, Washington, California, Virginia, and now make my home in Texas. My wife Lora and I have four grown children of whom we are justifiably proud, not because we were such good parents but because God is good.

I've written several novels and an illustrated book on the training of horses, in addition to authoring and/or contributing to numerous technical manuals and articles in various publications and periodicals.

As a horse trainer and clinician (I trained performance horses for twenty five years), I had occasion to travel extensively and I've been blessed to have worked with a variety of horses and people in amazing circumstances and locations.

I've herded cattle in Texas, chased kangaroos on horseback through the Australian Outback, guided pack-trips into the high Sierras and the Colorado Rockies, conditioned and trained thoroughbred race horses, galloped a warmblood on the bank of a canal surveyed by George Washington, and spent uncounted, delightful hours breaking bread with unique characters in diverse parts of the world.

At one (very brief) point I was one of the 3% of fine visual artists who earned their entire income from sales of their art. I'm a painter, sculptor and writer.

Under the name Daniel Roland Banks I write contemporary detective thrillers. I'm a member of American Christian Fiction Writers and Western Writers of America.

My book ANGELS & IMPERFECTIONS was selected as a finalist in the Christian Fiction category in the 2015 Reader's Favorites International Book Award contest.

In 2013, after 40+ years of searching, I found and got reacquainted with my half-brother and a host of relatives from my mother's side of the family.

I can't sing or dance, but I'd like to think I'm considered an engaging public speaker, an accomplished horseman and an excellent judge of single malt Scotch.

12934380R00184

Made in the USA
Lexington, KY
26 October 2018